Here is another magnificent space adventure by one of the greatest science fiction writers of our time, E. E. 'Doc' Smith. In some ways a book of prediction, definitely a book of provocative ideas, *Subspace Explorers* is a novel in the finest Smith tradition which will maintain his high reputation among his multitudes of fans, and win him many more.

E. E. 'Doc' Smith

Subspace Explorers

Panther

Granada Publishing Limited
First published in Great Britain in 1975 by
Panther Books Ltd
Frogmore, St Albans, Herts AL2 2NF

Published by arrangement with Canaveral Press Inc
Copyright © Edward E. Smith 1965
Made and printed in Great Britain by
Richard Clay (The Chaucer Press) Ltd
Bungay, Suffolk
Set in Linotype Plantin

Contents

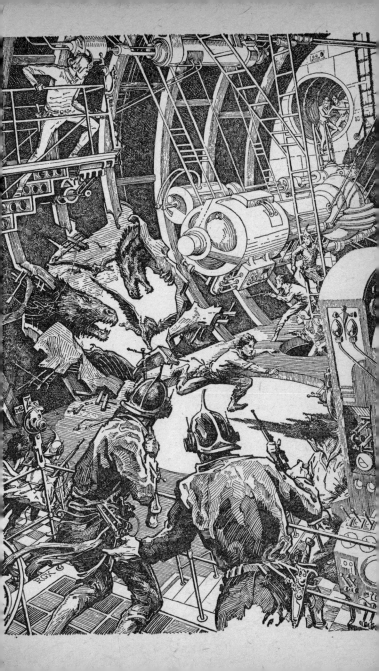

CHAPTER ONE

Catastrophe

At time zero minus nine minutes First Officer Carlyle Deston, Chief Electronicist of the starliner *Procyon*, sat attentively at his board. He was five feet eight inches tall and weighed one hundred sixty-two pounds. Just a little guy, as spacemen go. Although narrow-waisted and, for his heft, broad-shouldered, he was built for speed and maneuverability, not to handle freight.

Watching a hundred lights and half that many instruments; listening to four telephone circuits, two with each ear; hands flashing to toggles and buttons and knobs; he was completely informed as to the instant-by-instant condition of everything in his department during count-down. Everything had been and still was in condition GO.

Nevertheless, he was bothered; bothered as he had never been bothered before in all his three years of subspacing. He had always had hunches and they had always been right, but this one was utterly ridiculous. It wasn't the ship or the trip – nothing was yelling 'DANGER!' into his mind – it was something down in the Middle that was pulling at him like a cat tractor and it didn't make sense. He *never* went down into passenger territory. He had no business there and flirting with vac-skulled girls were not his dish.

So he fought his hunch down and concentrated on his job. Lift-off was uneventful; so was the climb out to a safe distance from Earth. At time zero minus two seconds Deston poised a fingertip over the red button, but everything stayed in condi-

11

tion GO and immergence into subspace was perfectly normal. All the green lights except one went out; all the needles dropped to zero; all four phones went dead; all signals stopped. He plugged a jack into the socket under the remaining green light and said

'*Procyon* One to Control Six. Flight eight four nine. Subspace radio test number one. How do you read me, Control Six?'

'Control Six to *Procyon* One. I read you ten and zero. How do you read me, *Procyon* One?'

'Ten and zero. Out.' The solitary green light went out and Deston unplugged,

Perfect signal and zero noise. That was that. From now until Emergence – unless some robot or computer called for help – he might as well be a passenger. He leaned back in his seat, lit a cigarette, and began really to study this wild hunch, that was getting worse all the time. It was all he could do to keep from calling his relief and going down there right then; but he couldn't and wouldn't do that. He was on until plus three hours. He couldn't possibly explain any such break as that would be, so he stuck it out.

At time zero plus one hundred seventy-nine minutes his relief appeared. 'All black, Babe?' the newcomer asked.

'As the pit, Eddie. Take over. You've picked out your girl-friend for the trip, I suppose?'

While taking the bucket seat, Eddie said, 'Not yet. I got sidetracked watching Bobby Warner ...'

A wave of psychic force hit Deston's mind hard enough almost to turn it inside out; but he clenched his teeth and held his pose.

'... and after seeing her just walk across the lounge once, all the other women looked like a dime's worth of catmeat. Talk about poetry in motion!' Eddie rolled his eyes, made motions with his hands, and whistled expressively. 'Oh, *brother*!'

'Okay, okay, don't blow a fuse,' Deston said, in what he hoped was his usual tone and manner. 'I know. You'll love her undyingly – all this trip, maybe.'

'Huh? How *dumb* can you get? D'you think I'd even *try* to play footsie with *Barbara Warner*?'

'You play footsie with the pick of the passenger list, so who's Barbara Warner, to daunt Don Juan Eddie Thompson, the Tomcat of Space?'

'I thought you knew *some* of the facts of life, Babe. She's Warner's only child, is all. Warner of WarnOil; the biggest in all space. Operates in every solar system known to man and never puts down a dry hole. All gushers that blow their rigs clear up into the stratosphere. Everybody wonders how come. The poop is, his wife's an oil-witch, is why he lugs her around with him all the time. Why else would he?'

'Maybe he loves her. It happens, you know.'

'Huh? After twenty-some years of her? Comet-gas! Anyway, would *you* have the sublime gall to make a pass at WarnOil's heiress, with more millions in her own sock than you've got dimes? If you ever made passes, I mean.'

'Uh-uh. Negative. For sure.'

'You nor me neither. But *what* a dish! *Brother,* what a lovely, luscious, toothsome *dish*!'

'Cheer up; you'll be raving about another one tomorrow,' Deston said callously, turning away.

'I don't know ... maybe; but even if I do, *she* won't be anything like *her*,' Eddie mourned, to the closing door.

Deston didn't go to his cabin; didn't even take off his side-arm. He didn't even think of it; the .41 automatic at his hip was as much a part of his uniform as his pants.

Entering the lounge, he did not have to look around. She was playing contract, and as eyes met eyes and she rose to her feet a shock-wave went through him that made him feel as though every hair he had was standing straight on end.

She was about five feet four. Her hair was a startlingly brilliant artificial yellow; her eyes a deep, cool blue. She could have made the Miss Western Hemisphere finals. Deston, however, did not notice any of these details – then.

'Excuse me, please,' she said to the other three at her table. 'I must go now.' She tossed her cards down onto the table and walked straight toward him; eyes still holding eyes.

He backed hastily out into the corridor, and as the door closed behind her they went naturally and wordlessly into each other's arms. Lips met lips in a kiss that lasted for a long time.

It was not a passionate embrace – passion would come later – it was as though each of them, after endless years of bootless, fruitless longing, had come at long last home.

'Come with me, dear, where we can talk,' she said finally, eyeing with disfavor the half dozen spectators; and, in her suite a few minutes later, Deston said:

'So *this* is why I had to come down into passenger territory. You came aboard at exactly zero seven forty-three.'

'Uh-uh.' She shook her head. 'A few minutes before that; that was when I read your name on the board. First Officer, Carlyle Deston. It simply unraveled me; I came completely unzipped. It's wonderful that you're so strongly psychic, too.'

'I don't know about that,' he said, thoughtfully. 'Psionics says that the map is the territory, but all my training has been based on the axiom that it isn't. I've had hunches all my life, but the signal doesn't carry much information. Like hearing a siren while you're driving a ground-car. You know you have to pull over and stop, but that's all you know. It could be police, fire, ambulance – *anything*. Anybody with any psionic ability at all ought to do a lot better than that, I should think.'

'Not necessarily. You don't *want* to believe it, so you've been fighting it; beating it down. So it has to force its way through whillions and skillions of ohms of resistance to get through to you at all. But I *know* you're very strongly psychic, or you wouldn't've come down here...' she giggled suddenly '... and you'd've jumped clear out into subspace when a perfectly strange girl attacked you. So ... aren't you going to ask me to marry you?'

'Of course I am.' He blushed hotly. 'Will you? Right now?'

'You can't without resigning, can you? They'd fire you?'

'What of it? I can get a good ground job.'

'But you wouldn't *like* a ground job!'

'What of that, too. A man grows up. Between you and any job in the universe there's no choice.'

'I knew you'd say that, Carl.' She hugged his elbow against her side. 'I'd *love* to get married right now...' She paused.

'Except for what?' he asked.

'I thought at first I'd tell my parents first – they're aboard, you know – but I won't. She'd scream and he'd roar and neither of them could make me change my mind, so we *will* do it right now.'

He looked at her questioningly; she shrugged and went on, 'We aren't what you could call a happy family. She's been trying to make me marry an old goat of a prince and I finally told her to go roll her hoop – to get a divorce and marry the foul old beast herself. And he's been pushing me to marry an oil-man – to consolidate two empires – that it makes me sick at the stomach just to look at! Last week he *insisted* on it and I blew up like an atomic bomb. I'd keep on finding oil and stuff for him, I said, but . . .' She broke off as Deston stiffened involuntarily.

'Oil?' he asked, too quietly. 'You're the oil-witch, then; not your mother. Besides having more megabucks in your own right than any . . .'

'Don't say it, dearest!' She seized both his hands in hers. 'I know how you feel. I don't like to let you ruin your career, either, but *nothing* can come between us now that we've found each other. So I'll tell you this.' Her eyes looked steadily into his. 'If it bothers you that much I'll give every dollar I own to some foundation or other. I swear it.'

He laughed shamefacedly as he took her into his arms. '*That's* knocking me for the well-known loop, sweetheart. I'll live with it and like it.'

Then, to get away from that subject, he explored with knowing fingers the muscles of her arms and back. 'You're trained down as fine as I am and it's my business to be – how come?'

'I majored in Phys. Ed. and I love it. And I'm a Newmartian, you know, so I teach a few courses . . .'

'Newmartian? But I thought – aren't the headquarters of all the big outfits, including WarnOil, on Tellus?'

'In a way. Management, yes, but very little property. Everything possible is owned on Newmars and we Warners have always lived there. The tax situation, you know.'

'I didn't know; taxes don't bother me much. But go ahead. You teach a few courses. In?'

'Oh, bars, trapeze, ground-and-lofty tumbling, acrobatics,

aerialistics, highwire work, muscle-control, unarmed combat – all that sort of thing.'

'Ouch! So if you ever happen accidentally to get mad at me you'll tie me up into a pretzel?'

She laughed. 'A pleasant thought; but you know as well as I do that a good big man can take a good little one every time.'

'But I'm not big. I'm just a little squirt.'

'You outweigh me by forty pounds and I know just how good space officers have to be. You're *exactly* the right size.'

'For the first time in my life I'm beginning to think so.' Laughing, he put his arm around her and led her up to a full-length mirror. 'We're a mighty well-matched pair ... I like us immensely ... well, shall we go see the chaplain? Or should we look for a priest – or maybe a rabbi?'

'We *don't* know each other very well, do we? But we'll have all the rest of our lives to learn the unimportant details. The chaplain, please. Let's go.'

They went; still talking. 'You'll live with me in the suite, won't you?' she asked. 'All the time you aren't on duty?'

'I can't imagine doing anything else.'

'Wonderful! Now I want to talk seriously for a minute. You'll never need a job, nor any of my money, either. Not ever. The thought of dowsing never even entered your mind, did it?'

'Dowsing? Oh, witching stuff. Of course not.'

'Listen, darling. All the time I've been touching you I've been learning about you – and you've been learning about me.'

'Yes, but ...'

'No buts, buster. You actually have tremendous powers; ever so much greater than mine. All I can do is feel oil, water, coal, and gas. I'm no good at all on metals – I couldn't feel gold if I were perched right on the ridge-pole of Fort Knox. But if you'll stop fighting that terrific power of yours and really *use* it I'm positive that you can dowse anything you want to. Even uranium.'

He didn't believe it, and the argument went on until they reached the chaplain's office. Then, of course, it was dropped automatically; and the next five days were deliciously, deliriously, ecstatically happy days for them both.

At the time of this chronicle starships were the safest means of transportation ever used by man; but there was, of course, an occasional accident. Worse than the accidents, however – but fortunately much rarer – were the complete disappearances: starships from which no distress signal was ever received and of which no trace was ever found.

And on the Great Wheel of Fate the *Procyon*'s number came up.

In the middle of the night Carlyle Deston came instantaneously awake – deep down in his mind a huge, terribly silent voice was roaring 'DANGER! DANGER! DANGER!' He did not take time to think or to reason; he grabbed Barbara around the waist and leaped out of bed with her.

'Trouble, Bobby! Get into your suit – quick!'

'But ... but I've *got* to dress!'

'No time! Snap it up!' He stuffed her into her suit; leaped into his own. 'Control!' he snapped into its microphone. 'Disaster! Abandon Ship!'

The alarm bells clanged once; the big red lights flashed once; the sirens barely started to growl, then quit. The whole vast fabric of the ship shuddered as though it were being mauled by a thousand and impossibly gigantic hammers.

And out in the corridor 'Come on, girl, sprint!' He put his hand under her arm and urged her along.

She tried, but her best wasn't good. 'I've never been checked out on sprinting in space-suits, so you'd better ...'

Everything went out. Lights, artificial gravity, air-circulation – everything.

'You've never been checked out on null-gee, either, so hang on and we'll travel.'

'Where to?' she asked, hurtling through the air faster than she would have believed possible.

'Baby Two – Lifecraft Number Two, that is – my crash assignment. Good thing I was down here with you – I don't think anybody'll make it from the Top. Next turn left, then right. I'll swing you.'

At the lifecraft he kicked a lever and a port swung open – to reveal a blaze of light and a startled gray-haired man who, half-floating in air, was hanging onto a fixture with both hands.

'What happened?' the man asked. 'I didn't know whether . . .'

'Wrecked. Null-gee and high radiation. I'll have to put you in the safe for a while.' Deston shoved the oldster into a small room, gave him a line, and turned to Barbara. 'My tell-tale reads twenty – pink – so we've got a few minutes. Wrap a leg around that lever there and I'll see if I can find some passengers and toss 'em to you. Or is null-gee getting to you too much?'

'I'm pretty gulpy, but I can take it.'

'Good girl – you may have to take a lot of it.'

The first five doors he tried were locked. The sixth was not; but the couple inside the room were very gruesomely dead. So was everyone else he could find until he came to a room in which a man in a space-suit was floundering helplessly in the air. He glanced at his tell-tale. Thirty-two. High red. Time to go.

In the lifecraft he closed the port, cut in the launcher, and slammed on a one-gravity drive away from the ship. Then he shucked Barbara out of her suit and shed his own. He unclamped a fire-extinguisher-like affair; opened the door of a tiny room. 'In here!' He shut the door behind them. 'Strip, quick!' He cradled the device and opened four valves.

Fast as he was, she was naked and ready for the gush of thick, creamy foam from the multiplex nozzle. 'Oh, Dekon?' she asked. 'I've read about it. I rub it in good, all over me?'

'That's right. Short for "Decontaminant, Complete; Compound, Absorbent, and Chelating; Type DCQ." It takes care of radiation, but speed is of the essence. All over you is right.' He placed the foam-gun on the floor and went vigorously to work. 'Eyes, too, yes. *Everywhere*. Just that. And swallow six big gulps of it . . . that's it. I slap a gob of it over your nose and mouth and you inhale once – hard and deep. One good one's enough, but if it isn't a good one you die of lung cancer, so I'll have to knock you out and give it to you while you're unconscious, and that isn't good – complications. So make it good and deep!'

'Will do. Good and deep.' She emptied her lungs.

He put a headlock on her and slapped the Dekon on. She inhaled, hard and deep, and went into paroxysms of coughing.

He held her in his arms until the worst of it was over; but she was still coughing hard when she pulled herself away from him.

'But – you? Lemme – help – you – quick!'

'No need, sweetheart. The old man won't need it – I got him into the safe in time – the other guy and I will work on each other. Lie down on the bunk there and take it easy for half an hour.'

Forty minutes later, while all four were still cleaning up the messes of foam, the chattering sender stopped sending and the communicator came on. Since everything about a starship is designed to fail safe, they were of course in normal space. On the screens many hundreds of stars blazed, in half the colors of the spectrum.

'Baby Three acknowledging,' the speaker said. 'Jones and four – deconned – who's calling and how's your subspace communicator?'

'Baby Two, Deston and three. Mine's dead, too. Thank God, Herc! With *you* to astrogate us maybe we'll make it. But how'd you get away? Not down from the Top, that's for sure.'

Vision came on; a big, square-jawed, lean, tanned face appeared upon the screen. 'We were in Baby Three already.'

'Oh.' Deston was quick on the uptake. 'You, too?'

'That's right. But the way the old man chewed you out, I knew he'd slap me in irons, so we hid out. We found three men before high red. I deconned Bun, then ...'

'Bun?' Barbara exclaimed. 'Bernice Burns? How *wonderful*!'

'Bobby!' The face of a silver-haired beauty appeared beside Jones'. '*Am* I glad you got away too!'

'Just a sec,' Deston said. 'Data for rendezvous, Herc. . . . Hey! My watch stopped – so did the chron!'

'Here too,' Jones said. 'So I'll handle it on visual.'

'But it's non-magnetic – and *nothing* can stop an atomi-chron!' Deston protested.

'But something did,' the gray-haired man said. 'A priceless datum. Observations of fact have already invalidated twenty-four of the thirty-eight best theories of hyperspace. I take it that none of you were in direct contact with the metal of the

19

ship at the time of disaster?'

'We weren't,' Deston said. Then, to the younger stranger, 'You? And identity, please.'

'I know *that* much. Henry Newman, crew chief normal space.'

'Your passengers, Herc?'

'Vincent Lopresto, financier, and his two bodyguards. They were sleeping in their suits. Grounders.'

'Just so,' the old man said. 'Insulated, we acquired the charge very gradually. What did the bodies look like?'

Deston thought for a moment. 'Almost as if they had exploded.'

'Precisely.' Gray-Hair beamed. 'That eliminates all the others except three – Morton's, Rothstein's, and my own.'

'You're a specialist in subspace, sir?'

'Oh, no, I'm not a specialist at all. I'm a dabbler; a...'

'In the College?' Deston asked, and the other nodded.

'With doctorates in everything from astronomy to zoology? I'm mighty glad you were using this lifecraft for an observatory when we got it, Doctor ...?'

'Adams. Andrew Adams. But I have only eight at the moment. Earned degrees, that is.'

'And you have a lot of apparatus in the hold?'

'Less than six tons. Just what I must have in order to...'

'Babe.' Jones' voice broke in. 'Got you figured. Power two, alpha eighteen, beta forty-three...'

Rendezvous with the *Procyon*'s hulk was made; both lifecraft hung motionless relative to it. No other lifecraft had escaped. A conference was held. Weeks of work would be necessary to determine the ship's condition. Hundreds of other tasks would have to be performed, and there were only nine survivors. Everyone would have to work, and work hard.

The two girls wanted to be together. So did the two officers; since, as long as they lived or until the *Procyon* made port, all responsibility rested: first, upon First Officer Carlyle Deston; and second, upon Second Officer Theodore Jones. Therefore Jones and Bernice came aboard Lifecraft Two and Deston asked Newman to go over to Lifecraft Three.

'Uh-uh, I like the scenery here a lot better.' Newman's eyes raked Bernice's five feet nine of scantily-clad sheer beauty from ankles to coiffure.

'As you were, Mister Jones!' Deston rasped, and Jones subsided. Deston went on, very quietly, 'As crew chief, Newman, you know the law. I am in command.'

'You ain't in command of *me*, pretty boy. Not out here where nobody has ever come back from. I make my own law – with *this*.' Newman patted his side pocket.

'Draw it, then, or crawl.' Deston's face was coldly calm; his right hand still hung motionless at his side.

Newman glanced at the girls, both of whom were frozen; then at Jones, who smiled at him pityingly. 'I . . . my . . . but yours is right where you can get at it,' he faltered.

'You should have thought of that sooner. I'm waiting, Newman.'

'Just wing him, Babe,' Jones said then. 'He's strong enough, except in the head. We may need his back.'

'Uh-uh. I'll have to kill him sometime, so it might as well be now. Square between the eyes. A hundred bucks I'm two millimeters off dead center?'

Both girls gasped and stared at each other in horror; but Jones said calmly, without losing any part of his smile, 'Not a dime; I've lost too much that way already,' – at which outrageous statement both girls realized what was going on and smiled in relief.

And Newman misinterpreted those smiles completely; especially Bernice's. The words came hard, but he said them. 'I crawl.'

'Crawl, what?'

'I crawl, sir.'

'Your first job will be to build some kind of a brute-force device to act as a clock. One more break will be your last. Flit.'

Newman flitted – fast – and Barbara, who had opened her mouth to say something, shut it. No, he would have killed the man; he would have had to. He still might have to. So she said, instead,

'Why'd you let him keep his pistol? The . . . the *slime*! And after you saved his life, too!'

'Typical of the type. One gun won't make any difference.'

'But you can lock up *all* their guns, can't you?'

'I'm afraid not. Lopresto's a mobster, isn't he, Herc?'

'If he's a financier I'm an angel – complete with wings and halo. They'll have guns hidden out all over the place.'

'Check. You and I'll go over and . . .'

'And I,' Adams said. 'I must tridi everything, and do some autopsies, and . . .'

'Of course,' Deston agreed. 'With a Big Brain along – oh, excuse that crack, please, Doctor Adams. It slipped out on me.'

Adams laughed. 'In context, I regard that as the highest compliment I have ever received. In these circumstances you need not "Doctor" me. "Adams" will do very nicely.'

'I'm going to call you "Uncle Andy",' Barbara said with a grin. 'Now, Uncle Andy, in view of what you just said, one of your eight doctorates is in medicine.'

'Naturally.'

'Are you any good at obstetrics?'

'In the present instance I feel perfectly safe in saying . . .'

'Wait a minute!' Deston snapped. 'Bobby, you are *not* . . .'

'I am too! That is, I don't suppose I *am* yet, but with him aboard I'm certainly *going* to. I *want* to, and if we don't get back both Bun and I will *have* to. Castaways' Code. So there!'

Deston started to say something, but Barbara forestalled him. 'But for right now, it's high time we all got some sleep.'

It was and they did; and next morning the three men wafted themselves across a few hundred yards of space to the crippled liner. Floodlights were rigged.

'What . . . a . . . mess.' Deston's voice was low and wondering. 'The Top especially . . . but the Middle and the Tail don't look too bad.'

Inside, however, devastation had gone deep into the Middle. Walls, floors, and structural members were sheared and torn and twisted into shapes impossible to understand or explain. And, even worse, there were *absences*. In dozens of volumes, of as many sizes and of shapes incompatible with any three-dimensional geometry, every solid thing had simply vanished – vanished without leaving any clue whatever as to how or where

22

it could possibly have gone.

It took four days to clean the ship of Dekon foam and to treat the hot spots that the automatics had missed. Four long days of heartbreaking labor in weightlessness and four too-short nights of sleep in the heavenly – to seven of them, at least – artificial gravity of the lifecraft. With the hulk deconned to zero (all ruptured radiators had of course been blown automatically at the time of catastrophe) Jones and Deston went over the engine rooms item by item.

The subspace drives were fused ruins. Enough normal-space gear was in working order, however, so that they could put on one gravity of drive, which was a vast relief to all. Then Jones began to jury-rig an astrogation set-up and Deston went to help Adams.

A few evenings later Adams said, 'Well, that covers all the preliminary observations I am equipped to make. Thanks a lot for your help, Babe, I won't bother you any more for a while.'

Deston grinned ruefully. 'You'll have to, Doc. I don't mean the routine – clean-up, bodies, effects, and so on – Lopresto's handling that. You've learned a lot of stuff that none of the rest of us can make head or tail of. That makes you the director; we're only the cheap help.'

'I've learned scarcely anything yet; only that when we approach any planet we must do so with extreme – I might almost say fantastic – precautions.'

'Blasting at normal, it'll be a mighty long time before we have to worry about that.'

'Not as long as you think, Babe,' Jones said. 'We're in toward the center of the galaxy somewhere; stars are a lot thicker here. It's only about a third of a light-year to the nearest one. Point three five, I make it.'

'But what's the chance of its having a Tellus-Type planet?'

'Oh, that isn't necessary,' Adams said. 'Any planet will, it is virtually certain, enable us to restore subspace communication.'

'It'll still be a mighty long haul,' Deston said. 'The shape the engines are in, I doubt if they'll stand up under more than about one gee on a long pull. We can't do much better than that anyway, because we've got no grav-control – the Q-converters are all shot and we can't fix 'em.'

'We'll travel at *one* gravity,' Barbara said. 'Babies; remember?'

'I'll figure it that way,' Deston said, and went to work with his slide-rule. A few minutes later he reported, 'Neglecting the Einstein Effect, which is altogether too hairy for a slapstick, I make it about fourteen months. But since velocity at turnover will be crowding six tenths of a light, that neglect makes it just a guess.'

'We'll compute it tomorrow morning,' Jones said. 'For your information, all, we're heading for that star now.'

CHAPTER TWO

The Zeta Field

The tremendous Chaytor engines of the *Procyon* were again putting out their wonted torrents of power. The starship, now a mere spaceship, was on course at one gravity. The lifecraft were in their berths, but the five and the four still lived in them rather than in the vast and oppressive emptiness that the liner then was. And outside of working hours the two groups did not mix.

In Lifecraft Three, four men sat at two small tables. Ferdy Blaine and Moose Mordan were playing cards for small stakes. Ferdy was of medium size, lithe and poised, built of rawhide and spring steel. Moose the Muscle was six feet five and weighed a good two sixty. The two at the other table had been planning for days. They had had many vitriolic arguments, but neither had made any motion toward his weapon.

'Play it my way and we've got it made, I tell you!' Newman pounded the table with his fist. 'Seventy-five *megabucks* if it's a dime! Heavier loot than your second-string syndicate ever even *thought* of in one haul! I'm almost as good an astrogator as Jones is and a better engineer, and at *practical* electronics I'm just as good as Pretty Boy Deston is.'

'Oh, yeah?' Lopresto sneered. 'How come you're only a crew-chief, then?'

'*Only* a crew-chief!' Newman yelled. 'D'ya think I'm dumb or something? Or don't know where the big moola is at? Or ain't in exactly the right spot to collect right and left? Or I ain't got exactly the right connections? With Mister Big himself? You ain't *that* dumb!'

'Dumb or not, before I make a move I've got to be *sure* that we can get back without 'em.'

'You can be *damn* sure. I got to get back myself, don't I? But paste this in your hat – *I* get the big platinum blonde.'

'You can have her. Too big. The little yellow-head's my dish.'

Newman sneered into Lopresto's hard-held face. 'But remember this, you small-time, chiseling punk. Rub *me* out after we kill them and you get nowhere. You're dead. Chew on that a while and you'll know who's boss.'

After just the right amount of holding back and objecting, Lopresto agreed. 'You win, Newman, the way the cards lay. So all that's left is – when? Tomorrow?'

'Not quite. Let 'em finish figuring course, time, distance, turnover – all that stuff. They can do it a lot faster and some better than I can. I'll tell you when.'

'Okay, and I'll give the signal. When I yell NOW we give 'em the business.'

Newman went to his cabin and the muscle called Moose said, 'I don't like that ape, boss. Before you gun him, let me work him over a little, huh?'

'We'll let him think he's top dog for a while yet; then you can have him.'

A few evenings later, in Lifecraft Two, Barbara said, 'You're worried, Babe, and everything's going so smoothly. Why?'

'Too smoothly altogether. That's why. Newman ought to be doing a slow burn and goldbricking all he dares, and he isn't. And I wouldn't trust Lopresto as far as I can throw a brick chimney by its smoke. I smell trouble. Shooting trouble.'

'But they couldn't do *anything* without you two!' Bernice protested. '*Could* they, Ted, possibly?'

'They could, and I think they intend to. Being a crew chief, Newman is a jackleg engineer, a good practical 'troncist, and a rule-of-thumb astrogator, and we're computing every element of the flight. And if he's what I *think* he is . . .' Jones paused.

'Could be,' Deston said. 'One of an organized ring of pirate-smugglers. But there isn't enough plunder that they could get away with to make it pay.'

'No? Think again. Not plunder; salvage. With either of us alive, none. With both of us dead, can you guess within ten megabucks of how much they'll collect?'

'*Blockhead!*' Deston slapped himself on the forehead. 'And they aren't planning on killing the girls until the last act.'

Both girls shrank visibly and Barbara said 'I see.'

Deston went on, 'They know they'll have to get both of us at once – the survivor would lock the ship in null-G and they'd be sitting ducks ... and it won't be until after we've finished the computations. We very seldom work together. If we make it a point *never* to be together on duty ...'

'And be sure to always have our talkies turned on,' Jones put in, grimly.

'Check. They'll have to think up some reason for getting everybody together, which will be the tip-off. Blaine will probably draw on me ...'

'And he'll kill you,' Jones said, flatly. 'You're fast, I know, but he's a professional – probably one of the fastest guns in all space.'

'Yes, but ... I've got a ... I mean I think I can ...'

Bernice, smiling now, stopped Deston's floundering. 'Why don't you fellows tell each other that you're both very strongly psionic? Bobby and I let our back hair down long ago.'

'Oh – so you'll have warning, too, Babe?' Jones asked.

'That's right; but the girls can't start packing pistols now.'

Bernice laughed. 'I wouldn't know how to shoot one if I did. I'll throw things – I'm very good at that.'

Jones didn't know his new wife very well yet, either. 'What can you throw hard enough and straight enough to do any good?'

'Anything that weighs less than fifty pounds,' she replied, confidently. 'In this case ... chairs, I think. Flying chairs are really hard to cope with. I'll start wearing a couple of knives in leg-sheaths, but I won't throw 'em unless I absolutely have to. Who will I knock out with the first chair?'

'I'll answer that,' Barbara said. 'If it's Blaine against Babe, it'll be Lopresto against Herc. So you'll throw your chair at that unspeakable oaf Newman.'

'I'd rather brain him than anyone else I know, but that would leave that gigantic gorilla to ... in that case, Bobby, you'll simply *have* to go armed.'

Barbara held out her hands. 'I always do.'

'Against a man-mountain like him? You're *that* good? Really?'

'Especially against a man-mountain like him. I'm that good. Really. And we should have a signal — an unusual word — so the first one of us to sense their intent yells "BRAHMS!" Okay?'

That was okay, and the four went to bed.

Three days later, the intended victims allowed themselves to be inveigled into the lounge. All was peace and friendship — until suddenly a four-fold 'BRAHMS!' rang out, an instant ahead of Lopresto's stentorian 'NOW!'

It was all a very good thing that Deston had had warning, for he was indeed competing out of his class. As it was, his bullet crashed through Blaine's head, while the gunman's went into the carpet. The other pistol duel wasn't even close and Newman didn't get to aim his gun at Adams at all.

Bernice, even while shrieking the battle-cry, leaped to her feet, hurled her chair, and reached for another; but one chair was enough. It knocked the half-drawn pistol from Newman's hand and sent his body crashing to the floor, where Deston's second bullet made it certain that he would stay there.

If Moose Mordan had had time to get set, he might have had a chance. His thought processes, however, were lamentably slow; and Barbara Deston was very, very fast. She reached him before he even began to realize that this pint-sized girl actually intended to hit him; thus his belly-muscles were still completely relaxed when her left fist sank half-forearm-deep into his solar plexus.

With an agonized 'WHOOSH!' he began to double up, but she scarcely allowed him to bend. The fingers of her right hand, tightly bunched, were already boring savagely into a spot at the base of his neck. Then, left hand at his throat and right hand pulling hard at his belt, she put the totalized and concentrated power of her whole body behind the knee she

28

drove into his groin.

That ended it. To make sure, however – or to keep Barbara from knowing that she had killed a man? – Deston and Jones each put a bullet through the falling head before it struck the floor.

Both girls flung themselves into their husbands' arms.

'Oh, I *killed* him, Carl!' Barbara sobbed. 'And the worst of it is, I really *meant* to! I *never* did anything like that before in . . .'

'You didn't kill him, Barbara,' Adams said.

'Huh?' She raised her head from Deston's shoulder; the contrast between streaming eyes and dawning relief was almost funny. 'Why, I did too! I *know* I did!'

'By no means, my dear. Nor did Bernice kill Newman. Fists and knees and chairs do not kill instantly; bullets through the brain do. The autopsies will show, I'm quite certain, that these four men died instantly of gunshot wounds.'

With the gangsters out of the way, life aboard ship settled down, but not into a routine. When two spacemen and two grounder girls are trying to do the work of a full crew, no routine is possible. Adams, much older than the others and working even longer hours, became haggard and thin.

'But this work is *necessary*, my dear children,' he informed the two girls when they remonstrated with him. 'This material is all new. There are many extremely difficult problems involved and I have less than a year left to work on them. *Less than one year*, and it is a task for many men and all the resources of a research center.'

To the officers, however, he went into more detail. 'Considering the enormous amounts of supplies carried; the scope, quantity, and quality of the devices employed; it is highly improbable that we are the first survivors of this type of catastrophe to set course for a planet.'

After some discussion, the officers agreed with him.

'While I can not as yet analyze or evaluate it, we are carrying an extremely heavy charge of an unknown nature; the residuum of a field of force which is possibly more or less analogous to the electromagnetic field. This residuum either is or is

29

not dischargeable to an object of planetary mass. I am now virtually certain that it is; and I am of the opinion that its discharge is ordinarily of such violence as to destroy the starship carrying it.'

'Good God!' Deston exclaimed. 'Oh – *that* was what you meant by "fantastic precautions"?'

'Precisely.'

'Any idea of what those precautions will have to be?'

'No. This is all *so* new ... and I know *so* little ... and am working with pitifully inadequate instrumentation ... however, we have months of time yet, and if I am unable to derive a solution before arrival – I don't mean a rigorous analysis, of course; merely a method of discharge having a probability of success of at least point nine – we will remain in orbit around that sun until I do.'

The *Procyon* bored on through space at one gravity of acceleration; and one gravity, maintained for months, builds up to an extremely high velocity. And, despite the Einstein Effect, that acceleration was maintained, for there was no lack of power. The *Procyon*'s uranium-driven Wesleys did not drive the ship, but only energized the Chaytor Effect engines that tapped the total energy of the universe.

Thus, in seven months of flight, the spaceship had probably attained a velocity of about six-tenths that of light. The men did not know the day or date or what their actual velocity was, since the brute-force machine that was their only clock could not be depended upon for either accuracy or uniformity. Also, and worse, there was of course no possibility of determining what, if anything, the Einstein Effect was doing to their time rate.

At the estimated midpoint of the flight the *Procyon* was turned end for end; and, a few days later, Barbara and Deston cornered Adams in his laboratory.

'Listen, you egregious clam!' she began. 'I *know* that Bun and I have been pregnant for at *least* eight months and we ought to be *twice* as big as we are. You've been studying us constantly with a hundred machines that nobody ever heard of before and all you've said is blah. Now, Uncle Andy, I want the *truth*. *Are* we in for a lot of trouble?'

'Trouble?' Adams was amazed. 'Of course not. None at all. Perfectly normal fetuses, both of them. Perfectly.'

'But for what *age*?' she demanded. 'Four months, maybe?'

'But that's the crux!' Adams enthused. 'Fascinating; and indubitably supremely important. A key datum. If this zeta field is causing it, that gives me a tremendously powerful new tool, for certain time vectors in the generalized matrix become parameters. Thus certain determinants, notably the all-important delta-prime-sub-mu, become manipulable by ... but you aren't *listening*!'

'I'm listening, pops, but nothing is coming through. But I'm *awfully* glad I'm not going to give birth to a monster,' and she led Deston away. 'Carl, have you got the *foggiest* idea of what he was talking about?'

'Not the foggiest – that was over my head like a cirrus cloud – but if you gals' slowness in producing will help the old boy lick this thing I'm all for it, believe me.'

Months passed. Two perfect babies – Theodore Warner Deston and Barbara Bernice Jones – were born, four days apart, in perfectly normal fashion. Adams made out birth certificates which were unusual in only one respect; the times, dates, and places of the births were to be determined later.

A couple of weeks before arrival Adams rushed up to Deston and Jones. 'I have it!' he shouted, and began to spout a torrent of higher – very *much* higher – mathematics.

'Hold it, Doc!' Deston protested. 'I read you zero and ten. Can't you delouse your signal?'

'W-e-l-l.' The scientist looked hurt, but did abandon the high math. 'The discharge *is* catastrophic; energy of the order of magnitude of ten thousand average discharges of lightning. I do not know what it is, but it is virtually certain that we will be able to discharge it, not in the one tremendous blast of contact with the planet, but in successive decrements by the use of long, thin leads extending downward toward a high point of the planet.'

'Wire, you mean? What kind?'

'The material is unimportant except in that it should have sufficient tensile strength to support as many miles as possible of its own length.'

'We've got dozens of coils of hook-up wire,' Deston said, 'but not too many *miles* and it's soft stuff.'

Jones snapped his finger. '*Graham* wire!'

'Of course,' Deston agreed. 'Hundreds of miles of it aboard. We'll float the senser down on a Hotchkiss ...'

'Tear-out,' Jones objected.

'Bailey it – and spider the Bailey out to eighteen or twenty pads. We can cannibal the whole Middle for metal.'

'Sure. But surges – backlash. We'll have to remote it.'

'No problem there; servos all over the place. To Baby Two.'

'Would you mind delousing *your* signal?' Adams asked, caustically.

' 'Scuse, please, Doc. A guy *does* talk better in his own lingo, doesn't he? Graham wire is used for re-wrapping the Grahams, you know.'

'No, I don't know. What are Grahams?'

'Why, they're the intermediates between the Wesleys and the Chaytors ... okay, okay; Graham wire is one-point-three-millimeter-diameter ultra-high-tensile alloy wire. Used for re-inforcing hollow containers that have to stand terrific pressure.'

'Such wire is exactly what will be required. Note now that our bodies will have to be grounded very thoroughly to the metal of the ship.'

'You're so right. We'll wrap up to the eyeballs in silver mesh and run leads as big as my arm to the frame.'

They approached their target planet. It was twice as massive as Earth; its surface was rugged and jagged; its mountain ranges had sharp peaks over forty thousand feet high.

'There's one more thing we must do,' Adams said. 'This zeta field may very well be irreplaceable. We must therefore launch all the lifecraft except Number Two into separate orbits, so that a properly-staffed and properly-equipped force may study that field.'

It was done; and in a few hours the *Procyon* hung motionless, a thousand miles high, directly above an isolated and sharp mountain peak.

The Bailey boom, with its spider-web-like network of grounding cables and with a large pulley at its end, extended two hundred feet straight out from the *Procyon*'s side. A twenty-five-mile coil of Graham wire had been mounted on the remote-controlled Hotchkiss reel. The end of the wire had been run out over the pulley; a fifteen-pound weight, to act both as a 'senser' and to keep the wire from fouling, had been attached; and the controls had been tested.

Now, in Lifecraft Two – as far away from the 'business district' as they could be – the human bodies were grounded and Deston started the reel. The whole coil ran out, as expected, with no action. Then, slowly and carefully, Deston let the big ship float straight downward. Until, suddenly, it happened.

There was a blast beside which the most terrific flash of lightning ever seen on Earth would have seemed like a firecracker. Although she was in what was almost a vacuum, the *Procyon* was hurled upward like the cork of a champagne bottle. And as for what it felt like – the sensation was utterly indescribable. As Bernice said, long afterward, when she was being pressed by a newsman, 'Just tell 'em it was the living end.'

The girls were unwrapped and, after a moment of semi-hysteria and after making sure that the babies were all right, were as good as new. Then Deston aimed his plate and gulped. Without saying a word he waved a hand and the others looked. The sharp tip of the mountain was gone: it had become a seething, flaming lake of incandescent lava.

'And what,' Deston managed, 'do you suppose happened to the other side of the ship?'

The boom was gone. So were all twenty of the grounding cables that had fanned out in all directions to anchorages welded to the vessel's skin and frame. The anchorages, too, were gone; and tons upon tons of steel plating and of structural members for many feet around where each anchorage had been. Many tons of steel had been completely volatilized; other tons had run like water.

'Shall I try the subspace radio now, Doc?' Deston asked.

'By no means. This first blast would of course be the worst,

33

but there will be several more, of decreasing violence.'

There were. The second, while it volatilized the boom and its grounding network, merely fused small portions of the anchorages. The third took only the boom itself; the fourth, only the dangling miles of wire. At the fifth trial nothing – apparently – happened; whereupon the wire was drawn in and a two-hundred-pound mass of steel was lowered into firm contact with solid rock.

'Now you may try your radio,' Adams said.

Deston flipped a switch and spoke into his microphone. '*Procyon* One to Control Six. Flight eight four nine. Subspace radio test number nine five – I think. How do you read me, Control Six?'

The reply was highly unorthodox. It was a wild yell, followed by words not addressed to Deston at all. 'Captain Reamer! Captain French! Captain Holloway! ANYBODY! It's the *Procyon*, that was lost over a year ago! *IT'S THE PROCYON!*'

'Line it up! If it's some damn fool's idea of a joke ...' a crisp authoritative voice grew louder as its source approached the distant pickup '... he'll rot in jail for a hundred years!'

'*Procyon* One to Control Six,' Deston said again. His voice was not quite steady this time; both girls were crying openly and joyfully. 'How do you read me, Frenchy old horse?'

'It *is* the *Procyon* – that's the Runt himself – hi, Babe! I read you nine and one. Survivors?'

'Five. Second Officer Jones, our wives, and Doctor Andrew Adams, a Fellow of the College of Study.'

'It can't be a lifecraft after this long – what shape is the hulk in?'

'Bad. Can't immerge. The whole Top is an ungodly mess and some of the rest of her won't hold air – air, hell! Section Fourteen won't hold shipping crates! The Chaytors are okay, but five of the Wesleys are shot, and all of the Q-converters. Most of the Grahams are leaking like sieves, and ...'

'Hold it, Babe. They want this on a recorder downstairs, too. The newshawks are knocking the doors down. This marriage bit. The brides – who are they?'

Deston told him. Just that; no more.

'Okay. They want a lot more than that; especially the sobbers, but that can wait. What happened?'

'I don't know. You'd better fly a Fellow of the College over there to talk to Doc Adams. Maybe he can explain it to another Big Brain, but I wouldn't bet, even on that.'

'Okay. Downstairs is hooked in and so is Brass. Give us everything you know or can guess at.'

Deston spoke steadily for thirty minutes. He did not mention the gangsters, nor psionics, nor the extraordinary long periods of gestation; otherwise his report was accurate and complete. When it was done, French said:

'Mark off. Off the air, Babe – nice job. Now, Herc, on the air. Mark on. Second Officer Theodore Jones reporting. You're orbiting the fourth planet of a sun. What sun? Where?'

'I don't know. Unlisted; we're in unexplored territory. Standard reference data as follows,' and Jones read off a long list of observations; not only of the brightest stars of the galaxy, but also of the standard reference points, such as S-Doradus, lying outside it. 'When you get that stuff all plotted you'll find a hell of a big confusion, but I hope there aren't enough stars in it but what you'll be able to find us sometime.'

'Mark off. Don't make me laugh, Herc; your probable center will spear it. If there's ever more than one star in any confusion *you* set up I'll eat all the extras. But there's a dozen Big Brains, gnawing their nails off to the elbows to talk to Adams. So put him on and let's get back to sleep, huh? They're cutting this mike now.'

'Hold it!' Deston snapped. 'I want some information too, dammit! What's your Greenwich?'

'Zero seven one four plus thirty-seven seconds. So go to bed, you night-prowling owl.'

'Of what day, month, and year?' Deston insisted.

'Friday, Sep...' French's voice was replaced by that of a much older man; very evidently that of a Fellow of the College.

After listening for less than a minute, Barbara took Deston's arm and led him away. 'Any at all of *that* gibberish is exactly that much too much, husband mine. So I think we'd better take Captain French's advice, don't you?'

Since there was only one star in Jones' 'confusion' (by the book, *Volume of Uncertainty*) finding the *Procyon* was no problem at all. High Brass came in quantity and the whole story, except for one bit of biology, was told. Two huge sub-spacegoing machine-shops also came, and a battalion of mechanics, who worked on the crippled liner for over three weeks.

Then the *Procyon* started back for Earth under her own subspace drive, under the command of Captain Theodore Jones. His first and only command for the Interstellar Corporation of course, since he was a married man. Deston had tendered his resignation while still a First Officer, but his superiors would not accept it until after his promotion 'for outstanding services' had come through. Thus Captain Carlyle Deston and his wife and son were dead-heading, not quite back to Earth, but to the transfer point for Newmars.

Just before that transfer point was reached, Deston went 'up Top' to take leave of his friend, and Jones greeted him with:

'I've been trying to talk to Doc again; but wherever he starts or whatever the angle of approach he *always* boils it down to this: "Subjective time is measured by the number of learning events experienced". I ask you, Babe, what in *hell* does that mean? If anything?'

'I know. Me, too. It sounds like it ought to mean *something*, but I'll be damned if I know what. However, if it makes the old boy happy and gives the College a toe-hold on subspace, what do *we* care?'

And at this same time Barbara had been visiting Bernice. They had of course been talking about the babies, and an awkward silence had fallen.

'Oh,' Barbara licked her lips. 'So you get those feelings too.'

'Too?' Bernice's face paled. 'But they're absolutely normal, Bobby. Perfect. Absolutely perfect in every respect.'

'I know . . . but once in a while . . . an aura or something . . . it scares me simply witless.'

'I have them too. Not often, but . . . well, they began even before she was born.'

'Oh? So did mine! But they *aren't* monsters, Bun! I just *know* they aren't!'

36

'So do I. Of course they aren't. They aren't even mutants. Look, Bobby, let's think instead of emoting. All four of us are very strongly psychic, but each of us got it from only one side of the family. With both parents psychic the effect would have to be intensified, wouldn't it?'

'It would, at that. That's the answer, Bun, you solved the mystery. They have the same thing we have, except more of it. But they *can't* have real powers without experience or knowledge, so when they grow up they'll be stronger than we are and we'll learn from them.'

'That's the way it is. I'm sure of it.'

'So am I, now. I feel a lot better, Bun. I've got to gallop. This isn't goodbye, dear – I'll see you soon and often – it's just so long.'

CHAPTER THREE

Deston the Dowser

For a week the Destons were busy settling down in their low, sprawling home on Newmars. Deston had not had time to think about a job, and Barbara did not intend to let him think about one. Wherefore, the first free evening they had, while they were sitting close together on a davenport near the fire-place in their living-room, she said:

'I know how much you really want to explore deep space. I do, too. I'm sure we could accomplish something worth while, and I'd like very much to leave a size five-bee footprint on the sands of time, too. There's a way we can do it.'

Deston stiffened. 'I'd like to believe that, pet. I'd give my right leg to the hip and one eye – but what's the use of kidding ourselves? Your last buck, even if I'd lay it on that kind of a line, wouldn't cover the nut.'

'The way things are now, no. But listen. What is the one single thing that all civilization needs most desperately?'

'Uranium. You know that as well as I do.'

'I know; but I want you to think very seriously about the reality, the intensity, and the importance of that need. So elucidate.'

'Okay.' Deston shrugged his shoulders. 'It's the *sine qua non* of interstellar flight; of running the Chaytor engine. While all the uranium does is trigger the power intake, the bigger the Chaytor the bigger its Wesley has to be and the faster the uranium gets used up. Uranium's so scarce that except for controls its price would be fantastic. Hence the black market, where its price *is* fantastic. Hence bribery, corruption, and so forth. Half of the deviltry and skulduggery on all ninety-six planets is due to the hard fact that the supply of uranium can not be made to equal the demand. Sufficient?'

'Sufficient. Now for it. I've been hinting, but you've been shying away from psionics as though it were something to be ashamed of, and it isn't. In space we were all too horribly busy to do anything about it, but now I'm going to slug you with it. Carl, I *know* that you're the first real metal-dowser that ever lived. Don't ask me how I know; I just know. If you'll just get serious and really *work* on your latent abilities you'll be able to find any metal you please as easily as I can find oil.'

Tightening his arm, he swung her around and stared into her eyes. 'I know all about things that way. Hunches. So how do I go about learning to dowse metal?'

'Like I did. I started on coal, holding a lump in my hand. I concentrated on it until I could sense everything about it, clear down to its atomic structure. Then, looking at a map and spreading it out, I could see every coal deposit on the planet. So here's a piece of copper tube and a blueprint of this house. Concentrate as hard as you possibly can; then you'll know what I mean.'

'Oh – so you've been laying for me.'

'Of course I have. This is the first time we've had any time.'

'Okay. I'll give it the good old college try.'

He tried it. He tried over and over again. For half an hour he put everything he had into the effort. Then, coming out of his near-trance, he wiped his sweating face and said, 'I can't swing it alone, pet. There must be *some* way for you to show me how the damn thing goes – if I've got what it takes.'

'Of *course* you have!' she snapped. 'Don't think for a single second you haven't – I *know* you have, I tell you!'

'If you know it, it's so and I believe it. But the question still is – *how*? But say, you can read my mind, can't you?'

Her eyes widened. 'Why, I don't know. I never tried to, of course ... but what good would *that* do?'

'Just a hunch. With that close a contact, maybe some of your knowledge will rub off onto me. Especially if you push.'

'I'll push, all right; but remember, no resistance. With such a chilled-steel mind as yours, *nothing* could get through.'

'No resistance. Just the opposite. I'll pull you in with every tractor I can bring to bear. Across a table?'

'Uh-uh, this is better. Closer.'

They gripped hands and stared into each other's eyes. For a long two minutes nothing happened; then Barbara broke contact. 'I got a little,' she said. 'You were fighting with a boy twice your size. A red-haired boy with a lot of freckles.'

'Huh? Spike McGonigle – that was twelve or fifteen years ago and I haven't thought of the guy since! But I got something, too. You were at a party, wearing a red dress cut down to here and emerald ear-rings. You put a slightly pie-eyed chicken colonel flat on his face because he wouldn't take "no" for an answer.'

'Not on his *face*, surely ... oh, yes, I remember. But *this* isn't what we wanted, at all. However, it's something; so let's keep on with it, shall we?'

They kept it up until bed-time, and went at it again immediately after breakfast next morning. Progress was maddeningly slow, but it was progress. Progress marked by a succession of stabbing, fleeting pains, each of which was followed by the opening of an entire vista of one-ness. They did not complete the operation that day, or in three more, or in a week; but finally, the last vista opened, they sat for minutes in what was neither ecstasy nor consternation, but something having the prime elements of both. For full mental rapport is the ultimate intimacy; more intimate by far than any other union possible.

Barbara licked her bloodless lips and said, not in words but purely in thought, 'Oh, Carl! So *this* is what telepathy really is!'

'Must be.' He was not speaking aloud, either. '*What* the people who talk about telepathy don't know about it!'

'Oh, this is *wonderful*! But it isn't what we were after, at all.'

'But it may very well be a prerequisite, hon. I won't be just watching you do it now; we'll be doing it as one. So break out your bottle of crude oil.'

'Oh, that won't be necessary. I know oil so well that we won't need a sample, not even a map. Look – it goes like this . . . see?'

'*See!* Listen, Bobby. How could anybody ever learn such an incredibly complex technique as that all by himself? How did you ever learn it?'

'Looked at that way . . . I guess maybe I didn't. I must have been born with it.'

'That makes sense. Now let's link up and take that copper atom apart clear down to whatever makes up its theta, mu, and pi mesons.'

But they didn't. Much to the dismayed surprise of both, their combined attack was no more effective than Deston's alone had been. He frowned at the sample in thought, then said, 'Okay. The thing's beginning to make sense.'

'What sense?' she demanded. 'Not to me, it isn't. Is this another of your hunches?'

'No. Logic. I'm not sure yet, but one more test and I will be. Water. You won't need a sample?'

'No more than with oil. It's just about the same technique. Like this . . . there. But it doesn't get me anywhere. Does it you?'

'Definitely. Look, Bobby. Water, gas, oil, and coal. Oxygen, hydrogen, and carbon. Oxygen, the highest, is atomic number eight. Maybe you can – what'll we call it? "Handle"? – handle the lower elements, but not the higher ones. So maybe both of us together can handle 'em all. If this hypothesis is valid, you already know helium, lithium, beryllium . . .'

'Wait up!' she broke in. 'I wouldn't recognize any one of them if it should stop me on the street and say hello.'

'You just think you wouldn't. How about boron, as in boric acid? Eye-wash, to you?'

Her mind flashed to the medicine cabinet in the bathroom. 'I *do* know it, at that. I've never handled it, but I can.'

'Nice. How about sodium, as in common salt?'

'Can do.'

'Chlorine, the other half of salt?'

'That hurt a little – took a little time – but I made it.'

'Fine! The hypothesis begins to look good. Now we'll

tackle calcium together. In bones – my thick skull, for instance.'

'*Ouch!* That really hurt, Carl. And you did it. I couldn't have, possibly, but I followed you in and I know it now. But golly, it felt like ... like it was stretching my brain all out of shape. Like giving birth to a child, something. I *told* you you're stronger than I am, Carl, but I want to learn it all. So go right ahead, but take it a little slower, please.'

'Slow it is, sweetheart,' and they went ahead.

And in a couple of days they could handle all the elements of the periodic table.

Then and only then did they go back to what they had started out to do. Seated side by side, each grasping the short length of metal, they stared at the blueprint and allowed – or, rather, impelled – their perception to pervade the entire volume of the house.

'We've *got* it!' Deston yelled, aloud. 'It *is* a new sense – a sixth sense – and *what* a sense!'

They could see – sense – perceive – every bit of copper in, under, and around the building; the network of tubes and pipes stood out like the blood-vessels in a plastic model of the human body. While the metal was not transparent in the optical sense, they could perceive in detail the outside, the inside, and the ultimately fine structure of the material of each component part of the whole gas-and-water-supply installation.

'Oh, you *did* it, Carl!'

'*We* did it – whatever it is. But I can do it alone now; I know exactly how it goes. This is really terrific stuff.' He lost himself in thought, then went on, 'And the cardinal principle of semantics is that the map is *not* the territory. Let's go in the library, roll out the big globe of Newmars, and give this planet a going-over like no world ever got before.'

'Oh, that'll be fun! Let's!'

'And you wouldn't, by any chance, just happen to have samples of uranium oxide, pitchblende, and so forth on hand, would you?'

'Not by chance, no. I done it on purpose. Here they are.'

There is no need to go into detail as to the exact fashion in which they explored the enormous volume of the planet, or as to exactly what they found. It is enough to say that they learned; and that, having learned, the techniques became almost automatic and the work itself became comparatively easy.

The next morning Deston made another suggestion. 'Bobby, what do you say about seeing what we can do with that forty-eight-inch globe of Tellus?'

'*Tellus!* Light-years and light-years from here? Are you completely out of your mind?'

'Maybe I'm a little mad with power, but listen. If the map actually is the territory it's scale that counts, not distance. It's inconceivable, of course, that there isn't a limit somewhere – but where is it? I've got an urge to spread our wings a little.'

'A highly laudable objective, I'd say, but I'll bet you a cookie that Tellus is 'way beyond that limit. Drag out the globe ... ah, there you are, sweet mother world of the race! Now watch out, Mom; ready or not, here we come!'

They went; and when they found out that they could scan and analyze the entire volume of Earth, mile by plotted cubic mile, as easily and as completely as they could that of Newmars on whose surface they were, they stared at each other, appalled.

'Well ... I ... that is ...' Barbara licked her lips and gulped. 'I owe you a cookie, I guess, Carl.'

'Yeah.' But Deston was not thinking of cookies. 'That tears it. It really does. Wide open. Rips it up and down and sidewise.'

'It does for a fact. But it makes the objective even more laudable than ever, I'd say. How do you think we should go about it?'

'There's only one way I can see. I said I'd never spend a dime of your money, remember? I take it back. I think we'd better charter one of WarnOil's fast subspacers and buy all the off-Earth maps, star-charts, and such-like gear we can get hold of.'

'Charter? Pfooie! We own WarnOil, silly, subspacers and everything else. In fee simple. So we'll just take one. I'll arrange that; so you can take off right now after your maps and charts and whatever. Scoot!'

'Wait up a bit, sweet. We'll have to have Doc Adams.'

'Of course. He'll be tickled silly to go.'

'And Herc Jones for captain.'

'I'm not so sure about that.' Barbara nibbled at her lower lip. 'A little premature, don't you think, to unsettle him and Bun – raise hopes that may very well turn out to be false – before we find out what we can actually do?'

'Could be. Okay, fellow explorer – the count-down is on and all stations are in condition GO.'

Of all the preparations for the first expedition into the unknown, only one is really noteworthy; the interview with Doctor Adams in his home. For months he had been concentrating on the subether and his zeta field; and when he learned what the purpose of the trip was, and that he would have a free hand and an ample budget, he became enthusiastic indeed.

To a mind of such tremendous power and range as his, it was evident from the first that his young friends had changed markedly since he had last seen them. This fact was of course a challenge. Adams was tall and lean and gray; and, although he was sixty years old, he almost never worked at a desk. He thought better, he said, on his feet. He had always reminded Deston of a lean, gray tomcat on the prowl for prey. He was on his feet now, pacing about.

Suddenly he stopped, clasped his hands behind his back, and stared at Deston through the upper sections of his gold-rimmed trifocals. 'You two youngsters,' he said flatly, 'are using telepathy. Using it consciously, accurately, and completely informatively – a thing that, to my knowledge, has never before been demonstrated.'

'Oh?' Barbara's eyes widened. 'When we thought we were talking did we sometimes forget to?'

'Only in part. Mainly because of a depth of understanding – deduced to be sure, but actual nonetheless – impossible to language.' Then, Adams-like, he went straight to the point. 'Will you try to teach it to me?'

'Why, of course!' Barbara exclaimed. 'That, Uncle Andy, was very much on the agenda.'

'Thank you. And Stella, too, please? Her mind is of precisionist grade and is of greater sensitivity than my own.'

'Certainly,' Deston assured him. 'The more we can spread this ability around the better it will be for everybody.'

Adams left the room then, and in a minute or so came back with his wife; a slender, graceful, gray-haired woman of fifty-odd.

Both Andrew and Stella Adams had been students all their lives. They knew how to study. They had the brain capacity – the blocked or latent cells – to learn telepathy and many other things. They learned rapidly and thoroughly. Neither of them, however, could or ever did learn how to 'handle' any substance. In fact, very few persons of their time, male or female, ever did learn more than an insignificant fraction of the Destons' unique ability to dowse.

In compensation, however, the Adamses had nascent powers peculiarly their own. Thus, before they went to bed that night, Andrew and Stella Adams were exploring vistas of reality that neither of the Destons would ever be able to perceive.

Out in deep space, the Destons worked slowly at first. They actually landed on Cerealia, the most fully surveyed of all the colonized planets; and on Galmetia, only a little less so, as it was owned *in toto* by Galactic Metals; and on Lactia, the dairy planet.

Deston worked first on copper; worked on it so long and so intensively that he could find and handle and tridi any deposit of the free metal or of any of its ores with speed and precision, wherever any such might be in a planet's crust. Then he went on up the line of atomic numbers, taking big jumps – molybdenum and barium and tungsten and bismuth – up to uranium, which was what he was after.

Barbara did not work with him on metals very long; just long enough to be sure that she could be of no more help. She didn't really like metals, and she had her own work to do. It was just as important to have on file all possible data concerning water, oil, gas, and coal.

They worked together, however, at perfecting their techniques. Any thought of determining the working limits of psionic abilities had been abandoned long since; they were

45

trying with everything they had to minimize the necessity of using maps and charts. They succeeded. Just as Barbara, while still a child, had become able to work without samples; so both of them learned how to work without maps. All they had to know, finally, was where a solar system was; they could fix their sense of perception upon any star they could see, and hence could study all its planets. They tried to work independently of star-charts – to direct their attention to any point in space at will – but it was to be years before they were able to reach that peak of ability.

Deston found many deposits of copper, one of them very large, on the colonized plants; but he was interested in copper only as a means, not as an end. What he wanted was a mountain of uranium; and uranium was just as scarce on all ninety-five colonized planets as it was on Earth.

He knew that his sensitivity to his wife's money was the only flaw in their happiness. He knew what Barbara thought about his attitude, with the sure knowledge possible only to full mental rapport. She did not like it; and she, who had never had a money problem in her whole life, could not fully understand it. He should be big enough, she thought deep down and a little disappointedly, not to boggle so at such an unimportant thing as money.

But that attitude was innate and so much a part of Deston's very make-up that he could not have changed it had he tried, and he would not try. Almost everyone who knew them had him labelled as a fortune-hunter, and that label irked him to the core. It would continue to irk him as long as it stuck, and the only way he could unstick it was to do something – or make money enough – to make him as important as she was. A mountain of uranium – even a small mountain – would do it two ways. It would make him a public benefactor and a multi-millionaire. So – by the living God! – he would find uranium before he went back to civilization.

Adams and his scientists and engineers had developed an ultra-long-range detector for zeta fields, and they had not been able to find any other hazards to subspace flight. Hence they had been constantly stepping up their vessel's speed. Originally a very fast ship, she was now covering in hours distances

46

that had formerly required days.

On and on, then, faster and faster, deeper and deeper into the unexplored immensities of deep space the mighty flyer bored; and Deston finally found his uranium. They landed upon a mountainous, barren continent of a lifeless world. They put on radiation armor and labored busily for nineteen hours.

Then Deston told the captain, 'Line out for Newmars, please, and don't drag your feet.'

And that night, in the Destons' cabin: 'Why so glum, chum?' Barbara asked. 'That's the best thing for civilization that ever was and the biggest bonanza there ever was. I'd think you'd be shrieking with joy – I've almost been – but you look as though you'd just lost your pet hound.'

Deston shrugged off his black mood and smiled. 'The trouble is, petsy, it's *too* big. Too damned big altogether. And *look* at our planet Barbizon. Considering the size of the deposits and what and where the planet is, nobody except Galactic Metals could handle the project the way it should be handled.'

'Well, would that be bad? To sell it or lease it to them?'

'Not bad, honey; impossible. All those big outfits are murder in the first degree. Before I could get anywhere with them – if they find out I found it, even – GalMet would own not only Barbizon, but my shirt and pants, too.'

Barbara laughed gleefully. 'How well I know *that* routine! Do you think they don't do it in oil, too? But WarnOil's legal eagles know all about skulduggery and monkey business and fine print – none better. So here's what let's do. File by proxy ... and maybe you and I had better incorporate ourselves. Just us two; Deston and Deston, say. Develop it by another proxy, making darn sure that they don't find any uranium at all and nothing else that's worth more than three or four dollars a ton ...'

'Huh? Why not?'

'Because GalMet's spy system, darling, is very good indeed.'

'All right, but we've *still* got to make the approach ... dammit, I'd give it to GalMet for *nothing* if it'd give us a half hour face-to-face with Upton Maynard, to show him what you

47

and I together can do.'

'Not free. Ever. Just a bargain that he can't possibly resist. You figure out what that would be and I'll arrange the face-to-face with His High Mightiness Maynard.'

'Oh? Could be, at that, since you're a Big Time Operator yourself. You could go through the massed underlings like a snow-plow, hurling 'em kicking, far and wide.'

'Oh, no, I won't go through channels at all with a thing as big as this is. Shock treatment – I'll hit 'em high and hard.'

'Fine, gal – fine! So I'll write to Herc; tell him he can start getting organized. He'll be tickled to death – he doesn't like flying a desk any better than I do.'

'Write? Call him up, right now.'

'I'll do that, at that. I'm not used yet to not caring whether a call is across the street or across half of space.'

'And I want to talk to Bun, anyway.'

The call was put through and Barbara talked to Bernice for some fifteen minutes. Then Deston took over, finding that Jones was anything but in love with his desk job. When Deston concluded, '... family quarters aboard. Full authority and full responsibility of station. Full captain's pay and rank plus a nice bonus in stock,' Captain Theodore Jones was fairly drooling.

CHAPTER FOUR

Organization of the Little Gem

In comparison with silicon or aluminum, which together make up almost thirty-six percent of the Earth's crust, copper is a very scarce metal indeed, amounting to only a very small fraction of one percent. Yet it is one of the oldest-worked and most widely useful of all metals, having been in continuous demand for well over six thousand Tellurian years.

Yet of all the skills of man, that of mining cuprous ores had perhaps advanced the least. There had been some progress, of course. Miners of old could not go down very deep or go in very far; there was too much water and not enough air. The steam engine helped; it removed water and supplied air. Electricity helped still more. Tools also had improved; instead of wooden sticks and animal-fat candles there was a complex gadgetry of air-drills and electric saws and explosives, and there was plenty of light.

Basically, however, since automation could not be economically applied to tiny, twisting, erratic veins of ore, the situation remained unchanged. Men still crawled and wriggled to where the copper was. Brawny men, by sheer power of muscle, still jackassed the heavy stuff out to where the automatics could get hold of it.

And men still died, in various horrible fashions and in callously recorded numbers, in the mines that were trying to satisfy the insatiable demand for the red metal that is one of the prime bases upon which the technology of all civilization rests.

And the United Copper Miners, under the leadership of its

president, Burley Hoadman, refused to tolerate any advancement whatever in automation. Also, UCM was approaching, and rapidly, its goal – the complete unionization of every copper mine of the Western Hemisphere of Earth.

A few months before the events recorded in the preceding chapter, then, in the Little Gem, a comparatively small copper mine in Colorado, a mile and a half down and some six miles in, Top Miner Grant Purvis half-lay-half-crouched behind a two-hundred-fifty-pound Sullivan Slugger air-drill operating under one hundred seventy-five pounds per square inch of compressed air. He was a big man, and immensely strong. He was six feet two inches tall; most of his two hundred thirty-five pounds was hard meat, gristle, and bone. His leather-padded right knee was jammed against the wall of his tiny work-space; the hobnail-studded sole of his left boot was jammed even more solidly into a foot-hole cut into the hard rock of the floor. With his right shoulder and both huge hands he was holding the Sullivan to its work – the work of driving an inch-and-a-quarter steel into the face. And the monstrous, bellowing, thundering, shrieking Slugger, even though mounted upon a short and very heavy bar, sent visible tremors through the big man's whole body, clear down to his solidly-anchored feet.

In his shockingly cramped quarters Purvis changed steel; shifted the position of his Sullivan's mounting bar; cut new foot-holes; kept on at his man-killing task until the set of powder-holes was in. Then he dismounted the heavy drill and, wriggling backwards, lugged it and its appurtenances out into the main stope to make room for the powderman.

As he straightened up, half paralyzed by the position and the strain of his recent labors, another big man lunged roughly against him.

'Wot tha hell – sock *me*, willya?' the man roared, and swung his steel-backed timberman's glove against Purvis' mouth and jaw.

Purvis went down.

'Whatcha tryin' ta pull off, Frank?' the shift-boss yelled, rushing up and jerking his thumb toward the rise. 'You know better'n that – fightin' underground. You're fired – go on top an' get yer time.'

'Wha'd'ya mean, fired?' Frank growled. 'He started it, tha crumb. He slugged me first.'

'You're a goddam liar,' the powderman spoke up, setting his soft-leather bag of low explosive carefully down against the foot of the hanging wall. 'I seen it. Purve didn't do nothin'. Not a goddam thing. Besides, he wasn't in no shape to. He didn't lift a finger. You socked him fer nothin'.'

'Oh, yeah?' Frank sneered. 'Stone blind all of a sudden, I guess? I leave it to tha rest of 'em —' waving a massive arm at the two muckers and the electrician, now standing idly by, '— if he didn't sock me first. They all seen it.'

All three nodded, and the electrician said, positively, 'Sure Purve socked him first. We all seen 'im do it.'

Purvis struggled to his feet. He shook off a glove, wiped his bleeding mouth, and stared for a moment at the blood-smeared back of his hand. Then, and still without a word, he bent over and picked up a three-foot length of inch-and-a-quarter steel.

'Hold it, Purve – hold it!' The shift-boss put both hands against the big man's chest and pushed, and the atrocious weapon dropped with a clang to the hard-rock floor. 'Thass better. They's somethin' damn screwy here. It just don't jibe.'

He crossed over to his telephone and dialed. 'Say boss, what do I do when I fire a nap fer startin' a fight underground an' he won't go out on top? An' three other bastards say somethin' I saw good an' plain with my own eyes didn't hap ... okay, I'll hold ... okay ... yeah ... but listen. Mr. *Speers*' office! Thass takin' it awful high up, ain't it, just to fire a nogoodnik that ... okay, okay, now you hold it.' Turning his head, the shift-boss said, 'They want us all up on top an' they wanta know if you wanta go up under yer own air or will they send down some guards an' drag y'all tha way up there by yer goddam feet?'

They did not want to be dragged, so Shift-Boss McGuire said, into the phone, 'Okay, we're on our way up,' and hung up.

The seven men wriggled down the rise – the steeply-sloping passage, about the diameter of a barrel, that was the only opening into the stope – to the tributary tunnel some three hundred feet below. As they were walking along this tunnel toward the main drift and its electric cars, Purvis said:

'You said it, Mac, about it's bein' a hell of a long ways up to have to take firin' a louse like him. What'd they say?'

'Nothin'.' McGuire said. 'Nothin' at all.'

'The higher the better,' the electrician – who had done most of the talking up in the stope – growled. 'The bigger the man we can get up to with this thing, the harder you three finkin' bastards are goin' ta get the boots put to ya. You ain't got a prayer. It's four ta three, see?'

'Hold it, Purve – I said *hold it*!' McGuire shouted, grabbing the miner's right arm with both hands and hanging on – and Purvis did stop his savage motion. 'Like I said, Purve, this whole deal stinks. It don't add up – noways. An' what surprised me most was that nobody up on top was surprised at all.'

'Huh?' the electrician demanded, with a sudden change in manner and expression. 'Why not? Why wasn't they?'

'I wouldn't know,' the shift-boss replied, quietly, 'but we'll maybe find out when we get up there. But I'm tellin' you four apes somethin' right now. Shut up and stay shut up. If any one of you opens his trap just one more time I'll let Purve here push a mouthful of teeth down his goddam throat.'

Wherefore the rest of the trip to the office of Superintendent Speers, the Big Noise of the Little Gem, was made in silence.

Charles Speers was a well-built, well-preserved man nearing sixty. His hair, although more white than brown, was still thick and bushy. His eyes, behind stainless-steel-rimmed trifocals, were a clear, sharp gray. His narrow, close-clipped mustache was brown. When his visitors were all seated he pushed a button on his desk, looked at the shift-boss and said:

'Mr. McGuire, please tell me what happened; exactly as you saw it happen.' McGuire told him and he looked at the powderman. 'Mr. Bailey, I realize that no two eyewitnesses ever see any event in precisely the same way, but have you anything of significance to add to or subtract from Mr. McGuire's statement of fact?'

'No, sir. That's the way it went.'

'Mr. Purvis, did you or did you not strike the first blow?'

'I did not, sir. I'll swear to that. I didn't lift a finger – not 'til after, I mean. Then I lifted a piece of steel, but Mac here stopped me before I could hit him with it.'

'Thank you. This is interesting. Very.' Speers' voice was as clipped as his mustache. 'Now, Mr. Grover C. Shields – or whatever your real name may be – as a non-participating witness and as spokesman apparent for the majority of those present at the scene of violence, please give me your version of the affair.'

'They're lyin' in their teeth, all three of 'em,' the electrician growled, sullenly. 'But what's that "real name" crack supposed to mean? An' say, are ya puttin' all this crap on a record?'

'Certainly. Why not? However, this is not a court of law and you are not under oath, so go ahead.'

'Not me. Not by a damsight, you fine-feathered slicker. Not without a mouthpiece, an' nobody else does, neither.'

'That's smart of you. And you're still sticking to the argot, eh, Mr. – ah – Shields?' The mine superintendent's smile was exactly as humorous as the edge of a cut-throat razor. 'Such camouflage is of course to be expected. Come over here to the desk, please. I would like to glance at your hands.'

'Like hell you will!' Shields snarled, leaping to his feet. 'We're gettin' tha hell outa here right now!'

'Mr. Purvis,' Speers said, quietly, 'I would like to look at that man's hands. Don't break him up any more than is necessary, but I want those hands flat on this desk, palms up.'

Since Shields was already on his feet, he reached the desk and spread his hands out flat before Purvis touched him, exclaiming as he did so, 'An' *that's* on record, too, wise guy!'

'I'm afraid it may not be,' Speers said, gently, shaking his head. 'This machine is not a new model; it misses an item occasionally. But you see what I mean?' Speers paused, and from the ceiling above there came the almost inaudible click of a camera shutter. 'When did those hands ever do any real work? Resume your seat, please.' The alleged electrician did so. 'I have here seven personnel cards, from which I will read certain data into the record. George J. McGuire, Shift-Boss, length of service twenty-four years, black spots – demerits, that is – nineteen. Clinton F. Bailey, Powderman, fifteen years, ten demerits. Grant H. Purvis, Top Miner, twelve years, eight demerits. Each of these three has four or five times as many stars as black spots.

'On the other hand, John J. Smith, Mucker, forty-three days and thirty-three demerits. Thomas J. Jones, Mucker, twenty-nine days and thirty-one demerits. Frank D. Ormsby Timberman, twelve days and twenty demerits. Grover C. Shields, Electrician, five days and eleven demerits. There are no stars in this group. These data speak for themselves. The discharge of Ormsby is sustained. I hereby discharge the other three – Shields, Smith, and Jones – myself. You four go back, change your clothes, pick up your own property, turn in company property, and leave. Your termination papers and checks will be in the mail tonight. Get out.'

They got.

Speers pressed a button and his secretary, a gray-haired, chilled-steel virgin of fifty, came in. 'Yes, sir?'

'Please take Mr. Purvis there,' he pointed, 'over across and let the doctors look at him.'

'Oh, this ain't nothin' . . .' the miner began.

'It would be if I had it.' Speers smiled; a genuine smile. 'You do exactly what the doctors tell you to do. Okay?'

'Okay, sir. Thanks.'

'And Miss Mills, he's on full time until they let him go back to work full time.'

'Yes, sir. Come with me, young man,' and she led the big miner out of the room.

Still smiling, Speers turned to the two remaining men. 'Are you wondering what this is all about, or do you know?'

'I could maybe guess, if there'd been any UCM organizers around,' McGuire said, 'but I ain't heard of any. Have you, Clint?'

'Uh-uh.' The powderman shook his head. 'I been kinda expectin' some, but there ain't been even a rumble yet.'

'Those four men were undoubtedly UCM goons. They will claim that Ormsby was assaulted and that all four of them were fired because of talking about unionization – for merely sounding out our people's attitude toward unionization. Tomorrow, or the next day at latest, the UCM will bottle us up tight with a picket line.'

'But it'd be a goddam lie!' Bailey protested

'Sure it would,' McGuire agreed. 'But they've pulled some awful raw stuff before now an' got away with it. D'you think they can get away with it here, Mr. Speers?'

'That's the jackpot question. With the Labor Relations Board, yes. Higher up, it depends ... but I want to do a little sounding out myself. When we close down, we'll try to place everyone somewhere, of course; but in the event of a very long shut-down, McGuire, how would you like to go out to one of the outplanets?'

'I couldn't. I don't know nothin' but copper-minin'.'

'I mean at copper mining.'

'Huh?' The shift-boss was so amazed as to forget temporarily that he was talking to the Big Boss. 'They ain't none. They ain't gonna be none. The UCM won't stand fer none.'

'But suppose there were some?'

'You mean a knock-down-'n'-drag-out fight with UCM?'

'Precisely.'

McGuire pondered this shockingly revolutionary thought for a long minute, his calloused right palm rasping against the stiff stubble on his chin. 'I still couldn't,' he decided, finally. 'Not just 'cause the union'd win, neither. I like it a hell of a lot better here on Earth. If I was young an' single, maybe. But I ain't so young yet —' he was all of forty-two years old, '— an' three of tha kids're still home yet an' my old woman'd raise hell an' put a chunk under it. Besides, me an' her both like ta know where we're at. So when they get us organized I'll join tha union an' work 'til I'm sixty an' then retire an' live easy on my pension an' old-age benefits. Thataway I'll know all tha time just where I'm at.'

'I see.' Speers' voice was almost a sigh. 'And you, Bailey?'

'Not fer me,' the powderman said, with no hesitation at all. 'George chirped it —' he jerked his left thumb at the shift-boss, '— about wantin' ta know where yer at. I got nothin' much against tha union. It costs, but between it an' tha outplanets I'll take the UCM any day in tha week. Hoady Hoadman takes care of his men, an' out on tha outplanets ya never know what's gonna happen. Yer takin' awful big chances all tha time. Too goddam big.'

'I see, and thanks, both of you. Call Personnel about replacements and go ahead as usual – until you run into a picket line. That is all for now.'

As the two men left Speers' office he flipped the switch of his squawk box. 'Get me GalMet, please. Maynard's FirSec, Miss Champ . . .'

'Miss *Champion*!' The switchboard girl committed the almost incredible offense of interrupting the Super. '*Herself?*'

'Herself,' Speers said, dryly. 'As I was about to say, the password in this case is as follows "Gem – Little – Operation". In that order, please.'

'Oh – excuse me, sir, please. I'll get right at it.'

It took seven minutes, but finally Miss Champion's face appeared upon Speers' screen; a face startlingly young and startlingly comely to be that of one of the top FirSecs of all Earth.

'Good afternoon, Mr. Speers.' Her contralto voice was as smooth and as rich as whipping cream. 'It has broken, then?'

'Yes. Four men made themselves so obnoxious that we had to discharge them just now. There has been no talk whatever of unionization as yet, but I expect a picket line tomorrow.'

'Thanks for letting us know so promptly, Mr. Speers. I can't get at him myself for fifteen minutes or so yet, but I'll tell him at the earliest possible moment.'

'That'll be fine, Miss Champion. Goodbye.'

CHAPTER FIVE

Counter-Organization

Miss Champion did not wait for Maynard to tell her what to do about the Little Gem situation. She acted. She sent out seven coded subgrams, to seven different planets. Then, on her own electric typewriter, she wrote two short notes, also in code. She addressed and sealed two envelopes – herself. She pushed a button. A girl came into her office. Miss Champion said, 'Here are two letters, Bessie. One is to Hatfield of In-Stell, the other to Lansing of WarnOil. Each is to be delivered by special messenger. Delivery is to be strictly-personal-signature-required. Thanks.'

So, within a very few days after UCM's picket line had sealed the Little Gem mine as tight as a bottle, fourteen men and one woman met in GalMet's palatial conference room in the Metals Building, in New York City on Earth. Men representing such a tremendous aggregate of power had never before met in any one room. Maynard called the meeting to order, then said:

'Many of you know most of the others here, but most of you do not know us all. Please stand as I introduce you. The lady first, of course. Miss Champion, my First Secretary.'

The lady, seated at a small desk off to one side of the great table, rose to her feet, bowed gracefully – not directly toward the camera – and resumed her position.

'Bryce of Metals.' A slender man of fifty, with an unruly shock of graying black hair, rose, nodded, and sat down.

'Wellington of Construction.' A tall, loose-jointed, sandy-haired man did the same.

'Zeckendorff of the Stockmen ... Stelling of Grain ... Killingsworth of the Producers ... Raymer of Transportation ... Holbrook of Communications ... these seven men are the presidents of the seven largest organizations of the Planetsmen – the organized production and service men and women of ninety-five planets.

'Will you stand up, please, Mr. Speers? ... Superintendent Speers, of the Little Gem, now being struck, one of the very few non-union copper mines in existence. Speers is sitting on a situation that very well may develop into the gravest crisis our civilization has ever known.

'Next, Admiral Guerdon Dann of Interstellar ... who may or may not, depending pretty largely upon the outcome of this meeting, become our Galaxians' Secretary of War.'

There was a concerted gasp at this, and Maynard smiled grimly. 'I speak advisedly. Each of us knows something, but not one of us knows it all. The whole, I think, will shock us all.

'DuPuy of Warner Oil ... represents the law; Interplanetary Law in particular.

'Phelps of Galactic Metals ... is our money man.

'Hatfield of Interstellar ... Lansing of Warner Oil ... and I, Maynard of Galactic Metals ... represent top management.

'Now to business. For almost two hundred years most managements have adhered to the Principle of Enlightened Self-Interest; so that, while both automation and pay-per-man-hour increased, production per man-hour increased at such a rate – especially on the planets – that there was no inflation. In fact, just slightly the opposite; for over a hundred and fifty years the purchasing power of the dollar showed a slight rising trend.

'Then, for reasons upon which there is no agreement – each faction arguing its case according to its own bias – the economic situation began to deteriorate and inflation set in. It has been spiralling. For instance, of the present price of copper, about two dollars and a half a pound, only twenty-five cents is ... Phelps?'

'Rate One, Anaconda, electrolytic, FOB smelter,' the

moneyman said, 'is two point four five seven dollars per pound. This breaks down into: labor, one hundred four point six cents; taxes, ninety-three point nine cents; all other costs, twenty-four point nine cents; mark-up, twenty-two point three cents.'

Almost everyone looked surprised; many of the men whistled.

Maynard smiled wryly and went on, 'Thanks, Desmond. Copper is of course an extreme case; *the* extreme case. That is because it is the only important metal, and one of the very few items of our entire economy, that is produced exclusively on Tellus. There are two reasons for this. First, automation can not be economically applied to copper mining on Tellus or anywhere else we know of; there are no known lodes or deposits big enough. Second, the UCM is the only union that has been able to enforce the dictum that its craft shall be confined absolutely to Tellus.

'So far, I have stated facts, with no attempt to allocate responsibility or blame. I will now begin to prophesy. Information has been obtained, from sources which need not be named . . .' Most of the men chuckled; only a few of them only smiled, '. . . which leads us to believe as follows:

'Burley Hoadman is in trouble in his UCM – internal trouble. There are several local leaders, one in particular being very strong, who do not like him hogging so much of the gravy for himself. They want to get their own snouts into the gravy trough, and are gathering a lot of votes. The best way he can consolidate his position is by making a spectacular play. The Little Gem affair is his opening wedge. If he can make us fight this issue very hard, he will pull a WestHem-wide copper strike. He will refuse to settle that strike for less than a seventy-five or one hundred percent increase in scale. Since the UCM's scale is already the highest in existence, that will make him a tin god on wheels.

'There hasn't been a really important strike for over fifty years; and this one will not be important unless we ourselves make it so by putting up a real fight. Gentlemen, we have two, and only two, alternatives; we can surrender or we can fight.

'If we surrender, every other union in existence will demand a similar increase and the Labor Relations Board will grant it – and I don't need to tell you that WestHem's corrupt judiciary and government will support the LRB. Neither do I need to dwell upon what these events will do to the already vicious spiral of inflation.

'It's easy to say "fight", but how far must we be prepared to go? The LRB will rule against us. We will appeal. While that appeal is pending, Hoadman will call all his copper miners out. That strike will be completely effective, and as all industry slows down the public will scream for GalMet's blood. All the mass media of WestHem will crucify me personally. As I said, we will lose the appeal – or perhaps even before that, the government will seize the mines and give Hoadman everything he wants. In either case, if we stop at that point, we will be in even worse shape than if we had surrendered without fighting at all.'

'But how much farther than that can we possibly go?' Zeckendorff demanded.

'I'm coming to that. If we fight at all, we must be prepared to go the full route. We'll drag the legal proceedings out as long as we can. Meanwhile we'll be developing copper mines on the planets. We have maps and your Metalsmen and Builders will be very good at that. We'll ram planetary copper down WestHem's collective throat. However, that ramming will not be easy. The government is very strong and it will do its utmost to block every move we make. So the most logical conclusion is that we will have to form a government of the planets and declare our complete independence of Tellus.

'We are already calling ourselves the Galaxians; that would be as good a name as any for the new government. That would probably involve a massive and effective blockade of Tellus, which in turn might cause the Nameless One of EastHem to launch his thermonuclear bombs. WestHem would retaliate, and it is distinctly possible that all Tellus might become a radioactive wasteland.'

The silence, which had been deepening steadily, was broken by an explosive '*Je-sus Christ!*' from peppery little Bryce of Metals.

'Precisely,' Maynard went on. 'That is why this meeting

was called. This is – at least I think it will become – the first meeting of the Board of Directors of the Galaxians, a government which is to adhere strictly to the Principle of Enlightened Self-Interest.

'What we can accomplish remains to be seen. We will have to exert extreme caution; we must keep ahead of the opposition; above all, we must be able at all times to pull up short of ultimate catastrophe to Tellus.

'Whether or not we fight at all depends absolutely upon the attitude of the Planetsmen. We must have solidarity. Hoadman expects the full support of Labor, even to the extremity of a general strike of all the unions of WestHem. This would necessitate the cooperation of the Planetsmen, and he expects even that. It is psychologically impossible for any man of Hoadman's stripe to understand that on the planets there is neither Capital nor Labor; that we Galaxians are all labor and are all capitalists. Hence it is clear that unless we are sure of virtual unanimity of all Galaxians we can not fight Hoadman at all.

'I now ask the supremely vital question – Do the Planetsmen, the most important segment by far of the Galaxians, want to go the route for a stable dollar, and all that it means? You seven may retire to a private room for discussion, if you like . . .'

'But I see you don't need to,' Maynard went on, as all seven men spoke practically at once; Holbrook of Communications being first by an instant. 'Peter Holbrook, president of the Associated Wavesmen, has the floor.'

Holbrook of Communications was the youngest man there. He was scarcely out of his twenties and was so deeply tanned that his crewcut, sun-bleached hair seemed almost white. He looked like a professional football player; or like the expert 'pole-climber' he had been until a year before. He stood up, cleared his throat, and said, 'You're right, Mr. Maynard, we don't need to discuss that point. We've thought about it and talked about it a lot. We have been and are highly concerned. But I'm not the one to talk about it here. I yield the floor to Mr. Egbert Bryce, President of the Society of Metalsmen, who has been coordinating us all along on this very thing.'

'*You*, Eggie?' Maynard asked, with a grin, and the tone of the meeting became less formal all of a sudden. 'And you never let me in on it?'

'Me,' the wiry, intense Bryce agreed. 'Naturally not. You're always beating somebody's ears down about presenting a half-developed program and ours isn't developed yet at all. But you've apparently made plans for a long time ahead.'

'Plenty of them, but they're all fluid. Nothing to go into at this point. Go ahead.'

'All right. On this basic factor there's no disagreement whatever. No doubt or question. Tellurian labor is a bunch of plain damned fools. Idiots. Cretins. However, that's only to be expected because everybody with any brains or any guts left Tellus years ago. There's scarcely any good breeding stock left, even. So about the only ones with brains left – except for the connivers, chiselers, boodlers, gangsters, and bastardly crooked politicians – and that goes for most Tellurian capitalists, too. Right?'

'Dead right, and we don't like it one bit better than you do. That's why so much Tellurian capital is all set to join us Galaxians when we leave Tellus.'

'Oh? You've gone that far? That's some of the stuff you'll go into later?'

'Yes. Go ahead.'

'All right. Every time I think of Tellurian labor it makes me so damn mad . . .'

'Eggie's the evenest-tempered man alive,' Wellington explained to the group at large. 'Mad all the time.'

'So what?' the bristly little man snapped. 'This is a thing to really get mad about. Slaves! Not slaves, either – slaves don't necessarily like slavery and they sometimes rebel. They're *serfs*. They *like* it that way. Dead level – advancement by seniority only – security – security, *hell*! No change – change scares the pants off of 'em. Don't want to think. Think? They *can't* think. One good thought would fracture their brainless damned skulls. And as long as they get a dollar an hour more than they're worth they don't give a cockeyed tinker's damn that their bosses are stealing everything in sight that isn't welded down – and sometimes even some of that. So you can paste it in your tall silk hat, Mayn, that the Planetsmen are free men, not brainless stupid serfs. Burley Hoadman won't get any help at all from us in stealing any more megabucks than he already has stolen. Not by seven thousand spans of Steinman truss.'

'Serf labor versus free men,' Maynard said, thoughtfully. 'Very well put, Eggie. In that connection, Speers of the Little Gem made a tape that shows the attitude of two of his best men. Will you play it, please, Miss Champion?'

She played it and Maynard went on, 'We have thousands of similar recordings. The serf attitude is characteristic of non-union, as well as of union labor, and also of white-collar people as a class. In fact, it is characteristic of Tellus as a planet. In contrast to that attitude, Zeckendorff of the Stockmen brought along a tape, of which we will hear the last few sentences. Scene, a meeting of Local 3856 of the Stockmen. Occasion, the voting upon a resolution presented by a Tellurian union organizer after weeks of work. Miss Champion?'

She flipped a switch and the speaker said, 'The vote is nine hundred seventy-eight against; none for. That kind of crap doesn't go on the planets, Gaylord, and if you had the brain God gave a goose you'd know it. That kind of security is what life-termers on the Rock have and we don't want any part of it. Nobody but ourselves is *ever* going to tell us what we can or can't do; so you'd better get the hell out of here and back to Tellus before somebody parts your hair with a routing iron.'

'I like that,' Maynard said. 'I like it very much. We knew in general what the sentiment is. However, pure Galaxianism – everybody pulling together harmoniously for the common good – is an ideal and as such can never be realized. The question is, can we approach it nearly enough to make it work?'

'We can try – and I think we can do it,' Bryce said. 'Anyway, Mayn, this first hurdle was the biggest one, and it's solid. We can guarantee that.'

'Wonderful!' Maynard said. 'Then we're in business – so let's get on with it.'

And the meeting went on; not only for all the rest of that day, but all day and every day for two solid weeks.

Shortly after the Deston Uranium Expedition got back to Newmars, the Deston family went to Earth and to the Warner-owned, luxury-type Hotel Warner; arriving there early of an evening.

Barbara was thoroughly accustomed to red-carpet treatment. She nodded and smiled; she used first names abundantly in greeting; to a few VIP's she introduced her 'husband and business partner, Carlyle Deston.' A retinue escorted them up to their penthouse suite; the manager himself made sure that everything was on the beam. Lock, stock, and barrel, the place was theirs.

Deston was not used to high life, but he made a good stab at it. Even when, at the imposing portals of the Deep Space Room, the velvet rope was whisked aside and the crowd of waiting standees was ignored. But when, at the end of the long and perfect meal and of the magnificent floor show, no check was presented for signature, Deston did reach for his wallet; to be stopped by a slight shake of Barbara's head.

'But no tip, even?' he protested, in a whisper.

'Of course not. The office takes care of everything. I never carry any money on Tellus.'

And next morning a Warner limousine took them across town to the immense skyscraper that was the Warner Building, where they were escorted ceremoniously up into WarnOil's innermost private office; a huge, luxuriously business-like office worthy in every respect of being the *sanctum sanctorum* of the second-largest firm in existence.

As has been said, Warner Oil was not a corporation. It was not even a partnership. It had been owned *in toto* by Barbara's parents as community property; it was now owned in the same way by Carlyle and Barbara Deston. Thus, it had no stock and no bonds and published no reports of any kind. It had no officers, no board of directors. It had one general manager and a few department heads; men who, despite the unimportance of their titles, were high on the list of the most powerful operators of Earth.

The Destons' first appointment was with General Manager Lansing; a big, bear-like man who picked Barbara up on sight and kissed her vigorously. '*Mighty* glad to see you again, Barbry. Glad to meet you, Carl.' He engulfed Deston's hand in a huge, hard paw. 'I apologize for thinking you were something that crawled out from under a rock. What you've been putting out is the damndest hairiest line of stuff I've seen since the old gut-cutting days when the old man and I were pups. But go ahead, Barbry.'

'First, I want to assure you, Uncle Paul, that neither Carl nor I will bother you any more than father did. Not as much, in fact, because neither of us has any delusions as to who is running WarnOil and we both want you to keep on running it.'

'Thanks, both of you. I was hoping, of course, but I got a little dubious when Carl here started showing so many long, sharp, curly teeth.'

'I understand. Second, I'm very glad that all of you – all that count, I mean – approve of Carl's program.'

'Should have incorporated long ago. As for the hell-raising – wow!' He slapped himself resoundingly on the leg. 'If we can push *half* of that stuff through it'll rock the whole damned galaxy on its foundations.'

'Third, how is the probate coming along?'

'I'd better call DuPuy in here for that, I . . .'

'Uh-uh, listen! We don't want two solid hours of whereases and hereinbefores. You talk our language.'

'We're steam-rollering 'em and it tickles me a foot up . . .' Lansing broke off and into a bellow of laughter. 'Every damn shyster the government has got is screaming bloody murder and threatening everything he can think of, including complete confiscation, but they haven't got a leg to stand on. They *can't* tax anything except what little stuff we have here on Tellus, and the inheritance tax on that will be only a few megabucks. Everything else belongs to Newmars, where there's no inheritance tax, no income tax, and hardly any property tax; and the fact that DuPuy writes Newmars' laws has nothing to do with the case. So after DuPuy and his crew get tired of quibbling and horsing around we'll pay it out of petty cash and never miss it.'

The Destons, during the next few days, held conference after conference, during which hundreds of details were ironed out; and as a by-product of which the news spread abroad that the heiress was very active indeed in the management of civilization-wide Warner Oil.

One morning, then, at nine o'clock, Barbara herself punched the series of letters and numerals that was the unlisted and close-held number of Doris Champion, the First Secretary of Upton Maynard, the president of Galactic Metals, the largest firm that civilization had ever known. Barbara's yellow-haired self appeared up on the FirSec's screen; Barbara saw a tall, cool, svelte brunette seated at something less than forty square feet of cluttered-seeming desk.

'Yes?' the FirSec asked, pleasantly, then stared – and lost a little of her cool poise. For every FirSec on Earth knew that yellow-haired woman by sight . . . and she was on the com *in person* and there had been nothing preliminary through channels, at all . . .

'That's right,' Barbara confirmed the unspoken thought. 'I'm Barbara Warner Deston of WarnOil. Please arrange a half-hour face-to-face for Mr. Deston and me with Mr. Maynard. There's no *great* hurry about it; any time today will do.'

'A half *hour*! *Today?* I'm terribly sorry, Mrs. Deston, but it's simply impossible. Why, he's booked solid for . . .'

'I know he's busy, Miss Champion. but so are we. Just tell him, please, that he is the first metals man we have called, and that tomorrow morning we will call Ajax.'

'Very well. If you'll give me a ten-second brief I'll see what we can possibly do and call you back.'

'No briefing. You have my private number. We'll be here until twelve o'clock.' Barbara's hand moved toward the cut-off switch; but Miss Champion, being a really smart girl, smelled a deal so big that even a top-bracket FirSec should duck – and *fast*. Wherefore:

'Hold the beam for fifty seconds, please, Mrs. Deston,' she said, and snapped down the button that made her office as tight as the vault of a bank. Then, 'I'm sorry to interrupt, Mr. Maynard, but Mrs. Deston of WarnOil is on.' She cut the audio then, but kept on speaking rapidly.

In thirty seconds the keen, taut face of Upton Maynard

appeared upon Barbara's plate. 'Good morning, Mrs. Deston. Something about metal, I gather? A little out of your line, isn't it?'

'That's right, Mr. Maynard,' Barbara agreed. She added nothing and for a moment he, too, was silent. Then:

'It'll have to be after closing,' Maynard said.

'That's quite all right. We'll fit our time to yours and you may name the place.'

'Seventeen ten. Your office. Satisfactory?'

'Perfectly. Thank you, Mr. Maynard,' and as Barbara's hand moved to cut com Maynard's voice went on:

'Get my wife, Miss Champion. Tell her I'll be late again getting home this evening.'

CHAPTER SIX

Maynard Buys the Package

At ten minutes past five Upton Maynard – a tall, lean, gray-haired man of fifty-odd, with a fringe of gray-brown hair on the sides and back of an otherwise completely bald head – was ushered into the Destons' private office.

'How do you do, Mister Maynard.' Barbara shook his hand cordially. 'You haven't met my husband. Carlyle Deston of Deston and Deston, Incorporated.'

As the two men shook hands, Maynard said, 'Incorporated, eh? This room is spy-proof, of course.'

'Solid,' Deston assured him.

'Okay, Mrs. Deston; what have you got?'

'Oh, it's Carl's party, really. My part of this project was just to bring you two men together,' and Deston took over.

'This is such a weirdie, Mr. Maynard, that I'll have to give it to you in stages.' He opened a bulging accordion-pleated case and began to spread its contents out over the table. 'Barbara and I discovered a planet that's thousands of parsecs beyond where any human being had ever been before. We named it "Barbizon". We did, by proxy, all the development work necessary to establish full ownership of the entire planet.

'Here's an envelope-full of astronautic and planetological data. Here's the file on registration, work, prove-up, transfer, and so on. Here's the certification, by Earth's most eminent firm of consulting engineers – Littleton, Bayless, Clifton, and Snelling itself, no less – that said planet Barbizon is a new discovery; that it is exactly where we said it was; that all required work has been done; that the bodies of manganese ore actually exist; that the *in situ* values run as high as three dollars and seventy-one cents per ton; that ...'

'*Suckered*, by God!' Maynard smacked his right hand flat down against the table's top. 'You *mouse-trapped* us – and that hasn't been done before for twenty-five years.' His sharp gray eyes bored into Deston's with rapidly-mounting respect. 'To skip the rest of the preliminaries for the moment, what have you two actually got?'

'I told you he's quick on the uptake, Carl,' Barbara laughed, and Deston said, 'Uranium, Mr. Maynard. Solid enough for full automation and enough of it to supply every possible demand of all civilization from now on.'

'My ... good ... God.' Maynard almost collapsed back into his chair. 'I knew it would have to be something big ... but *automated uranium* – okay. Go ahead. Somebody told you I like fully-developed presentations?'

'That's right. So here are the applications complete, and here are the final patents – not only from Tellus, but also from Galmetia and Newmars as well. All this is proof of ownership; with – according to DuPuy of WarnOil – no possibility whatever of successful challenge.'

The tycoon, who had begun to examine the documents, replaced them in the envelope and nodded approvingly. 'If Pete DuPuy says it's ironclad it really is. So I'm ready for Stage Two.'

'Here's a large-scale tri-di, in kilometers, of the largest orebody. There are a lot of others, but this whole plateau is one solid mass of jewelry ore. It isn't pure pitchblende or pure anything else; it's been altered down by heat and pressure to an average specific gravity of about ten point one. So it will run well over ten metric gigatons to the cubic kilometer, and you can read the cubage for yourself. Do you wonder that we wouldn't talk to anyone except you in person about it?'

'That's evident – quite.' For ten silent minutes Maynard scanned data with practised ease. Then, 'There are a few points that need clarification. I know that there are a lot of crackpot planetary claims allowed every year; on planets so worthless that they lapse into the public domain as soon as the crackpots lose interest, go broke, or die. Some of the discoverers, crackpots of the purest ray, even get *LitBay* certification for their junkballs. But how in *hell* did you mousetrap *LitBay* into certifying for worthless manganese ore a planet so reeking with radiation that any high-school girl with a handful of loose wire would have been shrieking "URANIUM!" half an hour before you landed? You know and I know that any field man of *theirs* who didn't read his scintillometer every time he goes into a strange restaurant for lunch would get fired right then.'

'That did take a little doing,' Deston admitted, and Barbara laughed again. 'Our development work was done by the stupidest people we could find, and the man we made foreman was the stupidest one of the whole lot. We didn't appear at any Bureau of Planets ourselves, of course. Our proxies were a couple of very good actors who had studied being crackpots until they were letter-perfect. Then we waited until all *LitBay's* field men were out on jobs. Our proxies were in such a tearing rush to get Barbizon nailed down that they opened negotiations by offering double fees – and you know what *LitBay's* usual fees are – for fast action. So since it was so obviously just another crackpot location, who was ever to know or care that it was a couple of office-boys who went out? And, some way or other, their scintillometers happened to get swapped temporarily for a pair of slightly finagled ones we had on board.'

'I see.' Maynard shook his head admiringly. 'So the thing never got upstairs in their office ... and I can't twit Littleton about it because it never got anywhere near me, either. Okay. Barbizon is of course lifeless – and the whole planet reeks – this ninety-hour limit on the manganese location is the coolest spot on the planet, I suppose.'

'That's right. We couldn't put anybody in armor, so we didn't let anybody work over ten six-hour days.'

'Refresh my memory.' Maynard flipped pages; came up with a single sheet of paper. 'Ah. All your men were over sixty-five – and the *LitBay* kids were on the ground only nine hours. So when this is over you'll notify them that they've had ten percent of a year's permissible radiation, I suppose.'

Barbara smiled meaningly. 'No, Mr. Maynard. It has just

occurred to me that you might like to tell Mr. Littleton about that yourself.'

'So he'll think I mousetrapped him?' Maynard blushed to the top of his bald head. 'And I'm small-souled enough to take advantage of that face-saving offer. Thanks. But to get on with it, there's a glaring vacancy in these data – about that incredible tri-di . . .'

'It's there, Mr. Maynard,' Barbara put in. 'It really is.'

'I know it is. With a planet whose radiation would trip a scanner at four or five astronomical units out, and what it has cost you to nail it down, faking would be completely pointless. No, the missing information is, how did you make that tri-di? We know of *one* honest-to-God oil-witch . . .' He paused and looked pointedly at Barbara, 'but I've never heard of anyone who ever witched enough virgin ore of any kind to load a shotgun shell. Do you, Deston, claim to be the first metal-witch? Excuse me – "warlock", I suppose I should have said.'

'I most emphatically do not. Such crackpot stuff as that? No: "Improved instrumentation and techniques" is the full explanation. Secret, of course – obviously. And whatever made you think Barbara is an oil-witch? They're sinking as many dry holes as anybody.'

'Yeah.' As Maynard said it, the word was the essence of disbelief. 'Lately. I've noticed. You don't want to get her shot. Smart boy – if I were you I wouldn't either.'

'But sir, I assure . . .'

'Yeah,' Maynard said again. 'I'm assured, and I don't leak. So go ahead with Stage Three.'

'Thank you. Stage Three is to sell you the planet Barbizon, lock, stock, and barrel, for the sum of one dollar and other valuable considerations.'

Maynard's whole body tensed, but his voice came calm and quiet as he asked, 'Such as?'

'Two million shares of today's Class B GalMet common at today's close; to be delivered when the net profit of Project Barbizon amounts to two megabucks more than the cost of the shares.'

'*What?*' Maynard was shaken, and this time he could not help showing it. 'Less than two hundred megabucks, paid *after*

71

we clear it ... You're telling me there *is* a Santa Claus, making us a free-gratis-for-nothing Christmas present of God-knows-how-many mega – hell, no; not megabucks, it'll be billions. With production equalling full demand and the price set by the PESI formula it'll be God-knows-how-many gigabucks over the long pull. So you'll have to do some more explaining, Deston.'

'I was going to; but first, who else could possibly handle a project that big the way it should be handled?'

'Granted. We're geared for it; no one else is. But you know and I know that with Barbizon nailed down tight you can set and get any royalty you please.'

'I know.' Deston smiled suddenly. 'We just did. We toyed with the idea of socking you, but everything was against it and nothing for it. First: we, too, adhere to the Principle of Enlightened Self-Interest.'

'I see.' Maynard relaxed and his mien lightened tremendously. 'That shaft, son, dead-centered the gold. Go ahead.'

'Second; since metal isn't our dish, our take will be pure gravy, and the easier the bite we put on you and the deeper you get into the planet Barbizon, the more convinced you will become that we know what we're doing.'

'It's beginning to make sense. All this will soften me up for the real whingo. So what will Santa Claus, as represented by Deston and Deston Ink, do then?'

'Having established the fact beyond question that we have, by means of our highly advanced instrumentation and techniques, found an immense amount of one highly desirable natural resource, we will ask you what you want next. We will look for it and we will probably find it.'

'And, having found it?'

'Are you sold, up to this point?'

'Definitely.' Maynard's fingers drummed lightly upon the soft plastic covering of the arm of his chair. 'If the stuff were not there you wouldn't be here: none of this would make any sense at all.'

'We will then prove to you that we have found whatever it was that you wanted. The next step will be to merge GalMet and WarnOil – Barbara thinks that "Metals And Energy" would be a good name for the new corporation. Now, considering . . .'

'You're leaving out one element, Carl,' Barbara put in.

'Not exactly. That's speculation, and at the moment I'm . . .'

'He'll be interested in that particular speculation,' Barbara broke in, 'so I'll tell him. Mr. Maynard, DuPuy say that while it is not yet politically feasible to even suggest including InStell in this proposed merger, he thinks that the present gentlemen's agreement would not only continue, but would become even more so.'

Maynard nodded. 'I was beginning to think along that same line myself. Go ahead, Deston.'

'Considering the size and scope of the proposed firm, and the fact that it would not have to explore, but would have at its command any amount of any natural resource – how fast could it grow?'

'*What* a program . . . what a *program*!' Rock-still, Maynard thought for minutes. 'I've always insisted on a fully-developed presentation, but *this* . . . the three biggest firms in existence, all pulling together and with everything they need . . .' He paused.

'Lansing and DuPuy both said the trouble would be to keep it from growing too fast – getting all porous and falling apart. But that you knew that as well as they did, and wouldn't expand any faster than you could get top-bracket people, and that such executives are damned scarce.'

'They're *so* right. However, I'm ready – I'll go into that later. It won't be as long as you think. What's WarnOil's thought on organization?'

'To have some widely-known VIP as president, with actual management staying right where it is now; with you running Metals and Lansing running Energy and both of you playing footsie with Hatfield of InStell – with the figurehead president not necessarily knowing quite everything that goes on.'

'That sounds good. Lansing's an operator, and so is Hatfield.'

'Last, the stock classes will be such, and Deston and Deston's payments will be such, that voting control will be . . . oh, yes, "conserved" was the word DuPuy used. That's all, sir.'

'Not by several stages that isn't all. You've done altogether too much work on this to have it stop at this point. Next stage, please.'

Deston looked baffledly at Barbara; who gave him an I-told-you-so smile and said, 'You knew darn well you'd have to tell him the whole wild thing, so go right ahead and do it.'

'You certainly will, son,' Maynard agreed. He had thought that Deston, like so many other space officers, had used the glamor of his status to marry money. That idea was out. He wasn't the type. Neither was Barbara; glamor-boys by the score had been trying to marry her ever since she was fifteen ... and they *could* find metal ... and this whole deal showed honest-to-God *brains*. After a very brief pause he went on, 'Neither of you cares any more about money *as money* than I do. So it's something else. I'm beginning to think, Barbara, that you were right in ascribing most of this to Carl, here.'

'Of course I was.' Barbara grinned wickedly; she had known exactly what Maynard had been thinking. '*My* mind doesn't work that way at all. It really doesn't.'

'Okay, okay; don't rub it in.' Maynard answered her grin, not her words. 'I'm sure we'll go along, but after all this you'll *have* to tell me what you're really after.'

'The trouble is, I can't, at all exactly.' Deston spread out both hands. 'Too much extrapolation – altogether too many unknowns – at this point the picture becomes ver-*ee* unclear.'

'Okay. Your thinking so far has been eminently precise; I'd like to hear your extrapolations and speculations.'

'Okay. MetEnge, or whatever the new firm turns out to be, will employ DesDes as consulting geologists; that is, we would work independently of, and eventually replace, your geological staff and your prospectors and wildcatters and so on. If you should wish to employ us on an exclusive basis ...?'

'That goes without saying.'

'We would require a very substantial annual fee, payable in MetEnge voting stock at the market. All of our new discoveries, including the find not theretofore revealed, will be leased, not sold, to MetEnge.'

'Ah. "Conserve" is right. Pete has a very fine Italian hand indeed. I'm going to like this. Not money at all, but power.'

'Not exactly – or rather, we want power back of us. We want to explore subspace and deep space in ways and to depths that have never even been thought of before. There must be thousands of things not only undiscovered, but not even imagined yet. Barbara and I want to go out after some of them; and, since nobody can have any idea whatever of what we may run into, it is clear that the highly special ship may turn out to be the smallest part of what we'll need. So we'll want the full backing of the biggest private organization it is possible to build. A firm big enough and strong enough to operate on a scale now possible only to governments – one able and willing to handle anything we may stir up. Our present thought is that when MetEnge gets big enough we will offer it a fifty-fifty share of the expedition, build the ship, and take off. As I said, there's nothing clear about it.'

'It's clear enough for me to like it. You'd be surprised at the way the first part of the program ties in with stuff I've been working on for a long time. As for the other – untrammeled research into the completely unknown – you realize, of course, that if MetEnge participates fifty-fifty, DesDes will be on a non-retainer basis all the time you are out and will have to split fifty-fifty.'

'But there isn't going to be anything the least bit commercial about it!' Barbara protested.

'You're wrong there, young lady. Research always has paid off big, in hard dollars. So I'll buy the package.' Maynard got up and shook hands with them both. 'I'll take this stuff along. WarnOil's legal department is acting for you, I suppose?'

'Yes.'

'In the morning we'll send them a check for one dollar, with a firm binder, by special messenger and start things rolling.'

'Oh, you don't think it's silly, then?' Barbara asked. 'I was awfully afraid you'd think this last part of it was.'

'Far from it. I'm sure it will be immensely profitable.'

'In that case we have some more news for you.' Both Destons were smiling happily. 'We also found a deposit of native copper and copper ores big enough and solid enough for full automation.'

'*Copper!*' Maynard yelled, jumping out of his chair. 'Why

the hell didn't you bring that up first?'

'When would this other thing have been settled if we had?'

'You've got a point there. Where is it?'

'Belmark. Strulsa Three, you know.'

'*Belmark!* We *prospected* Belmark – it's colonized – fairly well along. We didn't find any more copper there than anywhere else.'

'It'd be impossible to find by any usual method, and it's over five hundred miles from the nearest town. Our finding it was a ... not an accident, but a byproduct – while we were training for uranium. If we'd known then what we know now I'd've found you a big one, but we weren't interested in copper.'

'How big is this one?'

'It'll smelt something over a hundred million tons of metal. It'll tide you over, but I don't know about amortizing the plant.'

'We can cut the price in half and still amortize in months ... but amortization cuts no ice here ... let's see, production of primary copper runs about six million tons ... but if we cut the price to the bone, God knows what the sales potential is ...'

Maynard immersed himself in thought, then went on, 'Definitely. That's the way to do it. Hit 'em hard. Really slug 'em ... that is, if ... how sure are you, Carl, that you can find us another big deposit? Within, say a year?'

Deston's mind flashed back over the comparatively few copper surveys he had made. 'Copper isn't too scarce and it tends to aggregate. I'll guarantee to find you one at least three times that big within thirty days.'

'Good! Let's cut the chatter, then. I can use your com?'

'Of course,' Barbara said; but Maynard's question had been purely a matter of form. He was already punching his call.

'Miss Champion,' Maynard said, when his FirSec's face showed on the screen. 'I hope you don't have any engagements for tonight.'

'I have a date, but it's with Don, so he'll understand perfectly when I break it.' She did not ask any questions; she merely raised her perfectly-sculptured black eyebrows.

'I want him, too, so bring him downtown as soon as you can. And please get hold of Quisenberry and Felton and tell them to get to the office jet-propelled. That's all for now.'

'I'll get right at it, Mr. Maynard.'

Maynard punched off and turned to Deston. 'I almost forgot – what are you charging for this?'

'Nothing. Free gratis for nothing.'

'*Huh?*'

'We have no claim on it. Nobody has. It's never even been surveyed; so call it DesDes's contribution toward knocking Burley Hoadman and his UCM off of the Christmas tree.'

'You've got the dope on it here in your office?'

'Yes.' Deston went to his desk and brought back a briefcase. 'Here's everything necessary.'

'Thanks immensely. We'll own it shortly. As for your royalties, we've been accused of claim-stealing, but we usually pay discoverers' royalties and we'll be glad to on this one. *Brother*, will we be glad to! So Phelps will – no, he'd take it for nothing, the skinflint, and lick his chops. I'll have Don Smith take care of it tonight. And now that that's settled,' Maynard smiled as he had not smiled in weeks, 'about that trip of yours. I envy you. If we were twenty-five years younger I'd talk my wife into going along with you. I'd better call her; and I'd like to have her meet both of you.'

'Why, we'd be *delighted* to meet her!' Barbara exclaimed.

Mrs. Maynard proved to be a willowy, strong-featured, gracious woman with whom the years had dealt very lightly. She was as glad to meet the Destons, about whom she had heard so much, as they were to meet her. And so on.

'I'm very sorry, Mrs. Maynard,' Barbara said, finally, 'that we had to keep your husband so . . .'

'Think nothing of it,' Maynard interrupted, briskly. 'Just one of those things. If you'd like to come downtown to the office, Floss, I'll take you out to dinner sometime during the evening.'

'I would like to, Upton, thanks. I'll be down in an hour or so.'

The Destons escorted Maynard up to the roof and to his waiting aircar; and after it had taken off:

'What do you suppose he meant by that "just one of those things" crack?' Deston asked.

'Why, he was on a *com*, silly, so he was *afraid* to say anything! Even that he was going to work all night!' Barbara explained, excitedly. '*That's* how big he knows it is!' and the two went enthusiastically into each other's arms.

CHAPTER SEVEN

Project Engineer Byrd

Miss Champion was as efficient as she was ornamental, and all of GalMet's top people were on call every minute of every day on the calendar. Therefore she and Executive Vice-President Eldon Smith and Project Engineers Quisenberry and Felton got to GalMet's main office almost as soon as Maynard himself did. When the two engineers came in Maynard looked at them with the well-known expression of the canary-containing cat.

'Good evening, gentlemen,' he said, with a wide and cryptic grin. 'I trust that your hearts are in good shape? And your nerves? That you are both sufficiently well integrated to withstand the shock of your trouble-making young lives?'

'Try us,' Quisenberry said. He was a black-haired, black-eyed, deeply-tanned man, a little past thirty, who had worked himself up the hard way; clear up from the lowest low of a copper mine. He looked – if not exactly sullen, at least as though he was very sure that what he had been doing on his own was vastly more important than any piffling, niggling conference with THE BIG BOSS. 'I'll live through it, I'm sure.'

'Okay. Each of you take a table; you'll need lots of room. Quisenberry, here's everything you'll need on a deposit of copper. Felton, ditto, uranium. I want preliminary roughouts of those projects as fast as you can get them. Very rough: plus-or-minus twenty-five percent will be close enough. Now, Don and Miss Champion, what we'll have to do tonight is rough out a full operational on copper in the light of information that has just come to hand.'

After what may have been an hour Mrs. Maynard came in and Quisenberry came up for air. His table was littered with hand-books, machine-tapes of various kinds, graphs, charts, and wadded-up scratch-paper; much of which had overflowed onto the floor.

'But this is *incredible*, sir.' It was the first time either engineer had called Maynard 'sir' in over a year. 'Of course I can't say that it's absolutely impossible for any such deposit as this to occur, but . . .' Quisenberry paused.

Maynard grinned again, but pleasantly, this time. 'Do you think I'd have all that stuff faked up and then come down here and work all night myself just to put you two through the wringer?'

'Put that way, of course not . . . but . . .' Quisenberry paused again and Felton, who had stopped work and was listening with both ears, came in with:

'Quizz said it, Mr. Maynard, and mine's ten to the fourth as hard to swallow as his. I can't make myself believe that there's that much uranium in one place anywhere in the universe.'

'I know exactly how you feel,' Maynard assured them. 'I was flabbergasted myself. You may take it as a fact, however, that all that data is accurate to within the appropriate limits of error. I myself am so convinced of its reliability that I am going to give you two men all the authorization you'll need and full authority to build and to operate fully-automated plants. Satisfactory? That's what you've been getting ready for all this time, isn't it?'

'Yes, *sir*!' Quisenberry said, and:

'You *said* it, sir!' Felton agreed.

At seven-fifty-five Maynard asked the group at large, 'Everybody ready to eat? I'll call Beardsley's.'

Neither engineer would leave his job; so, after Miss Champion had ordered up two one-gallon hot-pots of coffee and a good spread of smorgasbord, the two couples went to Beardsley's for dinner – a dinner that lasted for an hour and a half and cost Maynard exactly forty dollars (including tip). Then a GalMet aircar took Mrs. Maynard home and another one took the other three back to the office.

Along toward morning Quisenberry stood up, stretched, looked with distaste at his umpteenth cup of coffee, and said, 'I've made some assumptions, boss, that I'd better check with you before I give you the bad news. Okay?'

'Okay.'

'Rush all possible. That means twenty-four hours a day, Saturdays, Sundays, and holidays. All the personnel that can work efficiently, all the time. Crash priorities on material, which means no time for competitive bidding, so we'll have to pay top prices and bonuses. Check to here?'

'Check and okay.'

'Plant capacity. Assuming that you want to cut the price down to somewhere between eleven and twelve cents...'

'You're right on the beam, Quizz. Nearer eleven, I think.'

'Extrapolating on that basis, my guessometer says that we'll have to be producing at the rate of fifteen million tons by the end of the first year. That's a mighty big plant, boss. That's one supreme *hell* of a big plant.'

'I know. I like those figures very much.'

'You won't like these next ones, I'm afraid. On this rush-and-bonus basis it'll take pretty close to twenty-five mega-bucks in the first couple of months, and the total – well, it's a very rough guess at this point. All I'm sure of is the order of magnitude, but the total to first pour will probably run some-where in the neighbourhood of seventy-five megabucks.'

'Thanks. That's close enough for now. Just so we don't get caught short of cash in the till.'

'But listen – sir – Phelps will have a litter of lizards!'

'He'll be amenable to reason when he finds out that we are entering a completely new era in metals. Felton, how about you?'

Felton – a brawny youth with butch-cut straw-colored hair and blue eyes – could not answer immediately because his mouth was full of *shrimp a la Creole*. He swallowed hastily, then said:

'Since this will have to be a crash-pri job, too, everything Quizz said will apply. Add high radiation to all that, and a hostile dead planet clear out to hellangone beyond anywhere, and the tab gets no smaller fast. My best guesstimate as of now is that the total will crowd a hundred megabucks.'

'Fair enough. Thanks a . . .'

'One thing first,' Felton interrupted. 'Are you sure enough of this – this super-bonanza – for me to roust Bassler out right now? Tell him to cut out all this ten-cent petty-larceny rock-scratching we're doing now, break out all the armor we've got and order more, and start – but quick – jassacking some of that high-grade out of there and hauling it to Galmetia?'

'An excellent idea. Splendid! If I'd thought of it I would have suggested it hours ago. Go ahead.'

Felton did so and Maynard went on, 'Since you fellows made these estimates in hours instead of weeks I'll give you plenty of leeway. Miss Champion, please issue two preliminary authorizations: Quisenberry, seventy-five megabucks; Felton, a hundred.'

Preliminaries! Not maxes! Staring at each other as though they could not believe their ears, the two engineers shook hands solemnly with each other, and then with all three of the others. Then they poured themselves two more cups of strong black coffee and went back to work.

Work went on until half past five. Then, since each would have to be on the job by nine o'clock, Maynard broke it up so that each could get three hours' sleep. All top-echelon private offices were equipped for that. Night work was an essential part of such man-killing jobs as theirs; a part that envious underlings knew nothing about. It had happened before and it would happen again. And again and again.

This entire episode was just another one of those things.

A couple of months later, Miss Champion showed Deston into Maynard's office. The tycoon, although showing the effects of too little sleep, was in very fine fettle indeed.

'Good morning, chief,' Deston said. 'We're about ready to cut gravs. How are the projects coming along?'

'Fine! Quizz is really rolling it, and no leaks. And we cut the price of uranium another half a buck yesterday.'

'Nice going. Are you sure we can stay out a few months? I'll locate enough copper while we're gone, of course, to last you for a thousand years.'

'Positive. We'll drop the price of copper to where Hoadman will think he's been hit by a pile-driver.'

'So solly ... and the effect on all industry of cheap and plentiful copper – added to your widely-advertised fact that in a few months everybody can buy all the uranium they want for less than thirty cents per pound – will take the curse off of the public image GalMet will get when you smash UCM flat?'

'Not quite all of it, perhaps, but it will certainly help.'

'That's for sure. Okay; what do you want firstest and mostest of, now that copper and uranium are out of the way?'

'I wish I could tell you.' Maynard's fingers drummed quietly on his desk. 'You thought it would be simple? It isn't. It's all fouled up in the personnel situation I told you I'd tell you about. We have six good people – damned good people – each of whom wants a planetary project so passionately that if I stack the deck in favor of any one of them, all the others will blast me to a cinder and run, not walk, to the nearest exit.'

Deston did not say anything and after a moment the older man went on, 'Platinum and iridium, of course. Osmium, tungsten ...'

'Tungsten isn't too scarce, is it?'

'For the possible demand, very much so. I'd like to sell it for fifteen cents a pound. Beryllium, tantalum, titanium, thorium, cerium – and, for the grand climax to end all climaxes – *rhenium.*'

'Huh? I don't think I've ever heard rhenium even mentioned since my freshman chemistry.'

'Not too many people have, but right now I'm as full of information as the dog that sniffed at the third rail. It's so rare that no mineral of it is known; it exists only as a trace of impurity in a very few minerals. Strangely enough practically only in molybdenite.'

'Just a minute.' Deston went to a book-case, took out a handbook, and flipped pages. 'Um ... um ... mm. Dwimanganese. *Not* usually associated with manganese. *Maybe* it occurs in molybdenite as the sulphide – ReS_2 and/or Re_2S_7 – commercial source, flue dust from the roasting of Arizona molybdenite ...'

'Right. We own the outfit. That's *why* we own it. It produces a few tons a *year* of Cottrell dust, which yields just about enough rhenium to irritate one eyeball. Production cost, five dollars and seventeen cents per gram.'

'But what's it *good* for? Contact points ... cat mass ... heavy duty igniters, it says here.' Deston tapped the page with his forefinger. 'No tonnage outlet there.'

'What would you think of an alloy that had a yield point – not ultimate tensile, mind you, but *yield* – of well over a million pounds, and yet an elongation of better than five percent?'

Deston whistled. 'I *would* have said it was a pure pipe dream. What else is in it?'

'Mostly tungsten. A lot of tantalum. Rhenium around ten percent. The research isn't done yet, but they're far enough along to know that they'll have something utterly fantastic. The problem, Byrd tells me, is to determine the optimum formula and environment for the growth and matting of single crystals of metal – tungsten "whiskers", you know – you know about them.'

'A little, of course, but not too much. I'm a 'troncist.'

'I know. Well, they're playing around now with soak-pit times and temperatures and fractional percentages of this and that. The curve is still rising.'

'So you'll need tungsten and tantalum, too, by the gigaton, since that's a thing that the Law of Diminishing Returns would apply to exactly.'

'I didn't think I'd have to plot you a graph. So now, apart from the personnel problem, what do you think?'

Before replying, Deston studied the handbook for minutes. Then: 'The three atomic numbers are in order; seventy-three, four, and five. But in the Earth's crust rhenium runs less than one part in billions. So if there is any big mass of it anywhere the others are apt to be there too, and a hell of a lot more of 'em.'

'All the better, even from a project standpoint. Two prime sources of anything are a lot better than one.'

'I didn't mean that. All that stuff is terrifically heavy, and it's got to be close enough to the surface to get at. I simply can't visualize what kind of a planet could possibly have what we want. It *won't* be Tellus-Type, that's for damn certain sure.'

'I couldn't care less about that. We can set up automation on anything that isn't hotter than dull red.'

'Okay. That brings us back, then, to personnel. This Byrd – has he got what it takes to run such a weirdie as this rhenium thing will almost have to be?'

'Definitely, but Doctor Cecily Byrd isn't a man. Very much the opposite, which is exactly what is thickening the soup. If we could get hold of as little as one megaton of rhenium, so as to add this new alloy leybyrdite to cheap uranium and copper, it would make MetEnge such a public benefactor that it'd be a case of "the King can do no wrong". But if I deal one card from the bottom of the deck to "Curly" Byrd all hell will be out for noon.'

'That sounds like something more than ordinary sex antagonism.'

'It is. Much more. She not only uses weapons men don't have – and she's got 'em, believe me – but she brags about it. She's a carrot-topped, freckle-faced, shanty-Irish mick, with the shape men drool about and itching to use it – with a megavac for a brain and an ice-cube for a heart. She's half cobra, half black widow, half bitch, and one hundred percent hell-cat on wheels.'

'She must be quite a gal, to add up to two hundred and fifty percent.'

'She adds up to all that. So do the others. I would have fired her a year ago – she hadn't been on the job three weeks before she started making passes at me – but I haven't been able to find anyone else nearly as good as she is.'

'That's a mighty tough signal to read.'

'It's a unique situation. I've been gathering those people for over two years, getting ready to expand, and we haven't found anything big enough to expand into. I had eight of them. They were hard enough to handle before I gave Felton and Quisenberry their projects, but ever since then the other six have been damn near impossible. Each has tremendous ability and drive; each is as good as either Felton or Quisenberry and knows it. All working at about ten percent load; with nowhere in the galaxy to go to do any better. Frustrated – tense – sore as boils and touchy as fulminate – knives out, not only for each other, but also for Smith and me. Four men and two women. Purdom hasn't got any sex-appeal at all; Byrd oozes it at every pore. So I tell you rhenium first and the sex-pot is first out. So the other five *know* she got it by sleeping with me, and she – the Goddamned bitch! – grins like the Cheshire cat and rubs it in that *she* has got what it takes to land the big ones.'

'That's a hell of a picture, chief. I simply can't visualize top-bracket executives acting that way.'

'You haven't handled enough people for years enough. They can't act any other way. What I've been wanting to do, every time she sticks her damned sexy neck out, is wring it ... wait a minute; that gives me an idea ... yes, that'll work. The minute they find out for sure – they must all suspect it already – that you're an honest-to-God metal-wizard I can kick their teeth right down their throats. They'll all tear into their jobs like that many hundred-ton cat tractors.'

'But listen! You *can't* tell 'em – we've got to keep it dark, the way we find the stuff.'

'From most people, yes; but from anybody with a brain? One, of course, could be luck. Two might – just barely – be coincidence. But the next one? I won't have to tell them, even now. I'll make the method certain the same way you did – by denying its possibility.'

'Could be, at that ... so maybe we'd better make it a straight tri-di survey for everything you're interested in. That would save time, in fact, over all. What kind of a list would that be?'

'Here.' Maynard reached into a drawer and sailed a sheet of paper across his desk. 'The full want list, which we boiled down to the must-haves.'

Deston caught the paper and read it. 'Is that all?'

'Isn't that enough? You're a brute for punishment.'

'I'm surprised, is all, that gold isn't on it.'

'*Gold!*' Maynard snorted. 'Besides currency base, jewelry, and show, what's it good for? We've never touched it and never intend to – produce a few tons too much and you upset the economy instead of benefiting it.'

86

'I never thought of it that way, but that's right. Okay, chief, we'll flit. I'll keep you posted. 'Bye.'

Deston strode out and Maynard flipped a switch. 'Please get Wharton, Bender, Camp, Byrd, Train, and Purdom and bring 'em into the conference room. No note-pads and no recorder.'

'Very well, sir,' Miss Champion said; and in a few minutes four men and three women were walking toward the long table at the head of which Maynard sat.

'I for one was *busy*, Mister Maynard!' Cecily Byrd snapped. She was something under thirty, five feet ten in her nylons, and beautifully built. She moved with the lithe grace of a trained dancer. Her thick, brick-red, medium-bobbed hair was naturally and stubbornly curly; with a curliness no hair-dresser had ever been able to subdue. Her untannable skin was heavily freckled and, except for a touch of lipstick, she wore no make-up. Her features, while regular enough, were too bold and too strong by far for prettiness. Her mien was sullen and defiant; her eyes – smoldering green fires – swept the bare expanse of table. 'What? No pads and pencils? No mikes? Isn't this conference going to be of such gravid and world-shaking import that its every word and nuance should be preserved for the edification of all ages to come?'

'Shut up, Byrd, and all of you sit down.'

The red-head gasped and all the others stared; for this was something new. President Maynard had never before spoken to any one of them except in formal terms. Wondering and silent, they all sat down and Maynard smiled at them wolfishly, one by one. After a long half minute of this he spoke.

'I've been looking forward to this moment for a long, long time,' he gloated. 'But first, I wonder if any one of you has any idea of why I put up with all eight of you so long? Such intractable, intransigent hellions; such knuckle-dusting, back-stabbing, rampaging jerks as you all have been?'

'That's easy!' the red-head snapped, before any one of the eager others could say a word. 'Hog-the-talent. Dog-in-the manger. Standard Operating Procedure.'

'Wrong. You're also wrong in claiming to be busy. Not one of you has even the remotest inkling of what the word means. But you are all going to find out. *How* you'll find out! As soon as this meeting is over each of you will be handed a planetary-project authorization and will . . .'

'*What?*' 'Huh?' 'Where?' 'How come?' Six voices shouted or shrieked almost as one.

'Whereupon each of you will proceed to design and staff a full-scale, optimum-tonnage plant, exactly as you want it. Each of you will have full authority and full responsibility . . .'

'Full authority. Yeah,' Percival Train broke in, bitingly. He was a big, handsome, hard-bodied young man, with bushy, crew-cut brown hair and highly cynical – at the moment – gray eyes. 'Except that I'll be told exactly what to do and exactly how to do it and then it'll be my fault when the whole damned operation goes stinko. Full authority, hell! I've heard that song, words and music, before.'

'From me?' Maynard asked, quietly.

'Well . . . no.'

'Nor will you. You'll be on your own; subject to Top Management only in matters of policy – such as no pirating of personnel from each other, for instance. That's so none of you can come around later, bitching and belly-aching that your flop was due to the way we cramped your style. If each of you does a job, and I hope you will; fine. Anybody who doesn't will get fired. I would enjoy firing you, Train, and Byrd. Any questions?'

The six looked at each other, almost in consternation. Even 'Curly' Byrd was mute. Finally Train spoke.

'Maybe . . . to be tossing out *that* kind of money . . . this, on top of Barbizon and Belmark, really blows the plug. But I still don't think that Mrs. Deston is a metal-witch. It doesn't make sense.'

'Of course she isn't,' Rose Purdom, a plumpish, fortyish blonde put in. 'Or she'd have done it before. It's a new talent. *Mister* Deston. Those huge finds were just to prove to a certain hard-nosed tycoon that he could do it. That's what's really back of this gigantic super-merger.'

'If any or all of you want to believe in that supernatural twaddle it's all right with me,' Maynard said, dryly. 'What I am authorized to say is that the firm of Deston and Deston

Incorporated has, by marked improvements in instrumentation and techniques, been able to take noteworthy strides in the science or art of locating large deposits of certain metals.'

'Comet-gas!' Train rasped. 'You're right, Rose, it's Deston. *Es macht mir garnichts aus* who finds the stuff, or how; but just one question, Mr. Maynard. Are you going to play this straight, on a first-found-first-out basis?'

'Absolutely. Thus, either Wharton or Camp will probably be first, the lady Byrd here last. Probably all of you, however, except Byrd, will have your locations before you're ready for them.'

'But if probability governs, I *might* come in first,' Cecily Byrd said, looking pointedly at Maynard.

'The possibility, although vanishingly small, does exist,' Maynard admitted. 'Therefore, *if* that event occurs, I want you all to know now as a fact that it will be because rhenium is discovered first in a non-selective survey, and *not* because . . .' He paused and his icy gray eyes scanned as much of a highly-sculptured green garment as was visible above the table's top, 'I repeat, *not* because of our Doctor Byrd's generosity with her charms; which, by the exercise of super-human self-control, I have managed so far to resist. Now go back to your offices, all of you, and start earning part of your pay.'

The red-head flushed hotly – it was the first time anyone there had seen her blush – but not even that blast could dampen the enthusiasm of the melee that followed. They shook hands all around; they whacked each other – including Maynard and Miss Champion – on the back; the men kissed the women – including Miss Champion – vigorously; and they all babbled excitedly. In fact, it took fifteen minutes for Maynard to get them out of the conference room.

And the six engineer-scientist-executives who finally left that room were very different from the six who had entered it such a short time before.

The Destons and MetEnge, on a fifty-fifty basis, had bought from InStell the *Procyon*'s hulk, as is, at its appraised value for machinery and scrap. InStell had been glad to sell her on that basis; for in the still-somewhat-superstitious public mind she was, and under any possible disguise would remain, an irreparably jinxed and hoodooed death-ship.

She was now completely reconditioned; not as a passenger liner, but as an armed and armored, completely self-contained, subspace-going independent worldlet with a population of just under a thousand people. There were no unmarried men or women aboard, and most of the couples had children. Every man and every woman had passed a series of physical, mental, and psychological examinations.

With this special ship, then, and with this super-special crew, the Destons set out.

In the con-room there was now a forty-foot tri-di of the galaxy, with an eight-inch, roughly globular cluster of red dots in a spiral arm, much nearer to one edge than to the center of the huge lens. The Destons sat at two bewilderingly-instrumented desks. Behind them stood big, hard, tough Captain Theodore Jones, with his platinum-blonde wife Bernice. Her left hand rested upon his right shoulder; her spectacular head rested thoughtfully upon her hand.

At Jones' left, toward the massed control-boards of the ship, his fifteen top officers stood at ease; at his right was a group of twenty-odd scientists.

'So *that's* what all explored space amounts to.' Jones pointed at the tiny globe in the enormous, discus-shaped, light-point-filled volume which represented the galaxy. 'I simply would not have believed it. Damn it, Babe, are you *sure* that thing is to scale?'

'To within one percent, yes. That's why Bobby and I are going to work fourteen hours a day instead of six. I'm not going to try to tell any of you what to do' – Deston's eyes swept both groups – 'because each of you knows more about his own job than I do. So let's get at it.'

The *Procyon* flashed to the nearest one of the ninety-five colonized planets and Carlyle and Barbara Deston taped their three-dimensional surveys; the man on metals, the woman on oil, coal, water, and natural gas. Nor was her part any less important than his. The use of fuels as such, while large, was insignificant in comparison with their use in petrochemistry. Led by Plastics, that industry had grown so fast that not even

WarnOil's fantastic expansion had been able to keep up with it.

Day after day, planet after planet, they surveyed the ninety-five colonized planets and all the virgin planets they had scanned so sketchily on their first trip. Deston found immense deposits of several of the 'wanted' metals, including copper, and Barbara found plenty of water and fuels. Tungsten and tantalum, however, were no more abundant on any of those planets than they were on Earth; and rhenium existed only in almost imperceptible traces. Therefore the *Procyon* set out, on an immensely helical course, toward the center of the galaxy.

On their first expedition the Destons had learned so much that they could work any planet whose sun they could see. Now, as their psionic powers kept on increasing, their astronomers had to push the *Procyon*'s telescopes farther and farther out into the immensity of space to keep them busy.

Days lengthened into weeks, and life aboard the immense sky-rover settled down into a routine. Adults worked, read, studied, loafed, and tuned in programs of entertainment and of instruction. Children went to school and/or played, just as though they were at home. In fact, they *were* at home. Except that physical travel outside the hull was forbidden, life aboard the starship was very similar to, and in many ways more rewarding than, life in any village of civilization.

Deston and Barbara, however, worked and slept and ate – and that was all. Fourteen hours per day every day of every week is a brutal shift to work, especially at such grueling tasks as theirs; but the entire expedition had been built around those two and they wanted to get the job done.

CHAPTER EIGHT

The Battle of New York Spaceport

Galactic Metals moved its main office from Earth to Galmetia. WarnOil's was already on Newmars. InStell moved to Newmars. Many other very large firms moved from Earth to various 'outplanets'. Thus, while there was a great deal of objection to the formation of such a gigantic 'trust' as METALS AND ENERGY, INCORPORATED, there was nothing that West-Hem's government could do about it. While GalMet was now a wholly-owned subsidiary of MetEnge, neither its name nor its operation had been changed in any way.

In GalMet's vast new building on Galmetia, President Upton Maynard sat at the head of a conference table. At his left sat Executive Vice-President Eldon Smith and Comptroller Desmond Phelps. At his right were Darrell Stearns, head of GalMet's legal staff, and Ward Q. Wilson, Chief Mediator of WestHem. Miss Champion sat at her desk, off to one side. Wilson was speaking.

'... no over-riding authority, of course, since MetEnge is a Newmars corporation and GalMet's legal domicile and principal place of business is here on Galmetia. While such tax evasion is not ...'

'Let's keep the record straight, Mr. Wilson,' Maynard said, sharply. 'Not evasion; avoidance. Avoidance of Earth's ruthlessly confiscatory taxation was necessary to our continued existence. Under such taxation our basic principle of operation, which the founders of GalMet inaugurated over two hundred years ago, could not possibly have remained implemented.

'Do you think it's accidental that we are the largest firm in existence? It isn't; it is due absolutely to the fact that, very unlike capital in general, we have adhered strictly to the Principle of Enlightened Self-Interest. Simply stated, that Principle is: Don't be a hog. You make more, over the long pull, by letting the other fellows make something, too. Most important, it's non-inflationary, even though the standard of living is continually rising. If we had stayed on Earth and gone along all these years with blind, stupid, greedy, grasping conventional Capital, what would the price of steel have been today? What would the dollar have been worth?'

'Nevertheless, there has been some inflation ...'

'How well we know it!' Phelps, the moneyman, broke in. 'Whose fault is it? Your government's deficit spending – cradle-to-grave security – reckless, foolhardy installment buying – the whole inflated credit situation. We, on the other hand, do not use credit. We have no bonds, no preferred stock, no indebtedness. We buy sight-draft-attached-to-bill-of-lading and sell the same way. Hard money and cash on the barrelhead. We have it before we spend it.'

'I'm not saying that your principle hasn't worked very well for you, up to now. You haven't had a real strike for half a century, until now. Not because of the stable dollar or of your principle of operation, however, but simply because no union was strong enough to fight you to a finish. Now there is one. The UCM controls all copper-mining and Burley Hoadman controls the UCM. The situation, gentlemen, is now desperate; it is a civilization-wide emergency. It is intolerable that all industry should come to a halt because of your refusal to settle this strike. You know that all industry must have at least some new copper to operate at all.'

'We do,' Maynard said. 'You are saying that since Hoadman will not settle for anything less than double the present scale – already tops – we must cave in and pay it? And surrender to all the other unions that will jump onto the gravy train? That the subsequent inevitable surge of inflation won't hurt? You know exactly what the spiral will be.'

Wilson glanced at his microphone and said nothing. Miss Champion entered a couple of pot-hooks in her notebook.

Maynard went on:

'Your opinion is not for the record. I understand. This is an election year, and because the dear pe-pul are getting out of hand the administration sent you over here to tell us to give Hoadman everything he wants – or else. They're junking financial stability completely to get themselves re-elected.'

'No, I was not going to . . .'

'Not so crudely, of course; but nobody has put any pressure at all on Hoadman.'

'We can't.' Wilson spread his hands out helplessly and Miss Champion made a few more marks in her book. 'All popular sentiment is for the union and against you. You are altogether too big.'

'Or not big enough – yet,' Maynard said, savagely.

'Also, in the public mind, the salaries of all you tycoons are altogether too high.'

'High, hell!' Smith snarled. 'How about Hoadman's take? He drags down more than all four of us put together!'

'Whether or not it is true, that point is irrelevant. The pertinent fact is that Senator Wrigley of California is preparing a bill to annex both Newmars and Galmetia to the Western Hemisphere.'

Smith whistled. '*Brother!* They went a hell of a long ways out *after* that one!'

Wilson said nothing.

Stearns stared thoughtfully at the mediator, then said, 'It's unconstitutional. Obviously. It violates every principle of Interplanetary law.'

'Better yet, it's unenforceable,' Smith said. 'Admiral Porter knows as well as we do that his handfull of tomato-juice cans wouldn't stand the chance of the proverbial nitrocellulose cat in hell.'

'One more thing,' Maynard said. 'Ninety-five other planets wouldn't like it, either. Have you thought about what a good, solid boycott would do to Earth?'

'The possibility has been considered, and the consensus is that there can be no effective boycott. Labor will hold . . .'

'Hold it!' Maynard snapped. 'You know – at least you should – that the organizations of the Planetsmen are no more like the labor unions of Tellus than black is like white. They are in favor of automation. They want change. They want advancement by ability, not seniority. As opposed to that attitude, what do your unions want, Mr. Wilson?'

Wilson pursed his lips in hesitation and Smith said, 'I'll answer that for you, then, Mr. Wilson. They want security, period, but they don't want to have to earn it. They want everything handed to them on a platter. Advancement by seniority only – all they have to do is stay alive. No changes allowed except more pay and more benefits for fewer hours of exactly the same work. Strictly serf labor and that's the way they like it. Security, hell! It's exactly the same kind of security, if they had brains enough to realize it, as they'd have in jail.'

'It has been computed,' Wilson said, ignoring Smith's barbed opinion, 'that in an emergency outplanet Labor will support that of Earth. Furthermore, public opinion is very strongly opposed to such gigantic trusts, combines, and monopolies as you are. And finally, at the worst, the inevitable litigation would take a long time, which would . . .?' Wilson paused, delicately.

'It would,' Maynard agreed, grimly. 'It would cramp us plenty and cost us plenty; and the administration could and would pull a lot of other stuff just as slimy.'

Wilson neither confirmed nor denied the statement and Maynard went on, 'Okay. We'll sign up for everything Hoadman demands; even the voice in management and the featherbedding. Also, we'll make the wage scales and fringe benefits retroactive to cover all hours worked on and after July first.'

'May I ask why? They might yield that one point.'

'Why should they?' Smith sneered. 'It's just out of the goodness of our hearts. You may quote me on that.'

'And that isn't all,' Maynard went on. 'We wanted a three-year contract, but Hoadman wouldn't add a day to his one-year position. So we'll do even better than that. Type a memo, please, Miss Champion. What we've said, and add, "Cancellable by either party on ten days notice in writing".'

'*What?*' The mediator was shaken out of his calm. When Maynard handed him the signed memorandum he handled it as though it might bite. 'Just what have you robber barons got up your sleeves?'

'Nothing but our arms,' Smith assured him. 'What *could* we have? Haven't your spies kept you informed of our every move?'

(No outsider as yet knew anything about Project Belmark, which was ready to go into full production.)

'I don't like this at all – not any part of it,' Wilson said, thoughtfully. 'I don't think I will recommend signing any contract containing a cancellation clause. Even though I can't see it, I know there's a hook in it somewhere ... and I think I know what it is ... but Hoadman is perfectly sure that...?'

'Go ahead, ask me,' Smith said. 'I'll answer – I'm not under oath. You smell something because you can think. Hoadman can't. Even if he could, and even if there were a hook in the thing, he'll grab it. He'll have to. If he doesn't, the miners will throw him out on his ear. Besides, he'll love it. Imagine the headlines – "BURLEY HOADMAN, GIANT BRAIN OF LABOR, BRINGS MIGHTY GALMET TO ITS KNEES".'

'Mr. Maynard,' Wilson said, 'please erase Mr. Smith's remarks and this sentence from the record.'

'By no means. Hoadman will of course listen to this supposedly top secret recording, and to hear this bit may – just conceivably – be good for what ails him.'

Wilson wriggled uncomfortably and Miss Champion wrote another line of shorthand.

Discussion continued for another hour or so, after which Wilson took his leave.

The union signed, in spite of Wilson's objections, because Burley Hoadman *knew* that copper mining could not be automated except at prohibitive cost. Then Hoadman announced to THE PRESS:

'This shows what a really tightly organized union can do. We are perfectly free to keep ahead of the cost of living and we'll keep it that way, since we can tie them up again any time we please.'

Everything remained quiet then – except for some rumblings in other unions, none of which had time to develop into serious strikes – for a couple of weeks. Then GalMet cancelled its contract with the UCM. Simultaneously it announced a reduction in the price of copper to eleven point three six one cents per pound FOB spaceport and began to supply all its competitors with all the copper they wanted. (It did not develop until later that Ajax, Revere, and all other large producers were merging with MetEnge.) All mines worked by United Copper Miners shut down. Salaried people were transferred. All machinery was scrapped. All properties and buildings were either sold or simply abandoned. Then Maynard talked to the reporters who had for many days been demanding a statement.

'In an economy subscribing fully to the Principle of Enlightened Self-Interest neither stupidly avaricious capital nor serf labor would exist. Nor would such a corrupt government as we now have. While it may be true that any people deserves the government it gets, this three-pronged blight now threatening all civilization is intolerable and something must be done about it. We have begun doing something about it by making an example of Burley Hoadman and his unconscionably greedy United Copper Miners, who . . .'

'One question, Mr. Maynard!' a reporter broke in. 'In using the word "we" do you claim to be represent . . .'

'I claim nothing!' Maynard snapped. 'I state as a fact that I am speaking for the Galaxians – the free men and women and the intelligent capital of the planets. These two component halves of production, eternally irreconcilable on Earth, work together on the planets for the best good of all. To resume: the closed copper mines will not be re-opened. There will never, in the foreseeable future, be any employment anywhere for the skilled craftsmen known as copper miners. We have deliberately automated the entire craft out of existence.

'We do not know whether Hoadman will believe this statement or not. Nor do we care. If he wishes to use up his union's funds in supporting the men in idleness rather than in expediting their absorption into other industries, that is his privilege.

'It has been threatened that other unions will, in spite of contractual obligations, walk out in sympathy with the UCM, to enforce Hoadman's demand that we pay four men double-scale wages to sit on cushioned chairs and play stud poker while one machine does the work. In reply to these threats I say now that we are prepared to cope with such retaliation at any level of action required.

'We are ready even for a complete general strike by all the unions of WestHem. In that case all imports to and all exports from Earth will stop. Earth will stew in its own juice until the vast majority of WestHem's people, the unorganized people, decide to get themselves out of the mess into which, by their own stupidity, laziness, and lack of interest, they got themselves.'

This blast was broadcast immediately; and in less than an hour Antonio Grimes, president of the Brotherhood of Professional Drivers, was on Miss Champion's com, demanding access to Maynard.

Since she was expecting the call, he was put on at once.

'Good morning, Mr. Maynard,' he began. He was a short man, inclined to fat, with heavy jowls and small, piercing eyes. At the table with him were his three major lieutenants and – not much to Maynard's surprise – WestHem's Secretary of Labor Deissner and Chief Mediator Wilson. 'You overlooked the fact that nothing can replace the truck and the freight-copter. The situation, however, is not beyond repair. For a nominal sum, say a quarter-mega, I might not pull the boys off tomorrow morning.'

'The trouble with you, Grimes,' Maynard said, quietly, 'is that while you're smart, clever, and cunning, you can't really think. You haven't got the brain for it.'

'That crack'll *cost* you, Big Shot!' Grimes roared, shedding in the instant his veneer of gentility. 'I'll *show* you who's got a brain, you . . .'

'Shut up and listen!' Maynard snapped. 'If you had had any fraction of a brain you would have known that we knew exactly what you would do.'

'Like hell you knew! If you did you wouldn't've . . .' Grimes paused; it became evident that his train of thought had all of a sudden been derailed.

'The only question is, how big a battle do you want for an opener? All over WestHem at once, or just one spaceport at first, to see what we have? If you can think at all you'd better start doing it, because the bigger a flop you make the deader you'll be when it's over.'

'Comet-gas! You can't scare *me*!'

'I can't? That's nice.'

'Who'd want to shoot the whole wad at once? One at a time; one day apart. Tomorrow morning I seal New York Spaceport so tight a cockroach can't get in or out.'

'And we'll open it. Here's your one and only warning. Before we send our freight-copters in ...'

'Just how do you think you'll get any copters off the ground?'

'Wait and see. Before a copter lofts we'll come in on the ground. East on Carter Avenue. Through Gate Twelve. Along Way Twelve to the *Cygnus*. I'm telling you this because I don't want our machines to kill anybody. They'll be fully automatic, so programmed that we won't be able to stop them ourselves. Hence any goons along that designated route who can't get out of the way in time will be committing suicide. If you shoot down any of our copters your gun-crews will be killed. That is all.'

'Hot dog!' Grimes gloated. 'Drawing us a map – handing it to us on a platter! What you'll run into along ...'

Miss Champion flipped a switch and the screen went blank.

Carter Avenue became a very busy street. The biggest and heaviest trucks available, loaded to capacity with broken concrete and rock, were jammed into that avenue, blocking it solidly – pavement, parkway, and sidewalk – from building wall to building wall for one full mile. Riflemen with magnums sat at windows; fifty-caliber machine-guns and forty-millimeter quick-firing rifles peered down from roofs; anti-tank weapons of all kinds commanded every yard of that soon-to-be-disputed mile.

Grimes and his strategists had expected a fleet of heavy tanks. What appeared, however, exceeded their expectations by ten raised to a power. They were – in a way – tanks; but tanks of a size, type, and heft never before seen on Earth. There were only two of them; but each one was twenty feet high, sixty feet wide, and a hundred and eighty feet long.

They were not going fast, but when they reached the barricade, side by side and a couple of feet apart, they did not even pause. Both front ends reared up as one, but they did not climb very high. Under that terrific tonnage the blocking trucks were crushed flat; the steel of their structures and the concrete and stone of their loads subsided noisily to form a compacted mass only a few feet thick.

Guns of all calibers yammered and thundered, but there was nothing to shoot at except blankly invulnerable expanses of immensely thick high-alloy armor-plate. Flame-throwers, flammable gels, and incendiaries were of no avail. Inside those monstrosities there was nothing of life, nor anything to be harmed by any ordinary heat. Nor did those monstrous tanks fight back – then.

Gate Twelve was narrower than the avenue; its anchorages were eight-foot square pillars of reinforced concrete. Nevertheless the two super-tanks did not slow down; and, after they had passed, the places where those hugely massive abutments had been were scarcely to be distinguished from the rest of the scarred and beaten way.

Suddenly there was a terrific explosion, followed by horizontal sheets of fiercely-driven pulverized pavement and soil. Then another, and fifteen more. But not even the heaviest mines could stop those land-going superdreadnoughts. They wallowed a little in the craters, but that was all. They were simply too big and too heavy and too stable to lift or to tip over; their belly-armor was twelve inches thick and was buttressed and braced internally to withstand anything short of atomic energy. Nor could their treads be blown; since all that was exposed to blast were their stubby, sharply pyramidal, immensely strong driving teeth.

Along Way Twelve the strike-breakers rumbled, and up to GalMet's subspacer *Cygnus*. They stopped. A GalMet copter began to descend, to pick up its load of copper. There was a blast of anti-aircraft fire. The copter disintegrated in air.

This time, however, GalMet struck back. Gun-ports snapped open along the nearer behemoth's grim side and a dozen one-hundred-five-millimeter shells lobbed in high arcs across the few hundreds of yards of intervening distance. They exploded, and a few parts recognizable as arms, legs, and heads, together with uncountable grisly scraps of flesh and bone, were mingled with the shattered remains of the anti-aircraft battery.

That ended it.

In Maynard's conference room this time there were, in addition to the GalMet men, Lansing and DuPuy of Warner Oil, Hatfield and Spehn of Interstellar, and seven other men. With Grimes and his minions, were, as before, Deissner and Wilson of WestHem.

Secretary of Labor Deissner looked once at the fourteen men seated at Maynard's table and his ruddy complexion paled.

'Have you had enough, Grimes, or do you want to go the route?' Maynard asked. 'You *may* be able to hold your Drivers after this one beating, but one more will plow you under.'

'You're *murderers* now and you'll hang!' Grimes snarled.

'What will you use for law, fat-head?'

'To hell with law. I've got WestHem's law in my pants pocket and you'll hang higher than ...'

'Close your fat mouth, Tony,' Deissner said, bruskly. 'With WarnOil, InStell, and all the labor of the outplanets in on this, it may be a little ...' He paused.

'You're wrong, Deissner, it'll be much worse,' Smith sneered. 'Your computations will all have to be recomputed.'

After a short silence Maynard said, 'Mr. Secretary; besides WarnOil and InStell, I see that you recognize the presidents of the seven largest organizations of the Planetsmen. Mr. Bryce, President of the Metalsmen, has something to say.'

And fiery little Bryce said it. 'This Committee of Seven, of which I am the chairman, represents the Planetsmen, the organized production and service personnel of the ninety-five planets of the Galactic Federation. Our present trip has two purposes. First, here on Galmetia, to tell you Tellurians that the organized personnel of the planets – not the *out*-planets, you will note, but the *planets* – will not support the purely Tellurian institution of serf labor. We do no featherbedding and we will not support the practice anywhere. We welcome any innovation that will produce more goods or services at lower cost by using our brains more and our muscles less.

'Our second objective is to let the people of Tellus know that there is plenty of room on the planets for any of them who want to advance by using their brains and their abilities instead of being coddled, protected, and imprisoned from the cradle to the grave.'

There was a moment of tense silence, then Maynard said, 'That was very well put, Egbert; thanks. Now, Grimes, as to your having WestHem's law in your pants pocket. You haven't, but the hoodlums, gangsters, and racketeers who are your bosses, do have it in theirs. We Galaxians – the combined personnel and capital of the planets – know exactly what WestHem's law is: a hood-bossed, hood-riddled mob of abysmally corrupt snollygosters. We also know that static, greedy capital is as bad as – yes, even worse than – serf labor. Therefore we Galaxians have formed a new government, the Galactic Federation; that, among other things, will not – I repeat, NOT – permit any spiral of inflation.'

'But *some* inflation is now necessary!' Deissner protested.

'It is not. We're not asking you; we're telling you. If you do not stabilize the dollar we will stabilize it for you.'

'Delusions of grandeur, eh? How do you think you can?'

'By isolating Earth until the resulting panic puts the dollar back where it belongs. Earth can't stand a blockade. The planets can, and would much rather have a complete severance from Earth than have a dollar that will not mail a letter from one town to the next. Hence we of the Galactic Federation hereby serve notice upon the governments and upon the peoples of Earth: it will be either a stable dollar or a strict blockade of every item of commerce except food. Take your choice.'

'Serve notice!' Deissner gasped. 'Surely you don't mean ... you can't *possibly* mean ...'

'We do mean. Just that.' Maynard smiled; a thin, cold smile. 'This has not been a secret meeting. You tell 'em, Steve.'

And Stevens Spehn, Executive Vice-President of vast Interstellar, told them. 'This whole conference has been on every

channel, line, wavelength and station that InStell operates —
ether and subether, radio and teevee, tri-di and flat, in black-
and-white and in color.'

And Miss Champion flipped her switch.

CHAPTER NINE

Rhenia Four

Far out in deep space although the *Procyon* was, her communications officers monitored all four of the most important channels, and everything that came in on 'I-S One' was taped off. Thus, even though the 'Battle of New York Spaceport' and the conference that followed it took place in the middle of the starship's 'night', both were played in full on the regular morning news program. So was one solid hour of bi-partisan and extremely heated discussion by the big-name commentators of Earth.

To say that this news created a sensation is the understatement of the month. Nor was sentiment entirely in favor of GalMet, even though all the men aboard except Deston, and many of the women, were salaried employees and the whole expedition was on MetEnge–DesDes business.

'Shocking!' 'Outrageous!' 'Cold-blooded murder!'

'Who murdered first?' 'Land-mines, Seventy-fives, and Bofors!' 'Shot down the copter and killed everybody aboard!'

'But they should have settled the strike!' 'GalMet was utterly lawless!'

'I suppose it's lawful to use land-mines and anti-aircraft guns and make a full-war-scale battlefield inside New York City?'

And so on.

The top echelon was, of course, solidly in favor of Maynard, and Captain Jones summed up their attitude very neatly when he said, 'What the hoodlums are bellyaching about is that they were out-guessed, out-thunk, and out-gunned in the ratio of a hundred and five millimeters to seventy-five.'

'But listen,' Bernice said. 'Do you think, Babe, that there were any men aboard that copter?'

'One gets you a thousand there weren't. Maynard didn't say there were any.'

'He didn't say there weren't any, either,' Barbara argued, 'like he did for the tanks. What makes you so sure?'

'He knew what was going to happen – he let them think it was manned, probably as a deterrent – so you can paste it in your Easter bonnet, pet, that the only brains aboard that copter were tapes.'

Time wore on; the strife on Earth, which did not flare into the news again, was just about forgotten. Deston found several enormous deposits of copper. He found all the other most-wanted metals except rhenium in quantity sufficient to supply even the most extravagant demand. But of rhenium he still found only insignificant traces.

Each tremendous deposit of metal had been reported as soon as it was found. Crew after crew had been sent out. Plant after plant had been built; each one of which would be not only immensely profitable, but also of inestimable benefit to humanity as a whole, since all those highly important metals would soon be on the market at a mere fraction of their former high prices.

Still rhenium did not appear. 'I don't believe there *is* any such damn thing, anywhere in the whole galaxy,' Deston said, over and over, but he did not give up.

The starship bored along on its hugely helical course, deeper and deeper into unexplored space toward the Center. Until, after weeks of futile seeking, Deston did find rhenium. After a quick once-over, without waiting to get close enough to the planet for the physical scientists to make any kind of a survey, he called Galmetia and Miss Champion.

'Hi, Doris!' he greeted her happily. 'I've got some good news for you at last. We found it.'

'Oh? Rhenium? In quantity? How wonderful!'

'Yes. Oodles and gobs of it. All anybody and everybody can ever use. So how about busting in on the Chief Squeeze, huh?'

To Deston's surprise, since he had *always* had instant access to Maynard, the girl hesitated, tapping her teeth with a pencil. 'I ... just ... don't ... know.' Indecision, in one of the top FirSecs of all space, was an amazing thing indeed. 'He's all tied up with Plastics, Synthos, Pharmics, and half a dozen others, and he told me ...'

'Okay, skip it and give me a buzz. It's been here for a couple of billion years, anyway, so another hour or ...'

'That's what *you* think. Usually, Babe – practically *always* – he gives me my head, but this time he swore he'd shoot me right through the brain and hang my carcass out of the window on a hook, if I cut in on him with anything whatever or anybody whoever until this brawl is over ... but I know *damn* well he'll boil me in oil if I hold *this* up for even a minute ... Well, I think I'd rather be shot. Wouldn't you?'

'It'd be quicker, anyway.'

'Well, a girl can die only once.' She shrugged her shapely shoulders and cut Deston in.

'What the *hell*, Champion!' Maynard blazed; then, as he saw what was on the screen, his expression and attitude changed completely. 'Okay. Tell you-know-who to roll. Cut.'

Deston's image flipped back onto Miss Champion's screen and breathed a deep sigh of relief. 'Believe me, Babe, that was one brass-bound toughie to guess.'

'Check. But you're a smartie, doll, or you wouldn't be holding *that* fort. So let's get you-know-who and tell her to cut her gravs, huh?'

'Cutting her shoulder-straps would be enough. *B-z-z-z-z-zzt!* She'd take off without an anti-grav, let alone a ship.'

'She's been taking it big?'

' "Immense" would be a much better word ... Doctor Byrd, they have found your rhenium. Here's Mister Deston.'

It was evident that 'The Byrd' had been fighting with someone and was still in a vicious mood. When she saw Deston, however, her stormy face cleared and she became instantly the keen, competent executive. 'Have you *really* found some?' she demanded. 'Enough of it to make a fully-automated plant pay out?'

'Well, since the stuff runs well over twenty billion metric

tons to the cubic kilometer and it's here by the hundreds of cubic kilometers in solid masses, what do *you* think?'

'Oh my God! What's the planet like? A stinker, as expected?'

'All of that. No survey yet, but it's vicious. Several gees. Super-dense atmosphere, probably bad. No listing for it or anything like it – mountains and mesas of solid metal. You'll need personal armor, anti-gravs, skyhooks – the works. Pretty much like theory, from this distance. Closer up, it may get worse.'

'Everything anybody has suggested is aboard. But Deston; they tell me you're Top Dog on this. Is it actually true that the sky's the limit? And that I'm running it without interference?'

'Not even the sky is the limit on this one. No limit. Yes, except in matters of policy, you are the Complete Push.'

She glanced at Miss Champion, who said, 'If Mr. Deston says so, it is so; he has over-riding authority in this. In two minutes you will be handed an *unlimited* authorization, Doctor Byrd – the first one I ever heard of.'

'Oh, wonderful! Thanks a million, both of you! Now if you'll transfer him over here, Miss Cham...' Deston's image appeared upon Byrd's screen, '... pion – thanks. Mr. Deston, if you'll give Astrogation, here, the coords, we'll ...' A hand phone rang; she snatched it up. 'Byrd ... Yes, Lew, good news. At last, thank God, they've found our rhenium and we're jetting. Activate the whole project. Get Crew One aboard the *Rhene* as though the devil was on your tail with a pitchfork ... I know it's sudden, but Goddamn it, what did you expect? ... You've all been under notice for a month to be ready to blast off on fifteen minutes' notice ... Me? I'll be aboard and ready in *ten* minutes!'

Wherefore it was not long until the giant starship *Rhene* joined the *Procyon* in orbit around the forbidding planet Rhenia Four; in such an orbit as to remain always directly above a tiny valley surrounded by torn and jagged bare-metal-and-rock mountains; and Cecily Byrd came aboard the exploring vessel.

'I'm very glad to meet you in the flesh, Doctor Byrd,' Deston said, and as soon as she was out of her space-suit they shook hands cordially.

'Doctor Livingstone, I presume?' She giggled infectiously. 'You'll never know how glad I am to be here.' There was nothing sullen or morose or venomous about her now; she was eager, friendly, and intense. 'And no formality, Babe. I'm "Curly" to my friends.'

'Okay, Curly – now meet the gang. My wife, Bobby ... Herc Jones and his wife, Bun ... Andy Adams, our Prime Brain, and his wife, Stella ... This planet is a tough baby; a prime stinker.'

'So I gathered, and the more you find out about it the tougher and stinkier it gets. We've fabricated all the stuff you suggested, for which thanks, by the way, so, unless there have been new developments in the last couple of hours, I'll go back and we'll go down. Okay?'

'Okay except for an added feature. Herc and I are going along as safety factors. We have built-in danger alarms.'

'Oh? Oh, yes, I remember now. Welcome to our city.'

Aboard the *Rhene*, Deston said, 'But as chief of the party, Curly, you ought to stay up here, don't you think?'

'Huh?' The woman's whole body stiffened. '*As* chief of the party, buster, I'm the best man on it. What would *you* do? Stay home?'

'Okay,' and preparations went on.

Extreme precautions were necessary, for this was a fantastic planet indeed. In size it was about the same as Earth, but its surface gravity was almost four times Earth's. Its atmosphere, which was at a pressure of over forty pounds to the square inch, was mostly xenon, with some krypton, argon, and nitrogen, with less than seven percent by volume of oxygen. Its rivers were few and small, as were its lakes. Its three oceans combined would not equal the Atlantic in area, and what was dissolved in those oceans no one knew. The sun Rhenia was a Class B7 horror, so big and so hot that Rhenia Four, although twice as far away from Rhenia as Mars is from Sol, was as hot as Mars is cold. Even at latitude fifty north, where the starships were, and at an altitude of over fifteen thousand feet, at which the floor of the little valley was, the noon temperature in the shade was well over forty degrees Centigrade.

And there was life. Just what kind of life it was, none of the biologists could even guess. They had been arguing ever since arrival, but they hadn't settled a thing. There were things of various shapes and sizes that might or might not be analogous to the grass, shrubs, and trees of the Tellus-Type planets; but no one could say whether they were vegetable, mineral, or metalo-organic in nature. There were things that ran and leaped and fought; and things that flew and fought – all of which moved with the fantastic speed and violence concomitant with near-four gees – but if they were animals they were entirely unlike any animals ever before seen by man.

No one aboard the *Procyon* had even tried to land, of course. They didn't have the equipment; and besides, it was 'Curly' Byrd's oyster and she had repeatedly threatened mayhem upon the person of anyone who tried to open it before she got there.

The personal armor of the landing party – or rather, the observation party, since they did not intend to land – was built of heavy gauge high-alloy steel, and each suit was equipped with drivers and with anti-gravs. Their craft was much more like a bathyscaphe than a space-to-ground vehicle. Its walls were two inches of hard alloy; its ports were five inches of fused silica. It could, everyone agreed, take anything that Rhenia Four could dish out. In view of that agreement, Cecily had protested against wearing armor of proof inside the shuttle, but Deston had put his foot down there. Something *might* happen.

Counting the pilot, five persons composed the party, Director Byrd and Assistant Director Leyton were completely encased. Deston and Jones, however, had left their hands bare, as each was carrying a .475 semi-automatic rifle. Magnums, these, of tremendous slugging power; and all their cartridges – each gunner had three extra fifty-round drums – were loaded with armor-piercers, not soft-nosed stuff. They went down, talking animatedly and peering eagerly, until two silent inner alarms went off at once.

'Hold it!' Jones yelled, and Deston's even louder command was, 'High it at max, fly-boy!'

The craft darted upward, but even at full blast she was not

fast enough to escape from a horde of flying things that looked something like wildcats' heads mounted on owls' bodies, but vastly larger than either. They attacked viciously; their terrible teeth and even more terrible talons tearing inches-deep gouges into the shuttle's hard, tough armor. As the little vessel shot upward, however, higher and higher into the ever-thinning atmosphere, the things began to drop away – they *did* have to breathe.

Several of them, however, stayed on. They had dug holes clear through the armor; out of which the shuttle's air was whistling. The creatures were breathing ship's air – and liking it! – and were working with ferocious speed and power and with appalling efficiency.

Deston and Jones began shooting as soon as the first two openings were large enough to shoot through, but even those powerful weapons – the hardest-hitting shoulder-guns built – were shockingly ineffective. Both monsters had their heads inside the ship and were coming in fast. The others had dropped away for lack of air.

'Hercules' Jones, big enough and strong enough to handle even a .475 as though it were a .30-30, put fifty hard-nosed bullets against one spot of his monster's head and thus succeeded in battering that head so badly out of shape that the creature died before gaining entrance. Died and hung there, half in and half out.

But Deston, although supremely willing, simply did not have the weight and sheer brute strength to take that brutal magnum's recoil and hold it steady on one point. Thus when his drum was empty the creature was still coming. It was dying, however, almost dead, because of the awful pounding it had taken and because there was almost no air at all left in the shuttle.

Both men were changing drums, but they were a few seconds late. The thing had life enough left so that as it came through the wall and fell to the floor it made one convulsive flop, and in its dying convulsions it sank one set of talons into Cecily Byrd's thigh and the other into the calf of Lewis Leyton's leg. The woman shrieked once and, for the first time in her life, fainted dead away. The man swore sulphurously.

110

By this time they were almost back to the *Rhene*. The landing craft was taken aboard and a team of surgeons tried for a few minutes to get those incredible talons out of the steel and the flesh; then for a few minutes more they tried to amputate those equally incredible feet. Then they anesthetized both victims and carried the inseparable trio into the machine-shop; where burly mechanics ground the beast's leg in two with high-speed neotride wheels and, using tools designed to handle high-tensile bar stock, curled those ghastly hooks back out of flesh and armor. Thence and finally to the sick-bay, where the doctors put everything they could think of into those deep, but not ordinarily dangerous, wounds.

As soon as the doctors became fairly sure that no alien germs were at work in the human flesh, Deston strode up to Cecily's bed.

'We'll get one thing straight right now, Curly,' he said, 'I'm all done suggesting; I'm telling you. You don't go down there again until I say so.'

She straightened up angrily; she was not too sore to fight. 'Think again, buster. We're on the job now, not at HQ. It's my job and I'll run it any way I damn well please.'

'At HQ or anywhere else, my curly-haired friend, my authority over-rides on matters of policy and this is a matter of policy. You'll take it and you'll like it.'

'Over-rides, hell! I'll...'

'You'll nothing!' he snapped. 'Did you ever get socked on the jaw hard enough to lay you out stiff for fifteen minutes?'

Instead of becoming even more furious at that, she relaxed and grinned up at him. 'No, I never did. That would be a brand-new experience.'

'Okay. Much more of this sticking out of your beautiful neck and you'll get that brand-new experience. Now let's do some thinking on what to do next. I shot in an order for a special elsie* ...'

'Can you ... those kittyhawks went through super-stainless like so much cheese. What plating – neotride?'

'That's right. Here's the funny-picture.' He spread a blueprint out on the bed. 'I didn't have much of anything to do

* Elsie – LC – Landing Craft. EES.

with it, though; it's mostly Lew's work.'

She studied the drawing for a couple of minutes. 'That ought to do it; it'd stop a diamond drill cold ... it'd hold a neotride drill for a while ... but what *are* those monstrosities, Babe? All that the croakers will give out with is gobbledegook, soothing syrup, and pure pap.'

'Nobody knows. All the biologists aboard are going not-so-slowly nuts. They can't do anything from up here.'

'All of us. Nice.' She bit her lip. 'Without rhenium we can't work down there and we have to work down there to get rhenium. Strictly circular progress.'

'It isn't that bad, Curly. There are dozens of nice big chunks of the clear quill – thousands of tons of it – right out in the open down there. That's the special elsie's job, to go down and get 'em and bring 'em out here to us. The chief wants a good mess of it rushed in to Galmetia, but there's plenty of it lying around loose to take care of him and build five of your installations besides.'

'Wonderful! That makes me feel a lot better, Babe – I'll talk to you now until the croakers throw you out.'

CHAPTER TEN

The Party

Cecily and Leyton were both up and at work, their wounds completely healed, when the special elsie arrived. This landing craft was special indeed, for the first abortive attempt to approach that fantastically inimical planet had made it perfectly clear that they would have to have hundreds of tons of rhenium before they could begin to work.

This little ship was to get it. Her inner layer of armor was four inches thick, forged of the stubbornest super-steel available. The outer layer, electronically fused to the inner, was one full inch of neotride, the synthetic that was the hardest substance known to man – five numbers Rockwell harder than the diamond.

The starship carrying the elsie also brought two formally-typed notices – things almost unknown in a day of subspace communicators and tapes. The one addressed to 'Cecily Byrd, Ph.D., Sc.D., F.I.A.' (Fellow of the Institute of Automation) read in part 'You are hereby instructed, under penalty of discharge and blacklist, to stay aloft until complete safety of operation has been demonstrated,' and the gist of Deston's was 'I can not give you orders, but if you have half the brain I think you have, you *know* enough to stay aloft until safety of operation has been demonstrated.'

Cecily's nostrils flared, then her whole body slumped. 'He'd do it, too, the damned old tiger ... and this is the biggest job I ever dreamed about ... and I suppose *you'll* go down anyway.'

'Uh-uh. He makes sense. Actually, neither of us should take

the chance. Anyway, the stuff is right out in the open, where they can sit right down on it and grapple it ... and besides, my mother told me it isn't sporting to kick a lady in the face when she's down. It isn't done, she said.'

'She did? How nice of her! Thanks, Babe, a lot,' and she held out her hand.

Thus it was that Assistant Director Leyton and Captain Jones led the down-crew. They both, and two other big, strong men as well, carried .475's; but this time the magnums were not needed. The neotride held up long enough. In spite of everything the rabidly hostile 'animals' could do, the elsie grappled five-hundred-ton chunks of the stuff and lugged them up into orbit.

In the meantime the metallurgists, by subjecting the teeth and claws of the dead kittyhawks to intensive study, had solved their biggest basic problem. Or rather, they found out that Nature had solved it for them.

'The composition at maxprop – to get the best mat of longest single crystals, you know – is extremely complex and almost unbelievably critical,' Leyton told Deston, happily. 'It would have taken us years, and even then we wouldn't have hit it exactly on the nose except by pure luck.'

'Well, how do you expect to do in a couple of years what it took Old Mother Nature millions of years? Billions even, maybe.'

'It's been done. Anyway, we're 'way ahead of Old Mother in one respect – heat-treating. We've got a growth-cycle already that makes the original look sick.'

The new and improved leybyrdite was poured, forged, neotride-ground, and heat-treated. A tailored-to-order mining head was built; and, in spite of the frantic and highly capable opposition of the local life-forms, was driven into the mountainside.

This first unit took a long time, since everyone had to work in armor and anti-grav. After it was in place, however, the job went much faster, as air was run in and the whole installation was gravved down to nine eighty – Earth-normal gravity – and people could work in ordinary working clothes.

Section after section was attached; the whole gigantic assembly was jacked forward, inch by inch.

Adams and his crew developed a super-flame-thrower which, instead of chemical flames, projected a plasma jet – the heat of nuclear, not chemical, reaction. Cecily had twenty of them made and installed at strategic points. It took a couple of weeks for the various fauna to learn that such heat was quickly and inevitably fatal; but, having learned the fact, they kept their distance and the work went easier and faster.

But the director brushed aside the scientists' pleas for elsies in which to study. 'I'm sorry, Adams, but first things have got to come first. When we get a full stream of rhenium coming out of that hole in the ground I'll build you anything you want, but until then absolutely *nothing* goes that isn't geared directly to production.'

And she herself was everywhere. Dressed in leybyrdite helmet, leather jacket, leather breeches, and high-laced boots, she was in the point, in the middle, in the tail, and in all stations, for whatever purpose intended. And, since no two operations are ever alike and this one was like nothing else ever built, she was carrying the full load. But she knew what she was doing, and hers was a mind that did not have to follow any book. She ordered special machinery and equipment so regardlessly of cost that Desmond Phelps almost had heart failure. When she wanted ten extra-special units, each of which would cost over a hundred thousand dollars to build, she ordered them as nonchalantly as though they were that many ballpoint pens; and Maynard okayed her every requisition without asking a single question.

She had her troubles, of course, but only one of them was with her personnel – the revolt of her section heads. Some of them resented the fact that she was a woman; some of them really believed that they knew more about some aspects of the job than she did. She called a meeting and told them viciously to do the job her way and quit dragging their feet – or else. Next day, in four successive minutes, she fired four of them; whereupon the others decided that Byrd was a hard-rock man after all and began to play ball.

She had her troubles, of course – what big job has ever gone strictly according to plan? – but she met them unflinchingly

115

head on and flattened them flat. She knew her stuff and she held her crew and her job right in the palm of her hand. Even Maynard was satisfied; not too many men could have run such a hairy job as smoothly as she was doing it.

The last element was installed. The last tape was checked, rechecked, and double-checked. Maynard, Smith, and Phelps, all in person – a truly unprecedented event, this! – inspected and approved the whole project. Project Rhenia Four, fully automatic, was ready to roll in its vast entirety.

Maynard stared thoughtfully at his project chief. Her helmet was under her left arm. She hadn't seen a hair-dresser for five months; her rebellious brick-dust-red curls were jammed into a nylon net. Her jacket, breeches, and boots were scuffed, stained, scarred, and worn. She had lost pounds of weight; faint dark rings encircled both eyes. But those eyes fairly sparkled; her whole mien was one of keen anticipation. Maynard had never seen her in any such mood as this.

'Okay, Byrd; push the button,' he said.

'Uh-uh, chief, you push it. It's your honor, really; nobody else in all space would have stood back of me the way you have.'

'Thanks. It'd tickle me to; I've never started a big operation yet,' and the whole immense project went smoothly to work.

Strained and tense, they watched it for half an hour. Then Maynard shook her hand.

'You *were* worth saving, Byrd. You're an operator; a real performer. I hope you've got over that ungodly insecurity complex of yours. You know what I'm going to do to you if you ever start that hell-raising again?'

She laughed. 'You and Babe both seem to have the same idea; he says he'll knock me as cold as ice-cream. You, too?'

'No, I don't think that's the indicated treatment. I'll get you pie-eyed on the best brandy in Beardsley's cellar.'

'Don't tempt me, chief!' She laughed again as Smith, Phelps, Leyton, Deston, Jones, and the others came up to add their congratulations to Maynard's.

They kept on watching the tremendous installation, less and less tensely and with more and more eating and sleeping, for fifty more hours, during which time a hundred freighters departed with their heavy loads. Then all tension disappeared. Having run this long, it would continue to run; with only normal supervision and maintenance.

'Now for the usual party,' Smith said. 'Unusual, it should be, since this is a highly unusual installation. How about it, everybody?'

'Let's have a big dance,' Barbara suggested. 'Dress up and everything.'

'Oh, let's!' Cecily almost squealed. She was still in her scuffed leathers, still ready for any emergency. Her hair was still a tightly-packed mop. 'We're all rested enough – I just had fourteen hours sleep and two big steaks. Let's go!'

'We're off, Curly.' Bernice took her arm. 'We'll help each other get all prettied up. Herc, how about locking the ships together, so we won't get all mussed up in those horrible suits?'

'Can do, pet.' Jones gave his wife the smile reserved for her alone; a smile that softened wonderfully his hard, craggy, deeply-tanned face. 'For beauty in distress we'd do even more than that.'

In about an hour, then, the party began. Bernice and Cecily were standing together when Jones and Leyton came up to them. The red-head was a good inch taller than tall Bernice; she would have stood five feet ten without her four-inch heels. Both gowns were as tight as they could be without showing stress-patterns; both were strapless, backless, and almost frontless; both hemlines bisected kneecaps.

The two men were just about of a size – six feet three, and twenty pounds or so over two hundred. Leyton was handsome; Jones very definitely was not. Leyton was the softer; it was not part of his job to keep himself at the peak of physical fitness. He was, however, by no means soft. Being 'softer' than Theodore Jones left a lot of room for a man to be in very good shape indeed, and Lewis Leyton was.

Both men stopped and Jones whistled expressively; a perfectly-executed wolf-whistle. '*This* must be *Miss* Byrd.' He smiled as he took her hand and bowed over it – and, as a space officer, he really knew how to bow. 'Miss Byrd, may I have the honor and the pleasure of the second number, please?'

She dipped a half-curtsy and laughed. 'You may indeed, sir,' and Leyton swept her away.

Jones danced first with his wife, of course; then led Cecily out onto the floor. For a minute they danced in silence, each conscious of what a superb performer the other was and of how perfectly they matched. She was the first to speak.

'You're looking at my hair. Don't, Herc, please. Nobody in all space can do anything with it, and I didn't have time to let your beauty-shop even try.'

'Do you really mean that, Curly, or are you just fishing?'

'Of course I mean it! Look at Bun's hair, or Bobby's, or *anybody's*! They can fix it any way they please and change it any time they please. But *this* stuff?' She shook her intractable mop. 'This carroty-pink-sorrel mess of rusty steel-turnings? Nobody can do anything with it whatever. I can't even bleach it or dye it – or even wear a wig. It's bad enough, the color and the way it is now, but with it anything else, with my turkey-egg face, I look just simply like the wrath of God. Honestly.'

'If that's really the way you look at it, I think I'll tell a tale out of school. You know Bun isn't the jealous type.'

'Of course she isn't. My God, with what *she's* got, why should she be? How *could* she be?'

'Okay. Since she met you she's told me a dozen times that if anybody in all space could make a hair-piece like that – nobody can, she says – she'd shave her head and get one tomorrow.'

Cecily leaned back – she had been dancing very close – far enough to look into his eyes. 'Why, you great big damn liar . . .'

'Ask her, next time you see her.'

'I'll do just that. In the meantime, for the prize-winning big lie of the year, tell me that next to Bun I'm the prettiest girl here; not a hard-boiled hard-rock man in a ball gown.'

'I'll tell you something a lot better than that. You've got stuff by the cubic mile that no merely pretty girl ever did have or ever will have.'

'Such as?' she scoffed.

'If you really don't know, take a complete inventory of yourself sometime.'

'I have, thousands of times.'

'Wrong system, then. Change it.'

She leaned still farther away from him. 'You sound as though you really mean that.'

'I do Scout's Honor. And Bun agrees with me.'

'She does? I'll bet she does. You've got a nice line, Herc.'

'No line, Curly; believe me.'

'It'd be nice if I could ... but Herc, the chief thinks I have a terrific case of inferiority complex ... except he called it "insecurity" ... and Babe said ... do you think so?'

'I'm no psych, so I wouldn't know. But why in all the hells of space should you have?'

She actually missed a step. 'Why *should* I have! Just *look* at me! Or can't you imagine what it's like, being the ugliest duckling in the pond all your life?'

'Can't I? You *have* got a complex. Look at *me*, you dumb ... what do you think *I've* been all my life?'

She stared at him in amazement. 'Why, *you're* positively distinguished-looking!'

'Comet-gas! I've always been the homeliest guy around, but I got so I didn't let it throw me.'

'Anyway, men don't have to be good-looking.'

'Neither do women. Look at history.'

'Let's look at Bun instead – one of the most beautiful women who ever lived. You wouldn't have...'

'I certainly would have. Beauty helps, of course – and I admit that I like it, that she's a beauty – but over the long route it isn't a drop in the bucket and you know it. She'll still be a charmer at ninety, and so will you. She's prettier than you are, but you've got a lot of stuff she hasn't. What did you think I was talking about, a minute ago?'

'Sex. Anybody can throw that around.'

'Not the way you can. But that wasn't it, at all; that's only one phase. It's the total personality that carries the wallop. You've got it. So has Bun. And Bobby. Who else aboard? Nobody.'

'I wonder...' They danced in silence for a time. 'You could be right, I suppose ... after all, you and Maynard and Babe are certainly three of the smartest men I know.'

'You know we're right. So why don't you cut the jaw-flapping and get down to reality?'

'Maybe you *are* right. Thanks, Herc, the thought is one to dwell on. You know what I'm going to do?' She giggled suddenly. 'I haven't done it since my Freshman Frolic.' She drew herself up very close to him, snuggled her head down onto his shoulder, and closed both eyes.

And thus they finished the dance. He brought her back to a place beside his wife, thanked her, and turned away toward Barbara.

Cecily stared after his retreating figure. 'That's a lot of man you have there, Bun,' she breathed, as Smith and Phelps came up to claim them.

'I know,' Bernice agreed.

Ten minutes later, in the improvised powder room, Bernice continued the conversation quite as though it had not been interrupted. 'You wouldn't by any chance have it in mind to do anything about it, would you, darling?'

Each woman studied the other. Both were tall and superb of figure. Each projected in quantity – and not only unconsciously – the tremendous basic force that is sex appeal. But there all resemblance ceased. Bernice, as has been said, was one of the most beautiful women of her time. And besides beauty of face and figure, besides strength of physique and of character, she had the poise and confidence of her status and of her sure knowledge of her husband's love. Cecily Byrd, on the other hand, radiated a personality that was uniquely hers and that made itself tellingly felt wherever she was. In addition, she had the driving force, the sheer will-power, and the ruthlessly competent brain of the top-bracket executive she had so fully proved herself to be.

'It'd be fun,' the red-head said, thoughtfully. 'That would really be a battle.'

'As Herc likes to say, you chirped it that time, birdie.'

'Ordinarily, that would make it all the more fun, but I'll be working like a dog yet for quite a while – I'll hardly have time enough in bed even to sleep. So let's take a rain-check on it, shall we, my dear?'

'Any time, darling. Any time at all. Whenever you please.'

Blue eyes stared steadily into eyes of Irish green.

Then Cecily shook her head. 'I'm not going to try, Bun. I think too much of both of you . . . and besides, I might not be able to . . . You know, Bun . . .' She paused, then went on, slowly, 'I never have liked women very much; they're such flabby, gutless things . . . but you're a lot of woman yourself.'

'We're a lot alike in some ways, Curly – there *aren't* very many women like you and me and Barbara – for which fact, of course, most men would say "Thank God!"'

'You're *so* right!'

Not being men, the two almost-antagonists did not shake hands; but at that moment the ice began definitely to melt.

'But listen,' Bernice said. 'There are hundreds of men around here. Good men and big ones.'

Cecily grinned. 'But not usually both; and just being big isn't enough to make me come apart at the seams. He has to have a brain, too; and maybe what Herc just called a "total personality".'

'That *does* narrow the field . . . just about to Lew, I guess . . . but I suppose Executives' Code cuts both ways.'

'It's supposed to, probably, but I wouldn't care about that if he weren't such a stuffed shirt . . . but I'm getting an idea. Let's go hunt Babe up.' Then, as Bernice looked at her quizzically, 'My God, no – who except a half-portion like Bobby would want him? I just want to ask him a question.'

They found Deston easily enough. 'Babe,' Cecily said, 'You said there's a lot of tantalum here. As much as on Tantalia Three?'

'More. Thousands of times as much. Why?'

'Then Perce Train ought to come out here and look it over. I'll tell the chief so. Thanks, Babe.'

'Perce Train?' Bernice asked, the next time they sat together. 'The boyfriend?'

'Not yet. We were knifing each other all over the place, back at HQ, but we're both on top now. He'll be good for what ails me. Wait 'till you see *him*, sister – and hang onto your hat.'

'I'll have no trouble doing *that*, I'm positive,' Bernice said, a little stiffly; just as Jones came up, again to dance her away.

Percival Train appeared in less than a week. He was, as has

been said, a big bruiser. He was just about Leyton's size, and even handsomer. As soon as he got over the shock of discovering what a hellish planet Rhenia Four was, he became enthusiastic about its possibilities. He also, Bernice was sure, became enthusiastic about Project Engineer Byrd.

'But there's nothing flagrant about it that I can see, pet,' Jones argued one night, just before going to sleep. 'What makes you think so except Curly's jaw flapping?'

'I just *know* they are,' Bernice said, darkly. 'She really meant it, and she's the type to. She ought to be ashamed of herself, but she isn't. Not the least little tiny bit.'

'Well, neither of 'em's married, so what's the dif? Even if they are stepping out, which is a moot point, you know.'

'Well ... maybe. One good thing about it, she isn't making any passes at *you*, and she'd better not. I'll scratch both her green eyes out if she tries it, the hussy – so help me!'

'Oh, she was just chomping her choppers, sweetheart. Besides, I'm as prejudiced as I am insulated. I've never seen anyone within seven thousand parsecs of being *you*.'

'You're a darling, Herc, and I love you all to pieces.' She snuggled up close and closed her eyes; but she did not drop easily, as was her wont, to sleep.

If that red-headed, green-eyed vixen – that sex-flaunting powerhouse – *had* unlimbered her heavy artillery ... but she hadn't ... and it was just as well for all concerned, Bernice thought, just before she did go to sleep, that that particular triangular issue had not been joined.

CHAPTER ELEVEN

Psiontists

Secretary of Labor Deissner was very unhappy. The United Copper Miners, as a union, had been wiped out of existence. Mighty Drivers' all-out effort at New York Spaceport had been smashed with an ease that was, to Deissner's mind, appalling. Worse, it was inexplicable; and, since no one else really knew anything, either, he was being buffeted, pushed, and pulled in a dozen different directions at once.

The Dutchman, however, was nobody's push-over. He merely set his stubborn jaw a little more stubbornly. 'I want *facts*!' he bellowed, smashing his open hand down onto the top of his desk. 'I've got to have *facts*! Until I get *facts* we can't move – I *won't* move!'

For weeks, then, and months, 'Dutch' Deissner studied ultraconfidential reports and interviewed ultra-secret agents – many of whom were so ultra-ultra-secret as to be entirely unknown to any other member of WestHem's government ... and the more he worked the less secure he felt and the more unhappy he became. He was particularly unhappy when, late one night and very secretly, he conferred with a plenipotentiary from EastHem.

'The Nameless One is weary of meaningless replies to his questions,' the Slav said, bruskly. 'I therefore demand with his mouth a plan of action and its date of execution.'

'Demand and be damned,' Deissner said, flatly. 'I will not act until I know what that *verdammte* Maynard has got up his sleeve. Tell Nameless that.'

'In that case you will come with me now.'

'You talk like a fool. One false move and you and your escort die where you sit. Tell Nameless he does not own me yet and it may very well be he never will. If he wants to talk to me I will arrange a meeting in South Africa.'

'You are rash. Are you fool enough to believe that he will condescend to meet you at any place of your choosing?'

'I don't care whether he does or not. If he knows as much as I do, he will.'

The messenger went away; and, a long time later, the Nameless One did meet Deissner – with due precautions on each side, of course – in South Africa.

'Don't you know, fool,' the dictator opened up, 'that you will die for this?'

'No. Neither do you. Glance over this list of the real names of some men who have died lately in accidents of various kinds.'

If the Slav's iron control was shaken as he read the long list, it was scarcely perceptible. Deissner went on:

'As long as it was to my advantage I let you think that I was just another one of your puppets, but I'm not. If you insist on committing suicide by jumping in the dark, count me out.'

'In the dark? My information is that...'

'Have you any information as to where those so-huge tanks came from? Where they could possibly have been built?'

'No, but...'

'Then whatever information you have is completely useless,' the Dutchman drove relentlessly on. 'Maynard has been ready. What more is he ready for? That thought made me think. How did he get that way? I investigated. Do you know that computers and automation to the amount of hundreds of millions of dollars have been paid for by and delivered to non-existent firms?'

'No, but what...?'

'From that fact I drew the tentative conclusion that Met-Enge has industrialized a virgin planet somewhere; one that we know nothing whatever about.'

'Ridiculous! MetEnge builds its own automation ... but to save time they might ... but such a planet would have to be staffed, and that could not be done tracelessly.'

'It was done tracelessly enough so that we did not suspect it. I find that about sixty thousand male graduate engineers and scientists, and about the same number of young and nubile females of the same types, have disappeared from the ninety-six planets.'

'So?' This information had little visible effect.

'So those disappearances prove beyond any reasonable doubt that my tentative conclusion is a fact. Maynard is not bluffing; he is ready. Now, if MetEnge has worked that long and hard in complete secrecy it should be clear even to you that you and your missiles are precisely as dangerous to them as a one-week-old kitten would be. Before we can act we must find that planet and bomb it out of existence.'

'It is impossible to hide so many people, especially young ...'

'Do you think my agents didn't check? They did, thoroughly, and could find ...'

'Bah! Your agents are stupid!'

'They were smart enough to put the arm on your men on that list, and if you think Maynard is stupid you had better think again. The worst fact is that twenty-eight of my agents have disappeared, too, all of whom had worked up into good jobs with MetEnge and any one of whom could have and would have built a subspace communicator had it been humanly possible. The situation is bad. Very bad. That is why I have not acted. I will not act until I have enough facts to act on.'

'*My* agents would have found that planet if it exists. I will send my own men and they will find it if it exists.'

'You think you've got a monopoly on brains?' Deissner sneered. 'Send your men and be damned. You'll learn. Here are copies of everything I have found out,' and he handed The Nameless One a bulging brief-case.

Nameless took it without thanks. 'In three months I will know all about everything and I will act accordingly.'

'You *hope*. In the meantime you must agree that a general strike is out of the question.'

'Until I investigate, yes. Harrassing tactics merely.'

'Exactly what I am doing. Plan M.'

'As good as any. Your status in my organization will depend upon my findings,' and the Nameless One of EastHem strode out.

The tremendous new starship, the *Explorer,* built of leybyrdite and equipped for any foreseeable eventuality, was ready to fly. The Destons and the Joneses were holding their last preflight conference. No one had said anything for a couple of minutes; yet no one had suggested that the meeting was over.

'Well, that covers it ... I guess...' Deston said, finally, 'Except maybe for one thing that's been niggling at me ... but it makes so little sense that I'm afraid to say it out loud. So if any of you can think of anything else we might need, no matter how wild it sounds ... I'm playing a hunch. Write it down on a slip of paper and put it face-down on the table ... here's mine ... it'll be three out of four, I think ... read 'em and weep, Bun.'

Bernice turned the four slips over. 'Four out of four. Perce Train and Cecily Byrd. But what in *hell* do we want 'em *for?*'

'Search me; just a hunch,' Deston said, and:

'Me neither; just intuition.' Barbara nodded her head. 'But why didn't we say anything ... oh, I see. You and I didn't, Babe, because we thought Bun wouldn't want her along. Bun didn't because she thought we'd think it was so she could kick her teeth out. Herc didn't because Bun might think he wanted her along for monkey business. Right?'

That was right, and Deston called Maynard. 'You can have 'em both and welcome,' was the tycoon's surprising reaction to Deston's request. 'They're the two hardest cases I ever tried to handle in my life, and I've got troubles enough without combing *them* out of my hair every hour on the hour. They did such good jobs on their projects that they haven't got enough to do. I'd like to fire them both – their assistants are a lot bettter for their present jobs than they are – but of course I can't. But listen, son. Why lead with your chin? If I can't handle those two damned kittyhawks, how do you expect to?'

'I don't know, chief; I'm just playing a hunch. Thanks a lot, and so-long.'

Percival Train and Cecily Byrd boarded the *Explorer* together. 'What can you four want of us?' the red-head asked, as soon as the six were seated around a table. 'Particularly, what can you *possibly* want of me?'

'We haven't the foggiest idea,' was Deston's surprising answer. 'But four solid hunches can't be wrong. So suppose you break down and tell us.'

'In that case I think I can. That must mean that you and Bobby are a lot more than just a wizard and a witch; and that both Herc and Bun are heavy-duty psionicists, too – I've more than suspected just that of Herc. Right?'

'That's right,' Barbara agreed. 'So you and Perce both are too.' Train's jaw dropped and he looked at Barbara in pop-eyed astonishment. 'Which I didn't suspect consciously for a second. How long have you had it, Curly – *known* that you had it, I mean?'

'Just since the dance. You gave me hell, Herc, remember? And before that, the chief and Babe had worked me over, too ...'

'I remember.' Jones began to grin. 'All I'm surprised at ...'

'Hush, you.' Cecily grinned back at him. 'I don't get these moments of truth very often, so you just listen. Anyway, after the dance I felt lower than a snake's feet. I didn't feel even like going over to my handbag after a cigarette, so I just sat there and looked at it and pretty soon I could see everything perfectly plainly and one jumped out of my case inside my bag and into my mouth and lit itself. Then I knew, of course, and started working on it and I got pretty good at it. Watch. I'm over here in the corner and now back in my chair. Now – count the cigarettes in your case, Babe.'

'He doesn't need to,' Train put in. 'Twelve King Camfields. Stainless steel case – not the one you carried on Rhenia, by the way – right-hand shirt pocket.' A king-size Camfield appeared between Cecily's lips and came alight. 'One gone, eleven left.'

'Oh?' 'Ah!' 'So!' came three voices at once; and Deston, after counting his cigarettes, said, 'Eleven is right. That's a neat trick, Curly – just a minute.'

Grasping his case he stared fixedly at it and a Camfield

appeared in his mouth, too; but it did not light up. 'How do you concentrate the energy without burning the end of your ...' He broke off as Barbara shot him a thought, then went on, '... yeah, that can come later. Go ahead Perce.'

'You four are using *telepathy*!' Train declared.

'Uh-huh. It's easy, we'll show you how it goes. Go ahead.'

'There's not much to tell. I've had it all my life, but I've never let on about it until now and I've never used it except on the job; I've been afraid to. I read up on psionics, but it's never been demonstrated scientifically and I didn't want the psychs to start with me. So I kept still. I knew you two were witches, of course – even though that is impossible, too – but I wasn't in your class, so I still kept still. Oh, I could see the stuff plainly enough when I knew exactly where to look, but that was all.'

'How do you know that was all? You've been fighting the whole concept, haven't you, the same way I was?'

'Could be, I guess ... maybe I *have* got something ... latent, I mean ... at that.'

'I don't suppose we really need to ask you two, then, if you want to come along with us.'

'I'll say you don't – and thanks a million for asking us,' Cecily breathed; and Train agreed fervently. He went on, 'You have room enough, I suppose? And when's your zero?'

'Plenty. Nineteen hours today was announced, but we can hold it up without hurting anything a bit.'

'No need to. That gives us over seven hours and we won't need half that. Except for our bags at the hotel all our stuff's in the shed. We'll be seeing you – let's jet, Curly.'

Train called an aircab and they were whisked across the city. Nothing was said until they were in the girl's room. He put both arms around her and looked straight into her eyes; his hard but handsome face strangely tender. 'This hasn't been enough, Sess. I asked you once before to marry me...'

'I'm glad you brought that up, Perce. I was just going to ask you if you still harbored the idea.'

There is no need to go into exactly what happened then. After a time, however, he said, 'I knew why you wouldn't, before.'

'Of course,' she replied, soberly. 'We would have been at each other's throats half the time – we would have hurt each other unbearably.'

'And this changes things completely,' he said, just as soberly. 'Exploring the universe with *those* four . . . as well as the unknown universe of psionics . . .'

'Oh, wonderful!' she breathed. 'Just the thought of it – especially that you're so strongly psionic, too – rocks me. It changes my whole world. And besides,' her expression changed completely; she gave him a bright, quick grin, 'children, especially such super-children as yours and mine, ought to have two parents. Married. To each other. You know?'

'Children!' Train gasped. 'Why, I didn't know . . . you didn't tell me you were . . .'

'Of course not, silly. I'm not. I'm talking about the ones we're *going* to have. Super-children. Half a dozen of 'em.'

'Oh.' Train gulped. 'Okay. But why the "super"?'

'Have you ever scanned Teddy Deston and Babbsy Jones?'

'No. Why should I have? Or any other little toddlers?'

'They aren't ordinary little toddlers, Perce. Not by seven thousand rows of apple trees. I got a flash once. Just a flash and just once, but I know *damn* well it was a mind-block. They scare me witless. Babe and Herc think they're ordinary babies, too, but Bobby and Bun know very well they aren't. They won't admit it, of course, even to themselves, to say nothing of to each other – Bobby and Bun, I mean, not the kids – so don't *ever* breathe a word of this to *anybody* – besides, they'd snatch you bald-headed if you did. So – *verbum sap.*'

'I *think* you're more than somewhat nuts, presh, but I'll be as verbum sappy as you say. Now, one for the road,' which turned out to be several, 'and we'll go hunt us up a preacher.'

'But we *can't*!' she wailed. 'I forgot – just thought of it. Three days – those blood tests and things!'

'That's right . . . but with the physicals we've been taking every ten days – proof enough of perfect health so they'll waive 'em.'

'One gets you ten they won't. Did you ever hear of a small-type bureaucrat cutting one inch of his damned red tape?'

'I sure have. All you got to have to push bureaucrats around is weight, and we're heavyweights here ... it'd be quicker, though, to do it the sneaky way – some starship's chaplain.'

'Oh, let's!' She squealed like a schoolgirl. 'I know you meant "sneaky" in its engineering sense, but I don't. She has as much cat blood in her as I have. Maybe more.'

'She?' Train raised his eyebrows. 'Better break that up into smaller pieces, presh. Grind it a little finer.'

'Comet-gas! You know who, and why. Bun. If you don't tell her who the chaplain was or what world he was from – registry, you know – she'll *never* find out when we were married.'

Train laughed 'I see, kitten – but I always did like cats, and I don't leak. Okay, little squirt – let's jet.'

Long before nineteen hours, then, the Trains and their belongings arrived at the *Explorer*'s dock. Leaving her husband at the freight hoist, Cecily went up in the passenger elevator and looked Bernice up. 'Where's our room, Bun?' she asked, in a perfectly matter-of-fact tone and without turning a hair.

Bernice started to say something; but, as she saw the heavy, plain, yellow-gold band – Cecily had never worn a ring on either hand – she said instead, 'Why, I didn't know you were – when did *this* happen?'

'Oh, we've been married quite a while. We didn't want it to get out before, of course, but I thought sure you'd guessed.'

'I guessed something, but not that. I'm awfully sorry, Curly, really, but ...'

'You needn't be, Bun, at all; you had every right to. But I'll tell you one thing right now that I really mean – there'll be no more monkey-business for me. Ever.'

'Oh, I'm *so* glad, Curly,' and this time the two women did kiss each other. This was the beginning of a friendship that neither had thought would ever be.

At exactly nineteen hours the *Explorer* cut gravs. No one aboard her knew where they were going. Or what they were looking for. Or how long they would be gone.

When Maynard told Deston that he did not have time to cope with two such trouble-makers as Train and Byrd, he was stating the exact truth; for he was busier than even he had ever been before. It was a foregone conclusion that the opposition, which included the most corrupt and farthest-left government WestHem had ever known, would not and could not accept its two minor defeats as having decided the issue.

The crucial question was: would they call one more local, single-business strike – in an industry that could not possibly be automated – before taking the supreme gamble of a general strike?

The Galaxians had been trying for a long time to answer that question. As has been said, GalMet's spy system (officially, it did not exist; actually, it was an invisible division of the Public Relations Department) was very good. So was WarnOil's; and InStell's, by the very nature of things, was better than either. And, long before, Maynard had engineered a deal whereby Stevens Spehn had been put in charge of the combined 'Information Services' of the Galactic Federation – and it is needless to say what kind of coverage this new service provided.

Six men now sat at Maynard's conference table. Maynard, as usual, was at its head. Lansing of WarnOil sat at his left. Spehn sat at his right. Next to Spehn was a newcomer to the summit table – Vice-President Guerdon Dann, the Admiral of InStell's far-flung fleet of private-police battleships. In full uniform, he was the typical officer of space: big, lean, hard, poised, and thoroughly fit. While older, of course, than a line officer, his stiff, crew-cut red hair was only lightly sprinkled with gray and he did not as yet wear lenses. Side by side, below Lansing, sat two other newcomers, Feodr Ilyowicz and Li Hing Wong, Russian and Chinese directors on the Board.

'Yes, it'll be milk,' Spehn was saying. 'Impossible to automate, easy to make one hundred percent effective, and of extremely high emotional value.'

'Right,' Maynard agreed. '*How* the sobbers will shriek and scream about our starving helpless babies to death by the thousands. Any idea yet as to time?'

'Nothing definite, but it'll be fairly soon and the general strike won't be. They're holding that up while they're looking for our base, and nobody is even close yet to suspecting where

131

Base is. Deissner and Nameless are all steamed up about the vanishing boys and girls and automation, but they're looking for them on a new planet out in space somewhere, not on an island on Galmetia. Are the kids still happy in Siberia?'

'Very much so; the bonuses take care of the isolation angle very nicely. They're making a game of being Siberians. They know it won't be too long and they know why we have to be absolutely sure that a lot of stuff stays hush-hush.'

'Good. Next, Dutch Deissner is making independent noises and is getting big ideas. Full partnership, no less.'

'He'll get himself squashed like a bug.'

'Maybe, but so far he's been doing most of the squashing, and Mister Big is burning like a torch.'

'Umm . . . um . . . mm.' Maynard thought for a moment. 'So you think EastHem actually will bomb?'

'They're sure to.' Spehn glanced across the table at Ilyowicz and Li, who both nodded. 'Not too long, I think, after the general strike is called – especially when we foul it up. Extra-heavy stuff on all our military installations, and really dirty stuff – one-hundred-percent-lethal nerve gas – on all our biggest cities. Wait a couple of months and take over.'

'But retaliation – oh, sure, evacuation of the upper strata, they figure they have too many people, anyway.'

'Check. They figure on losing millions of peasants and workers. They plan on getting a lot of people away, but I can't get even an inkling as to where. Do either of you fellows have any ideas on that?'

Li shook his head and Ilyowicz said, 'No. I do not believe it can be a developed planet; I do not think that such a project could have been carried out so tracelessly. My thought is that it is a temporary hide-out merely, on some distant virgin planet.'

'That makes sense,' Spehn said. 'How are you making out on the subs and the big jets, Guerd?'

'Satisfactory,' the admiral replied. 'Everybody with half a brain is with us. We'll be ready as soon as those missile-killers come through. How are they doing on them, Mr. Maynard?'

'It took a long time to develop controls rigid enough to stand the gravs, but they're in full production now. You can start picking them up at Base next Thursday morning.'

'Fine!' Dann glanced at the two Asiatics. 'How are you two doing? Your jobs are tougher than ours.'

'Different, but easier, if anything,' Ilyowicz said, and Li nodded twice. 'All really intelligent persons are opposed to government by terrorism. A surprisingly large number of such persons proved to have enough psionic ability so that our so-called mystics could teach them to receive and to transmit thought. Thus we have no cells, no meetings, the absolute minimum of physical contact, and no traceable or detectable communications. Thus, the Nameless One has not now and will not have any suspicion that he and five hundred seventy-three of his butchers will die on signal.'

The Westerners gasped. East was vastly different from West. 'But if you can do that, why . . .?' Dann began, but shut himself up. That was their job, not his.

'Right.' Maynard approved the unspoken thought. 'Well, does that cover it?'

'Not quite – one thing bothers me,' Spehn said. 'The minute we blockade Earth the whole financial system of the galaxy collapses.'

'You tell him, Paul,' Maynard said. 'You're Deston and Deston.'

'Covered like a sucker's bet.' Lansing laughed and slapped himself zestfully on the leg. 'That's the prize joker of the whole business. GalBank – the First Galaxian Bank of New-mars – opens for business day after tomorrow. Have you got any idea of what a solid-cash basis even one installation like Project Barbizon is? Or especially Rhenia Four, that's bringing in a net profit of a megabuck an hour? And DesDes owns 'em by the dozen. Hell, we could fight an interstellar war out of petty cash and never miss it from the till. Son, if Dutch and Slobski had any idea of how much hard-cash money we've got it'd scare the bastards right out of their pants.'

'I see.' Spehn thought for a moment. 'I never thought of it before, but the way leybyrdite is taking everything over, no ordinary bank could handle it, at that. And Maynard, I've studied the material you gave us on your board-of-directors government of the Galactic Federation and I'll vote for it.

133

Nothing else has ever worked, so it's time something different was tried.'

'It won't be easy, but I'm pretty sure it can be made to work. After all, there have been quite a few self-cleaning boards of directors, that have lasted for generations; showing substantial profits, yet adhering rigorously to the Principle of Enlightened Self-Interest. Examples, the largest firms in existence.

'To succeed, our board must both adhere to that Principle and show a profit – the profit in this case being in terms of the welfare of the human race as a whole. Is there anything else to come before this meeting?'

There was nothing else.

'That's it, then. Round it off neatly, Miss Champion – the adjournment and so forth – as usual.'

CHAPTER TWELVE

Higher Education

Andrew Adams had what was probably the finest mind of any strictly human being of his age. He had a voracious and insatiable appetite for knowledge; his brain was an unfilled and unfillable reservoir. He was without prejudice, inhibition, or bias. He could, and frequently did, toss a laboriously-developed theory or hypothesis of his own down the drain in favor of someone else's – *any*one else's – that gave even slightly better predictions than did his own.

Being what he was, it was inevitable that when the Destons gave Adams his first real insight into telepathy and, through it, into the unimaginably vast and theretofore almost hermetically sealed universe of psionics, he dropped his old researches in favor of the new. He and his wife studied, more and ever more intensively, the possibilities and potentialities of the mind as *the mind*. Scholar-like, however, they needed to analyze and digest all the information available having any bearing upon the subject. Therefore, since there was no esoterica of that type in the *Procyon*'s library, they went back to Earth.

The Adams apartment was a fairly large one; five rooms on the sixteenth floor of Grantland Hall in Ann Arbor, overlooking the somewhat crowded but beautifully landscaped campus of the University of Michigan. Their living-room was large – seventeen by twenty-five feet – but it was the Adams, not the ordinary, concept of a living-room. Almost everything in it was designed for books and tapes; everything in it was designed for study.

First, they went through their own library's stores of philosophy, of metaphysics, of paraphysics, of occultism, of spiritualism, of voodooism, of scores of kinds of cultism and even more kinds of crackpotism, from Forteanism up – or down. They studied thousands of words to glean single phrases of truth. Or, more frequently, bits of something that could be developed into truth or into something having to do with truth. Then they exhausted the resources of the University's immense library; after which they requested twenty-two exceedingly rare tomes from the Crerar Library of Chicago. This was unusual, since scholars usually came to the Crerar instead of vice-versa, but Adams was Andrew Adams of the College; one of the very biggest of the Big Brains. Wherefore:

'It can be arranged, Dr. Adams,' Crerar's head librarian told him, as one bibliophile to another. 'These are replicas, of course – most of the originals are in Rome – and not one of them has been consulted for over five years. I'm glad to have you study these volumes, if for no other reason than to show that they are not really dead wood.'

Thus it came finally about that Andrew and Stella Adams sat opposite each other, holding hands tightly across a small table, staring into each other's eyes and thinking at and with each other in terms and symbols many of which can not be put into words.

'But it *has* to be some development or other of Campbell's Fourth Nume,' she insisted. 'It simply *can't* be anything else.'

'True,' he agreed. 'However, Campbell had only a glimmering of a few of the – facets? Basics? – of that nume. So let's go over the prime basics again – the take-off points – the spring-boards – to see if possible where our thinking has been at fault.'

'Very well. Fourth Nume, the – Level? Region? Realm? – of belief, of meaning, of ability to manipulate and to understand – of understanding of and manipulation of the phenomena of reality existing in the no-space-no-time continuum of ...'

'A moment,' Adams broke in. 'Non-space-non-time is preferable, I believe. And aren't those symbols contradictory and mutually exclusive?'

'By no means. In the totality of universes it is not only possible but necessary to manipulate both the immaterial and the material aspects of energy without reference to either time or space. Like this —' and her symbology went far beyond language.

'I see. My error. I was fouling it up. Shall we try again?'

'Not yet. We may find more. Non-space-non-time manipulation, then, and also n-s-n-t attributes, phenomena, and being. Most important – the *sine qua non* – is the ultimate basic of sex. Prerequisite, a duplex pole of power; two very-strongly-linked and very powerful poles, one masculine and one feminine ...'

'A moment, Stella, I'll have to challenge that nuance of thought. If we are dealing with pure, raw, elemental force – as I think we are – we've been thinking too nicely-nicey on that, especially you. The thought should be, I'm pretty sure, neither masculine and feminine nor manly and womanly, but starkly male and just as starkly female.'

'You're probably right, Andy ... you *are* right. So I'll think starkly female; as starkly so as an alley cat in heat. Shall we ... no, let's finish checking the list.'

They finished checking, and neither could perceive any other sources of error in the nuances of their thoughts. They tried it again, and this time it – whatever it was – clicked. Or rather, the result was not a click, but a sonic boom. Both bodies went rigid for seconds, then each drew a tremendously deep breath; as much from relaxation of tension as from realization of accomplishment. Then, poring over a street map of Calcutta, they went mentally to India; to the home of Mahatma Rajaras Molandru, who was one of the greatest sages then alive and who was also a Fellow of the College of Study.

'Is it permitted, Mahatma, that we converse with you and learn?' the fused minds asked.

So calm, so serene was the Great Soul's mind that he neither showed nor felt surprise, even at this almost incredible full meeting of minds. 'You are very welcome, friends Andrew and Stella. You have now attained such heights, however, that I have little or nothing to give you and much to receive from you.'

While the old Mahatma did get much more than he gave, the Adamses got enough new knowledge from him so that when they left India they no longer needed maps. Their linkage had a sureness and a dirigibility that not even the Destons were to match for many years.

From India they went to China, where they had a long and somewhat profitable interview with Li Hing Wong. Thence to Russia and Feodr Ilyowicz; where results were negligible.

'Andy, I never did like that man,' Stella said, when the short and unsatisfactory interview was over. 'And on such contact as this I simply can't stand him. Secretive – sly – he wouldn't really open up at all – all take and no give – that is *not* the way a good psiontist should act.'

'I noticed that; but the loss is really his. It made it impossible for us to give him anything ... but that attitude is perhaps natural enough – his whole heritage is one of secretiveness. Where next, my dear?'

They went to Tibet and to the Gobi and to Wales and to Rome and to Central Africa and to Egypt and to various other places where ancient, unpublished lore was to be found. They sifted this lore and screened it; then, after having sent a detector web of thought throughout the space and subspace of half the galaxy, they found and locked minds with Carlyle and Barbara Deston.

'Do not be surprised, youngsters,' the Adams duplex began.

'Huh?' Deston yelped. 'Clear to hellangone out here? And in subspace besides?'

'Distance is no longer important. Neither is the nature of the environment. Moreover, we are about to visit you in person.'

'Without a locus of familiarity? You can't.'

'That is no longer necessary, either. Here we are.' Seated side by side on a love-seat facing the Destons, the Adamses spoke the last three words aloud, in perfect unison.

Deston did not jump clear off of the davenport – quite. 'Out here into the middle of subspace and we're doing God-knows-how-many megaparsecs a minute relative to anything? So you've mastered absolute trans-spatial perception?'

'By no means. We have, however, been able to enlarge significantly our hyper-sphere of action. We have learned much.'

'That's the understatement of the century. But before you try to teach us any such advanced stuff as that, there's something simple – that is, it *should* be simple – that's been bothering me no end. You got a little time now, Doc?'

'Lot's of it, Babe. Go ahead.'

'Okay. Well, since I never got beyond calculus, and not very advanced calc at that, I don't know any more about high math than a pig does about Sunday. But you and I both know what we mean by plain, common, ordinary, every-day reality. We know what we mean when we say that matter exists. Check, to here?'

'In the sense in which you are using the terms "reality" and "matter", yes.'

'Okay. Matter exists in plain, ordinary, three-dimensional space. Matter is composed of atoms. Therefore *atoms* must exist and must have reality in three-dimensional space. So why can't any atomic physicist tri-di a working model of an atom? One that will work? One that human eyes can *watch* work? So that the ordinary human mind can understand how and why it works?'

'That's rank over-simplification, my boy. Why, the very concept of subatomic phenomena and of subspace is so . . .'

'I know it is. That's exactly what I'm bitching about. Basically, nature is simple, and yet you Big Brains can't handle it except by inventing mathematics so horribly complex that it has no relationship at all to reality. You can't understand it yourselves. You don't – at least I'm pretty sure you don't – really understand – like I understand that chair there, I mean – time or subspace or space or anything else that's really fundamental. So do you mind if I stick my amateur neck 'way out and make a rank amateur's guess as to why and why not?'

'I'm listening, Babe, with my mind as well as my ears.'

Barbara grinned suddenly. 'Out of the mouths of babes – one Babe in this case – *et cetera*,' she said.

'Okay, little squirt, that'll be enough out of you. Doc, I think there's one, and probably more than one, fundamental basic principle that nobody knows anything about yet. And that when you find them, and work out their laws, everything will snap into place so that even such a dumbster as I am will be able to see what the real score is. So you think I'm a squirrel food, don't you?'

'By no means. Many have had similar thoughts...'

'I know that, too, but now we jump clear off the far end. Do you read science fiction?'

'Of course.'

'You're familiar, then, with the triangle of electro-magnetics, electro-gravitics, and magneto-gravitics. That's just a wild stab, of course, but one gets you a hundred that there's something, somewhere, that will tie everything up together – subspace, hunches, telekinetics, witches, and all that stuff.'

Adams leaned forward eagerly. 'Have you done any work on it?'

'Who, *me*? What with?' Deston laughed, but there was no trace of levity in the sound. 'What would I be using for a brain? That's *your* department, Doc.'

Adams smiled and started to say something, but broke off in the middle of a word. His smile vanished. He sat immobile, eyes unfocused, for minute after minute. He sat there for so long that Deston, afraid to move, began to think that he had suffered some kind of a seizure.

Finally, however, Adams came out of his trance. He and Stella got up as one and, without a word, turned to leave the room.

'Hey!' Deston protested. 'Wait up, Doc! What gives?'

Adams licked his lips. 'I can't tell you, Babe. I'd be the laughing-stock of the scientific world – especially since I can't conceive of any possible instrumentation to test it.'

'After that, you've *got* to talk. So start.'

'The trigger was your flat statement – axiomatic to you – that the atom exists in three dimensions. Since that alleged fact can not be demonstrated, it probably is not true. If it is not true, the reverse – the Occam's-Razor explanation – would almost have to be that space possesses at least four physical dimensions.'

'Hell's ... flaming ... afterburners ...' Deston breathed.

'Exactly. The fact that this theory – to my knowledge, at least – has never been propounded seriously does not affect its validity. It explains every phenomenon with which I am familiar and conflicts with none.'

There was a long silence, which Deston broke. 'Except one, maybe. According to that theory, psionic ability would be the ability to perceive and to work in the fourth physical dimension of space. Sometimes in time, too, maybe. But in that cause, if anybody's got it why hasn't everybody? Can you explain that?'

'Quite easily. Best, perhaps, by analogy. You'll grant that to primitive man it was axiomatic that the Earth was flat? Two-dimensional?'

'Granted.'

'That belief became untenable when it was proved conclusively that it was "round". At that point cosmology began. The Geocentric Theory was replaced by the Heliocentric. Then the Galactic. Where are we now? We don't know. Note, however, that with every advance in science the estimated size of the physical universe has increased.'

'But what has that got to do with psionics?'

'I'm coming to that. While *intelligence* may not have increased very greatly over the centuries, mental *ability* certainly has. My thought is that the process of evolution has been, more and more frequently, activating certain hitherto-dormant portions of the brain; specifically, those portions responsible for the so-called "supra-normal" abilities.'

'Oh, *brother*! You really went out into the wild blue yonder after that one, professor.'

'By no means. It may very well be that not all lines of heredity carry any of the genes necessary to form the required cells, even in the dormant state, and it is certain that there is a wide variation in the number and type of those cells. But have you ever really considered Lee Chaytor? Or George Wesley?'

'Just what everybody knows. They were empiricists – pure experimenters, like the early workers with electricity. They kept on trying until something worked. The theory hasn't all been worked out yet, is all.'

' "Everybody knows" something that, in all probability, simply is not true. I believed it myself until just now; but now I'm almost sure that I know what the truth is. They both were

141

– they must have been – tremendously able psiontists. They did not publish the truth because there was no symbology in which they *could* publish it. There still is no such symbology. They concealed their supra-normal abilities throughout their lives because they did not want to be laughed at – or worse.'

Deston thought for a minute. 'That's really a bolus . . . what can we – any or all of us – do about it?'

'I'm not sure. Data insufficient – much more work must be done before that question can be answered. As we said, Stella and I have learned much, but almost nothing compared to what is yet to be learned. To that end – but it is long past bedtime. Shall all eight of us meet after breakfast and learn from each other?'

'It'll be a one-way street, professor,' Deston said, 'but thanks a million for the compliment, anyway. We shall indeed.'

The Adamses left the room and Carlyle Deston stared unseeingly at the doorway through which they had passed.

And next morning after breakfast the four couples sat at a round table, holding hands in a circle.

Very little can be said about what actually went on. It can not be told in either words or mathematics. There is no symbology except the esoteric jargon of the psiontist – as meaningless to the non-psionic mind as the proverbial 'The gostak distims the doshes' – by the use of which such information can be transmitted.

Results, however, were enormous and startling; and it must be said here that not one of the eight had any suspicion then that the Adams fusion had any help in doing what it did. Andrew Adams' mind was admittedly the greatest of its time; combining with its perfect complement would enhance its power; everything that happened was strictly logical and only to be expected.

The physical results of one phase of the investigation, that into teleportation, can be described. Each pair of minds was different, of course. Each had abilities and powers that the others lacked; some of which were fully developable in the others, some only partially, some scarcely at all. Thus, when it came to the upper reaches of the Fourth Nume, even Adams was shocked at the power and scope and control that flared up instantly in the Trains' minds as soon as the doors were opened.

'Ah,' Adams said, happily, 'That explains why you would not start out without them.'

'And *how*!' Deston agreed; and it did.

It also explained why Cecily had always been, in Bernice's words, 'such a sex-flaunting power-house'. It accounted for Train's years of frustration and bafflement. At long, long last, they had found out what they were for.

'You two,' Adams said, 'have, among other things, a power of teleportation that is almost unbelievable. You could teleport, not merely yourselves, but this entire starship and all its contents, to any destination you please.'

'They could, at that,' Deston marveled. 'Go ahead and do it, so Bobby and I can see how much of the technique we can learn.'

'I'm afraid to.' Cecily licked her lips. 'Suppose we – I, my part of it, I mean – scatter our atoms all over total space?'

'We won't,' Train said. Although he had not known it before, he was in fact the stronger of the two. 'Give us a target, Babe. We'll hit it to a gnat's eyeball.'

'Galmetia. GalMet Tower. Plumb with the flagpole. One thousand point zero feet from the center of the ball to our center of gravity.'

'Roger.' The Trains stared into each other's eyes and their muscles set momentarily. 'Check it for dex and line.'

Deston whistled. 'One thousand point zero *zero* feet and plumb to a split blonde hair. You win the mink-lined whatsits. Now back?'

'As we were, Sess,' Train said, and the starship disappeared from Galmetia's atmosphere, to reappear instantaneously at the exact point it would have occupied in subspace if the trip had not been interrupted.

The meeting went on. There is no need to report any more of its results; in fact, nine-tenths of those results could not be reported even if there were room.

An hour or so after the meeting was over, Adams sat at his desk, thinking; staring motionlessly at the sheet of paper upon which he had listed eighteen coincidences. He knew, with all his mathematician's mind, that coincidence had no place in reality; but there they were. Not merely one or two, but *eighteen* of them ... which made the probability a virtually absolute certainty.

There *was* an operator. The babies? Barbara? Of all the people he knew, they were ... but why should it be anyone he knew, or any given one or thing in this or any other galaxy? There were no data. A mutant, hiding indetectably behind his own powers? An attractive idea, but there was no basis whatever for any assumption at all ... anything to be both necessary and sufficient must of necessity be incomprehensible. Anything ... anywhere ... anywhen ...

At this point in his cogitations Barbara knocked on his door and came in, with her mind-blocks full on. He knew what was on her mind; he had perceived it plainly during the wide-open eight-way they had just held. Nevertheless:

'Something is troubling you, my dear?'

'Yes.' Barbara nibbled at her lip. '... it's just ... well, are you positively *sure*, Uncle Andy, that the babies are ... well ...' She paused, wriggling in embarrassment.

'Normal? Of course I'm sure, child. Positive. I have a file four inches thick to prove it. Have you any grounds at all for suspecting that they may not be?'

'Put that way, no, I haven't. It's just that ... well, once in a while I get a ... a *feeling* ... Indescribable ...' she paused again.

'It is possible that there is an operator at work,' he said, quietly. The girl's eyes widened, but she didn't say anything and he went on, 'However, I can find no basis whatever for any assumption concerning such a phenomenon. It is much more logical, therefore, to assume that these new and inexplicable "feelings" are in fact products of our newly enlarged minds, which we do not as yet fully understand.'

'Oh?' she exclaimed. '*You* have them, too? *You've* been working on it? Watching it?'

'I have been and am working on it.'

'Oh, wonderful! If there's anything to it, then, you'll get it!' She hugged him vigorously, kissed him on the ear, and ran

144

out of the room.

Adams stared thoughtfully at the closed door. That let Barbara out – or did it? It did not. Nor did it put her in any deeper. The operator, if any, was supernormal; superpsionic. The problem was, by definition, insoluble; one more of the many mysteries of Nature that the mind of man could not yet solve. Therefore he would not waste any more time on it.

He shrugged his shoulders, crumpled the sheet of paper up into a ball, dropped the ball into his wastebasket, and went to work on a problem that he might be able to solve.

CHAPTER THIRTEEN

The Outplanets

While no one knows when man first appeared upon Earth, it is generally agreed that it required many hundreds of thousands of years for the human population of Earth to reach the billion mark, which it probably did sometime in the eighteen twenties. In the next scant century, however, it doubled. In another seventy-five or eighty years it doubled again, to four billions. Then, due to limitation of births in most cultures and to famine and pestilence in the few remaining backward ones, the rate of increase began to drop; and early in the twenty-second century Earth's population seemed to be approaching seven billions as a limit.

Although cities had increased tremendously in size there was still much farmland, and every acre of it – including the Sahara, irrigated by demineralized and remineralized water from the ocean – was cultivated and fertilized to the maximum possible constant yield. There were also vast hydroponics installations. Complete diet had been synthesized long since; hence Earthly fare for many years had been synthetic for most, vegetarian-and-synthetic for almost all of the upper twenty percent. Cow's milk and real meat were for millionaires only.

The dwindling of Earth's reserves of oil and coal had forced the price of hydrocarbons up to where it became profitable to work oil shale, and it was from the immense deposits of that material that most of Earth's oil was being produced. Very little of this oil, however, was being used as fuel; almost every ton of it was going into the insatiable conversion plants of the plastics and synthetics industries.

Of power, fortunately, there was no lack. It was available everywhere, at relatively low cost and in infinite amount.

Infinite? Well, not quite, perhaps. Inexhaustible, certainly. Also incalculable, since no two mathematicians ever agreed even approximately in estimating the total kinetic energy of the universe. And that super-genius Lee Chaytor, in developing the engine that still bears her name – the engine that taps that inexhaustible source of energy – gave to mankind one of the two greatest gifts it has ever received. The other, of course, was Wesley's Subspace Drive; by virtue of which man peopled the planets of the stars.

However, it was only the bold, the hardy, and the independent, and the discontented who went. Nor was there at first any such thing as Capital: the bankers of Earth were, then as now, highly allergic to risking their money in any venture less certain than a fifty-percent-of-appraised-value first mortgage upon a practically sure thing. Hence everything was on shares.

Elbridge Warner, Barbara Deston's great-great-great-and-so-on grandfather, a multi-millionaire oil man and a rabid anti-union capitalist, was the first big operator to go off-Earth. Following the 'hunches' that had made him what he was, he hired a crew of the hardest, toughest, most intransigent men he could find and sniffed out a fantastically oil-rich planet, theretofore unknown to man. He named this planet 'Newmars' and claimed it *in toto* as his own personal private property.

Then, having put down a tremendously productive well, he built and populated a balanced-economy colony. He then put down a few more gushers and built an arms plant and a couple of battleships, after which he: 1) Moved everything he owned that was movable from Earth to Newmars, and 2) Fired every union man in his employ. The United Oil Workers struck, of course, whereupon he made or stole – the record is not clear upon this point – some Chaytor super-fusers and destroyed every Warner well on Earth. Destroyed them so thoroughly (everyone has seen a tri-di of what a super-fuser does) that not one of them could be made to produce again for years, if ever. He then sat back on his wholly-owned, self-sufficient, fortified planet and waited.

The result was inevitable. Even with Warner Oil at full production, the demand had been crowding the supply. And, because of the meagerness of Earth's reserves and because the shale-oil people would not expand their plants – they knew that Warner could under-sell them by any margin he chose – Earth had to make terms with Elbridge Warner. The Chamber of Commerce and the government of the United States of America forced the United Oil Workers to surrender; whereupon Warner graciously allowed fleets of tankers to haul oil from Newmars to Earth – at shale oil's exact delivered price.

Elbridge never did put down another well on Earth. In fact, as far as is known, he did not even visit Earth throughout the remainder of his hundred years of life. He was not bitter, exactly; he was stubborn, hard-headed, fiercely independent, and contumaceous; and he surrounded himself by preference with people of his own hard kind. Which, with that start and with Warner Oil always dominating the business, is why the oil-men of the planets have never been a gentle breed.

The Asteroid Mining Company followed WarnOil's lead. Iron and nickel, of course, and a few other metals, were available in plenty in Sol's asteroid belt; but a great many other highly important metals, particularly the heavier ones, were not. Wherefore the Asteroid Mining Company changed its name to Galactic Metals, Incorporated, and sent hundreds of prospectors out to explore new solar systems. These men, too – hard-muscled, hard-fighting, hard-playing hard-rock men all – were rugged, rough, and tough.

They found a sun with an asteroid belt so big and so full of chunks of heavy metal that it was all but unapproachable along any radial line anywhere near the plane of the ecliptic. This sun's fourth planet, while it was Tellus-Type as to gravity, temperature, water, air, and so forth, was much richer than Earth in metals heavier than nickel. Whereupon Galactic Metals pre-empted this metalliferous planet, named it 'Galmetia', and proceeded to stock it with metalsmen – a breed perhaps one number Brinnell harder even than Elbridge Warner's oil-men.

With colonization an actuality, and productive of profits far beyond anything possible on Earth, a few of the most venturesome capitalists of Earth decided to dip into this flowing fountain for themselves. Lactia Incorporated, the leading milk-and-meat producer, was the first banker-backed, consumer-oriented firm to take the big plunge. Knowing that it could fly a fifty-thousand-ton tanker from an outplanet to Earth in little more time and at little more expense than was required to ship a five-gallon container from Trempealeau, Wisconsin, to Chicago, Illinois, it found and claimed a Tellus-Type planet whose tremendous expanses of fertile plains and whose equable climate made it ideal for the production of milk and meat. It named its planet Lactia. Then Lactia the firm colonized Lactia the planet with feed-raisers, dairymen, and stockmen, and began to spend money hand over fist.

It required years, of course, to build up the herds, and an immense amount of money, but when many hundreds of millions of cattle lived upon hundreds of millions of fertile acres, the retail price of milk had come down from twenty-five dollars a pint to the mythically-old figure of twenty cents per quart. Beef, pork, and mutton were available in every marketplace. Clothing of real wool and of real leather was being sold at prices almost anyone could afford. For, then as now, the businessmen of the planets adhered as closely as they possibly could to the Law of Diminishing Returns.

Dozens of other industries followed Milk's lead. Wheatfields were measured by the 'square' (one hundred square kilometers) instead of by the acre and bread again became a basic food. Rice became available in full supply and at low cost. Breakfast cereals reappeared upon the shelves of even the smallest foodstores. All of this came about because, with all due respect to the biochemical engineers, natural food tasted better than synthetic and 'felt' better in the mouth and vast numbers of consumers were willing to pay a premium for it.

(With increasing automation, ever-mounting demand, and ever-increasing production as costs were lowered, planetary agriculture eventually, of course, put the synthetic-food industry completely out of business.)

These subsidiary planets, unlike Newmars and Galmetia, were at first dependent upon Earth. However, each one grew in population at an exponential rate. For, despite all the automation that is economically feasible, it takes a lot of men to work even as small a holding as a hundred squares of land. Men need women and women go with their men. Men and women have children – on the planets, as many children as they want. Families need services – all kinds of services – and get them. Factories came into being, and schools – elementary schools, high schools, colleges, and universities. Stores of all kinds, from shoppes to supermarkets. Restaurants and theaters. Cars and trucks. Air-cars. Radio, teevee, and tri-di. Boats and bowling lanes. Golf, even – on the planets there was *room* for golf! And so on. The works.

At first, all this flood of adult population came from Earth; drawn, not by any urge to pioneer, but by that mainspring of free enterprise, profit. Profit either in the form of high wages or of opportunity to enlarge and to advance, each entrepreneur in his own field. And not one in a hundred of those emigrants from Earth, having lived on an outplanet for a year, ever moved back. 'Tellus is a nice place to visit, but *live* there? If the Tellurians like that kind of living – if they call it living – they can have it.'

But the lessening of Earth's population was of very short duration. Assured of cheap and abundant food, and of more and more good, secure jobs, more and more women had more and more children and cifies began to encroach upon what had once been farmland.

One of the most important effects of this migration, although it was scarcely noticed at the time, was the difference between the people of the planets and those of Earth. The planetsmen were, to give a thumbnail description, the venturesome, the independent, the ambitious, the chance-taking. Tellurians were, and became steadily more so, the stodgy, the unimaginative, the security-conscious.

Decade after decade this difference became more and more marked, until finally there developed a definite traffic pattern that operated continuously to intensify it. Young Tellurians of both sexes who did not like regimentation – and urged on by the blandishments of planetary advertising campaigns – left Earth for good. Conversely, a thin stream of colonials who preferred security to competition flowed to Earth. This condition had existed for over two hundred years. (And, by the way, it still exists.)

For competition was and is the way of life on the planets. The labor unions of Earth tried, of course; but the Tellurian brand of unionism never did 'take', because of the profoundly basic difference in attitude of the men involved. Some Tellus-Type unions were formed in the early years and a few strikes occurred; only one of which, the last and the most violent and which neither side won, will be mentioned here.

The Stockmen's Strike, on Lactia, was the worst strike in all history. Some three thousand men and over five million head of stock lost their lives; about eight billion dollars of invested capital went down the drain. Neither side would give an inch. Warfare and destruction went on until, driven by the force of public opinion – affected no little by the virtual absence of meat and milk from civilization's every table – the massed armed forces of all the other planets attacked Lactia and took it by storm. Martial law was declared. Capital was seized. Labor either worked or faced a firing squad. This condition would continue, both Capital and Labor were told, until they got together and worked out a formula that would work.

Experts from both sides, in collaboration with a board of the most outstanding economists of the time, went to work on the problem. They worked for almost a year.

Capital must make enough profit to attract investors, and wants to make as much more than that minimum as it can. Labor must make a living, and wants as much more than that minimum as it can get. Between those two minima lies the line of dispute, which is the locus of all points of reasonable and practicable settlement. Somewhere on that line lies a point, which can be computed from the Law of Diminishing Returns as base, at which Capital's net profit, Labor's net annual income, and the public's benefit, will all three combine to produce the maximum summated good.

Thus was enunciated the Principle of Enlightened Self-Interest. It worked. Wherever and whenever it has been given a chance to work, it has worked ever since.

The planets-wide adoption of this Principle (it never did gain much favor on Earth) ended hourly wages and full annual

151

salaries. Every employee, from top to bottom, received an annual basic salary plus a bonus. This bonus varied with the net profit of the firm and with each employee's actual ability. And the Planetsmen, as the production and service personnel of the planets came to be called, liked it that way. They were independent. They were individualists. Very few of them wanted to be held down in pay or in opportunity to any dead level of mediocrity just to help some stupid jerks of incompetents hang onto their jobs.

The Planetsmen liked automation, and not only because of the perennial shortage of personnel on the outplanets. And, week after week, union organizers from Earth tried fruitlessly to crack the Planetsmen's united front. One such attempt, representative of hundreds on record, is quoted in part as follows:

Organizer: 'But listen! You Associated Wavesmen are organized already; organized to the Queen's taste. All you have to do is use your brains and join up with us and it wouldn't take hardly any strike at all to ...'

Planetsman: 'Strike? You crazy in the head? What in hell would we strike for?'

Org: 'For more money, of course. You ain't dumb, are you? You could be getting a lot more money than you are now.'

Plan: 'I could like hell. I'd be getting less, come the end of the quarter.'

Org: 'Less? How do you figure that?'

Plan: 'I don't. I don't have to. We've got expert computermen figuring for us all the time, and they keep Top Brass right on the peak of the curve, too, believe me. You never heard of the Law of Diminishing Returns, I guess.'

Org: 'I did so; but what has that got to do with ...?'

Plan: 'Everything. It works like this, see? My basic is six thousand – and say, how much do Tellurian pole-climbers get?'

Org: 'Well, of course we would ...'

Plan: 'Not with our help you won't. You'll dig your own spuds, brother. Anyway, say we strike – and that's saying a hell of a lot – ever hear of Lactia? But say we do, and say they

152

raise our basic to – and that's saying a hell of a lot, too, believe me – but say they do, to – hell, to anything you please. Okay. So costs go up, so Top Brass has to raise prices . . .'

Org: 'Uh-uh. Let 'em take it out of their profits.'

Plan: 'They ain't makin' that much. Anyway, it'd stack up the same, come to the end of the quarter. The point would slide off of the peak and my bonus would get a bad case of the dropsy and I'd wind up the year making less than I will the way things are now.'

Org: 'Well, skipping that for just a minute, how about this automation that's putting so many of you men out of jobs?'

Plan: 'It ain't, that are worth a damn. If a man can't keep on top of the machines, to hell with him. Let him take a lower-basic job or go to Tellus and live on security. The more automation we can make work the more production per man-hour and the bigger my bonus gets. And pretty quick I can jump a level and raise my basic, too. It's just that simple. See?'

Org: 'I see that it don't make sense. What you don't see is that Capital has been suckering you all along. They've been giving you the business. Feeding you the old boloney and giving you the shaft clear to the hilt and you're dumb enough to take it.'

Plan: 'Not by seven thousand tanks of juice, chum, and needling won't make us let you lean on us a nickel's worth, either. We get the straight dope and our officers don't dip into the kitty, either, the way yours do. So what you'd better do, meathead, is roll your hoop back to Tellus, where maybe you can make somebody believe part of that crap.'

Aboard the *Explorer*, the Adamses and the Destons were discussing the course of civilization. Adams had prepared tables of figures, charts, and graphs. He had determined trends and had extrapolated them into future time. His conclusions were far from cheerful.

'This unstable condition has lasted far longer than was to have been expected two centuries ago,' Adams said, definitely. 'The only reason why it has lasted so long is because of the stabilizing effect of the planets siphoning off so many of Earth's combative and aggressive people. The situation is now, however, deteriorating; and, considering the ability, the quality, and the state of advancement of the Planetsmen, it will continue to deteriorate at an ever-increasing rate to the point of catastrophe.'

'Huh?' Deston asked. 'Grind that up a little finer, will you, professor?'

'It's inevitable. The original aim of Communism was to master all Earth. It failed. It also failed to gain any foothold upon any of the outplanets because the basic tenets of Communism are completely unacceptable to the independent and self-reliant peoples of the planets. The fact is, therefore, that Communism is bottled up on something over half of the land surface of one planet, while we "contemptible capitalist warmongers" are spreading at an exponential rate over a constantly increasing number of planets. The question is, what will this present Nameless One of EastHem – who is none too stable a character – do about this state of affairs?'

Deston whistled, and after a short silence Barbara said, 'He will bomb, I suppose you mean.'

'Could be, at that,' Deston agreed. 'Especially since East-Hem never will catch up with our production technology. The most important thing, as I see it, is when.'

'Within a very few years, I think,' Adams said. 'By these charts, five years at most, and probzbly much less than that.'

'Nice,' Deston said, and thought for moments. 'And he won't stick around for the fallout. He and the hard core of the Party will take off for some unknown planet – maybe they've been working on it for years – with the idea of bombing *all* our planets. Is that your idea?'

'That is one of many, but I do not have enough data to give a high probability to any one of them.'

'But Uncle Andy,' Barbara put in, 'Since you never have been anybody's professional crepe-hanger, you've already decided what to do about it. So give.'

'I have been able to find only one solution having a probability of success of point nine nine. In psionics, I think, lies the only possible answer. Such masters as Li Hing Wong and the mahatmas can do much, but not nearly enough. What we should do is find and train all the latent psionists we can. I

154

know of many who are not so latent, either – Maynard, Smith, and Champion of GalMet; Lansing and DuPuy of WarnOil; Hatfield, Spehn, and Dann of InStell; to name only a few of those whom I know personally. There must be thousands of others, none of whom any one of us has ever heard of. Such a force would almost certainly be able to cope with EastHem and its bombs; therefore it seems to me that the best course to pursue is to set up a school for psionic development.'

'Sounds good to me,' Deston approved. 'Have you got it going? We'll all get behind it and push.'

'How could we have, young man? Even starting in a small way, such a school would require an investment of at least a hundred thousand dollars – which might as well be a million, as far as the Adams resources are concerned.'

'A megabuck wouldn't more than start it, the way it ought to be.' Deston glanced at Barbara, who nodded. He took a sheet of paper out of a drawer, wrote a couple of lines and went on, 'Doc, for a man with your brains, you've got absolutely the least sense of anybody I know. *Any* nitwit would know that DesDes would back any such project as that clear up to the hilt. Here, give this to Lansing. It's for twenty-five megabucks now, and as much more as you want, whenever you want it.'

CHAPTER FOURTEEN

The General Strike

In their suite, Percival Train put his arm around his wife's supple waist, swung her around, and kissed her lingeringly. 'Let's sit down and talk this thing out. We both scanned both kids. We agree that they're both normal – apparently so, anyway – now. So what? Shoot me the load of what's bothering you.'

'So a hell of a lot.' A cigarette appeared between Cecily's lips, lit itself, and she burned a quarter of it in one long inhalation. 'I'll give you both barrels. They *had* mindblocks. Both of them did. Now they either haven't any or are able to hide the fact that they have and I know damn well which one it is. Now. How could a baby who can scarcely walk yet – to say nothing of two of them – have anything to hide or want to? Or be able to if they did? Here's how. They were both conceived in subspace . . .'

'So what? Don't you think that ever happened before?'

'Not in any ship that ever picked up a zeta charge, it didn't. No woman ever lived through *that* before to become a mother. And both periods of gestation were impossibly long. And all four parents were powerful psiontists; just how powerful you and I don't know and can't guess. And they both, at an age when normal babies are completely dependent, have supernormal intelligence and super-normal powers . . .'

'Hold it, presh, you're just guessing at that.'

'Guessing, your left eyeball! Look at what happened! Could any normal man alive, of his own ability, do what we know Upton Maynard did? Or Eldon Smith? Or Guerdon Dann? And look at Steve Spehn. You know as well as I do, Perce, that it's starkly *impossible* to hide an operation as big as that from a spy system as good as EastHem's. And look at me. I never had even a trace of psionic ability before — how did I get it? And so all of a sudden? And those are only a few of the stickers, big boy; if you aren't convinced yet I can go on for half an hour.'

Train, his face set hard in concentration, thought for minutes; then said, 'I'm convinced that...'

'Good! I didn't expect you to admit it.'

'Hold on, Sess! I'm convinced that there's an operator. I never thought about those things before in that way, but the way you pile them up leaves no room for doubt. But you got off on the wrong foot and never corrected yourself — so you went clear out to the Pleiades, by way of Canopus, Rigel, and S-Doradus, to hit Venus next door. Didn't you ever hear of Occam's Razor?'

'Why, of course, but...'

'Use it, then, and that functional as well as beautiful red-thatched head of yours.'

It took her only a couple of seconds. 'Why, it's *Barbara*!' she shrieked then. 'It's been *Barbara* all the time!'

'Right. So let's examine Barbara. She's been an honest-to-God witch all her life. The greatest and probably the only one-hundred-percenter ever. She's known it and worked at it. That much we know for sure. What else she is we'll never know, but we can do some freehand guessing. She's had her own way all her life. How? Yet it never spoiled her. Why not? Even as a teen-ager, nobody's line ever fooled her. Why not? Above all, why wasn't she ever shot or strangled or blown up with dynamite?'

Cecily nodded her spectacular head. 'Competition *must* have tried. That has always been the cut-throatingest of all cut-throat games. And, underneath, she really *is* hard.'

'Hard! She's harder than the superneotride hubs of hell itself! Whenever she has wanted anything she has taken it. Including Carlyle Deston. And speaking of Deston, look at what happened to him — and me. He didn't used to have any more psionic ability than I did — not as much. Then, all of a sudden — both of us — *bam-whingo!* And you can't say the kids did that — not to him, anyway. Not only they weren't born yet — you might claim they could work pre-natally — they weren't conceived yet . . . probably, that is . . .'

She laughed. 'You can delete the "probably", Perce. They got married right after their first meetings, you know. Anyway, virgin brides or not, they certainly were not pregnant ones. They both knew the facts of life.'

'Okay. She made full-scale, high-powered psionic operators out of Herc and Bun, too; long before the kids were born and probably before they were conceived. So, for my money, it was Bobby who worked all of us over and pulled the strings on the Adamses and on Maynard And Company and did everything else that was done.'

'But those babies are *not* normal babies, Perce . . .' She paused, then went on, 'But of course . . .' She paused again.

'Of course,' he agreed 'With cat-tractor-psiontist parents on both sides, how could they be? Especially with said parents working on them — just like we'll be working on ours — from the day they were born? Or maybe even before? I'll buy it that they have a lot more stuff than any normal kids could possibly have; up to and including mind-blocks and even the ability to hide them. When they grow up they'll probably have a lot more stuff than any of us. But now? And *that* kind of stuff? Uh-uh. No sale, presh; wrap it back up and put it back up on the shelf.'

'I'll do just that.' She drew a deep breath of relief and wriggled herself into closer and fuller contact. 'Just the thought of such little monsters as that simply petrified me.'

'I know what you mean. You almost gave me goose-flesh there for a minute myself.'

'But we can understand Bobby's doing it and play along.'

'You're so right. Actually, we owe her a vote of thanks for what she's done for us.'

'We certainly do. I'd tell her so myself, too, if it wouldn't . . . but say . . . s'pose she's reading us right now?'

The man stiffened momentarily, then said, 'We haven't said a word I wouldn't want her to hear. If you *are* on us, Bobby, I say this – thanks; and you can put it down in your book that we're both with you until the last clang of the gong. Check, Cecily?'

'*How* I check!' She kissed him fervently. 'You were right; I should have talked to you before. I didn't have a leg to stand on.'

'*That* allegation I deny.' He laughed, put his right hand on her well-exposed left leg, and squeezed. 'This, in case nobody ever told you before – I thought I had – is one of the only perfect pair of such ever produced.'

She put her hand over his, pressed it even tighter against her leg, and grinned up at him; and for a time action took place of words. Then she pulled her mouth away from his and leaned back far enough to ask, 'You don't suppose she's watching us *now*, do you?'

'No. Definitely not. She's no Peeping Thomasina. But even if she were – now that you're you again, my red-headed bundle of joy, we have unfinished business on the agenda. And anyway, you're not exactly a shrinking violet.'

'Why, I am too!' She widened her eyes at him in outraged innocence. 'That's a vile and base canard, sir. I'm just as much of a Timid Soul as you are, you Fraidy Freddie, you – why, I'm absodamlutely the shrinkingest little violet you ever laid your cotton-pickin' eyes on!'

'Okay, Little Vi, let's jet.' He got up and helped her to her feet; then, arms tightly around each other and savoring each moment, they moved slowly toward a closed door.

The cold-war stalemate that had begun sometime early in the twentieth century had become a way of life. Contrary to the belief of each side over the years, the other had not collapsed. Dictatorship and so-called democracy still coexisted; both were vastly stronger than they had ever been before. Each had enough super-powerful weapons to destroy all life on Earth, but neither wanted a lifeless and barren world; each wanted to rule the Earth as it was. Therefore the Big Bangs had not been launched; each side was doing its subtle best to outwit, to undermine, and/or to overthrow the other.

WestHem was expanding into space; EastHem, as far as

159

WestHem's Intelligence could find out, was waiting, with characteristic Oriental patience, for the capitalistic and imperialistic government of the west to fall apart because of its own innate weaknesses.

This situation existed when the Galactic Federation was formed; specifically to give all the peoples of all the planets a unified, honest, and just government; when Secretary of Labor Deissner, acting through Antonio Grimes, called all the milk-truck drivers of Metropolitan New York out on strike.

At three forty-five of the designated morning all the milk-delivery trucks of Depot Eight – taking one station for example; the same thing was happening at all – were in the garage and the heavy steel doors were closed and locked. The gates of the yard were locked and barricaded. The eight-man-deep picket line was composed one-tenth of drivers, nine-tenths of heavily-armed, heavy-muscled hoodlums and plug-uglies. They were ready, they thought, for anything.

At three fifty a fleet of armored half-tracks lumbered up and began to disgorge armored men. Their armor, while somewhat reminiscent of that worn by the chivalry of old, was not at all like it in detail. Built of leybyrdite, it was somewhat lighter, immensely stronger, and very much more efficient. Its wide-angle visors, for instance, were made of bullet-proof, crack-proof, scratch-proof neo-glass. Formation was made and from one of the trucks an eighty-decibel voice roared out:

'Strikers, attention! We are coming through; the regular deliveries are going to be made. We don't want to kill any more of you than we have to, so those of you with only clubs, brass knucks, knives, lead pipes, and such stuff, we'll try to only knock out as cold as frozen beef. You guys with the guns, every one of you who lets go one burst will get shot. Non-fatally, we hope, but we can't guarantee it. Now, you damn fool bystanders' – it is remarkable how quickly a New York crowd can gather, even at four o'clock in the morning – 'keep right on crowding up, as close as you can get. Anybody God-damned fool enough to stand gawking in the line of fire of fifty machine guns *ought* to get killed – so just keep on standing there and save some other fool-killer the trouble of sending you to the morgue in baskets. Okay, men, give 'em hell!'

160

To give credit to the crowd's intelligence, most of it did depart – and at speed – before the shooting began. New Yorkers were used to being chivvied away from scenes of interest; they were *not* used to being invited, in such a loud tone of such savage contempt, to stay and be slaughtered. Of the few who stayed, the still fewer survivors wished fervently, later, that they had taken off as fast as they could run.

Armored men strode forward, swinging alloy-sheathed fists, and men by the dozens went down flat. Then guns went into action and the armored warriors fell down and rolled haphazardly on the pavement; for no man, however strong, can stand up against the kinetic energy of a stream of heavy bullets. Except for a few bruises, however, they were not injured. They were not even deafened by the boiler-shop clangor within their horribly resounding shells of metal – highly efficient ear-plugs had seen to that.

Those steel-jacketed bullets, instead of penetrating that armor, ricocheted off in all directions – and it was only then that the obdurately persistent bystanders – those of them that could, that is – ran away.

The machine-gun phase of the battle didn't last very long, either. In the assault-proof half-tracks expert riflemen peered through telescopic sights and .30-caliber rifles barked viciously. The strikers' guns went silent.

Leybyrdite-shielded mobile torchers clanked forward and the massed pickets fled: no man in his right mind is *ever* going to face willingly the sixty-three-hundred-degree heat of the oxyacetylene flame. The gates vanished. The barriers disappeared. The locked doors opened. Then, with an armored driver aboard, each delivery truck was loaded as usual and went calmly away along its usual route; while ambulances and meat-wagons brought stretchers and baskets and carried away the wounded and the dead.

Nor were those trucks attacked, or even interfered with. It had been made abundantly clear that it would be the attackers who would suffer.

But what of the source of New York's milk? The spaceport and Way Nineteen? Pickets went there, too, of course; but what they saw there stopped them in their tracks. Just inside the entrance, one on each side of the Way, sat those two tremendous, invulnerable, enigmatic super-tanks. They did not do anything. Nothing at all. They merely sat there; but that was enough. No one there knew what those things could or would do; and no one there wanted to find out. Not, that is, the hard way.

Nor did the Metropolitan Police do anything. There was nothing they could do. This was, most definitely, not their dish. This was war. War between the Galaxians on one side and Labor, backed by WestHem's servile government, on the other. The government's armed forces, however, did not take part in the action. At the first move of the day, Maynard had taken care of that.

'Get the army in on this if you like,' he had told Deissner, flatly. 'Anything and everything you care to, up to and including the heaviest nuclear devices you have. We are three long subspace jumps ahead of anything you can do, and the rougher you want to play it the more of a shambles New York will be when it's over.'

Therefore, after that one brief but vicious battle, everything remained – on the surface – peaceful and serene. Milk-deliveries were regular and punctual, undisturbed by any overt incident. The only difference – on the surface – was that the milk-truck drivers wore leybyrdite instead of white duck.

Beneath that untroubled surface, however, everything seethed and boiled. Grimes and his lieutenants raved and swore. Deissner gritted his teeth in quiet, futile desperation. The Nameless One of EastHem, completely unaccustomed to frustration and highly allergic to it, went almost mad. He now knew that the Galaxians had the most powerful planet in the galaxy and *he could not find it*.

This situation was, of course, much too unstable to endure, and Nameless was the first to crack. He probably went completely mad. At any rate, his first move was to liquidate both Secretary of Labor Deissner and Chief Mediator Wilson. Nor was there anything of finesse about these assassinations. Two multi-ton blockbusters were detonated, one in each of two apartment hotels, and the fact that over three thousand persons died meant nothing to EastHem's tyrant. His second move was

162

to make Antonio Grimes the boss of all WestHem. Whereupon Grimes called a general strike; every union man of the Western Hemisphere walked out; and all hell was out for noon.

The union people, however, were not the only ones who walked out. Executives, supervisors, engineers, and top-bracket technicians did too, in droves, and disappeared from Earth; and they did not go empty-handed. For instance, the top technical experts of Communications Incorporated (a wholly-owned subsidiary of InStell) worked for an hour or so apiece in the recesses of their switch-banks and packed big carrying-cases before they left.

Grimes knew and counted upon the fact that WestHem's economy, half automated though it was, could not function without his union men and women at work. He must also have known the obverse; that it could not function, either, without the brains that had brought automation into being in the first place and that kept it running – the only brains that understood what those piled-up masses of electronic gear were doing. He must also have known that in any fight to the finish Labor would suffer with the rest; hence he did not expect a finish fight. He was superbly confident that Capital, this time as always before, would surrender. He was wrong.

When Grimes found every one of his own communications channels dead, he tried frantically to restore enough service to handle Labor's campaign, but there was nothing he or his union operators could do. (They were still called 'operators', although there were no longer any routine manual operations to be performed.)

These operators, although highly skilled in the techniques of keeping the millions of calls flowing smoothly through the fantastically complex mazes of their central exchanges, were limited by their own unions' rules to their own extremely narrow field of work. An operator reported trouble, but she must not, under any conditions, try to fix it. Nor could if she tried. No operator knew even the instrumentation necessary to locate any particular failure, to say nothing of being able to interpret the esoteric signals of that instrumentation.

There were independent experts, of course, and Grimes found them and put them to work. These experts, however, could find nothing with which to work. The key codes, the master diagrams, and the all-important frequency manuals had vanished. They could not even find out what, or how much, of sabotage had been done. It would be quicker, they reported, to jury-rig a few channels for Labor's own use. They could do that in a day or so; in just a little longer than it would take to fly technicians to the various cities he wanted in his network. Grimes told them to go ahead; but before the Labor leaders could accomplish much of anything, EastHem launched every intercontinental ballistic missile it had.

WestHem's warning systems and defenses were very good indeed. The Department of Defense had its own communications system, which of course was not affected by the strike. In seconds, then, after the first Eastern missile left the ground, the retaliatory monsters of the West began to climb their ladders.

And in minutes the Nameless One and hundreds of the hard core of the Party died; and thousands of his lesser minions were in vehicles hurtling toward subspacers which had for many months been ready to go and fully programmed for flight.

CHAPTER FIFTEEN

The University of Psionics

Earth as such did not have a space navy; there was no danger of attack from space and, as far as Earth was concerned, the outplanets could take care of themselves. Nor did either WestHem or EastHem; with their ICBM's they did not need or want any subspace-going battleships. Nor did any of the planets. Newmars and Galmetia were heavily armed, but their armament was strictly defensive.

Thus InStell had been forced, over the years, to develop a navy of its own, to protect its far-flung network of merchant traffic lines against piracy; which had of course moved into space along with the richly-laden merchantmen. As traffic increased, piracy increased; so protection had to increase, too. Thus, over the years and gradually, there came about a very peculiar situation:

The only real navy in all the reaches of explored space – the only law-enforcement agency of all that space – was a private police force not responsible to any government!

It hunted down and destroyed pirate ships in space. It sought out and destroyed pirate bases. Since no planetary court had jurisdiction, InStell set up a space-court, in which such few marauders as were captured alive were tried, convicted, and sentenced to death. For over a century there had been bitter criticism of these 'high-handed tactics', particularly on Earth. However, InStell didn't like it, either – it was expensive. Wherefore, for the same hundred years or so, InStell had been trying to get rid of it; but no planet – particularly Earth – or no Planetary League or whatever – would take it over. Everybody wanted to run it, but nobody would pick up the tab. So InStell kept on being the only Law in space.

This navy was small, numbering only a hundred capital ships; but each of those ships was an up-to-the-minute and terribly efficient engine of destruction, bristling with the most modern, most powerful weapons known to man.

High above Earth's surface, precisely spaced both vertically and horizontally, hung poised the weirdest, the motleyest fleet ever assembled. InStell's entire navy was there, clear down to tenders, scouts, and gigs; but they were scarcely a drop in the proberbial bucket. InStell's every liner, freighter, lofter, and shuttle that could be there was there; MetEnge's every ore-boat, tanker, scout, and scow that could possibly be spared; all the Galaxians' every available vessel of every type and kind, from Hatfield's palatial subspace-going private yacht down to Maynard's grandsons' four-boy flitabout. More, every space-yard of the planets had been combed; every clunker, and every junker not yet cut completely up, was taken over. Drives and controls had been repaired or replaced. Hulls had been made air-tight. Many of these derelicts, however, were in such bad shape that they could not be depended upon to stay air-tight; hence many of those skeleton crews worked, ate, and slept in spacesuits complete except for helmets – and with those helmets at belts at the ready.

But each unit of that vast and ridiculously nondescript fleet could carry men, missile-killers, computer-coupled locators, and launchers, and that was all that was necessary. Since there was so much area to cover, it was the number of control stations that was important, not their size or quality. The Galaxians had had to use every craft whose absence from its usual place would not point too directly at Maynard's plan.

The fleet was not evenly distributed, of course. Admiral Dann knew the location of every missile-launching base on Earth, and his coverage varied accordingly. Having made formation, he waited. His flagship covered EastHem's main base; he personally saw EastHem's first Inter-Continental Ballistic Missile streak upward.

166

'This is it, boys, go to work,' he said quietly into his microphone, and the counter-action began. A computer whirred briefly and a leybyrdite missile-killer erupted from a launcher. Erupted, and flashed away on collision course at an acceleration so appallingly high that it could not be tracked effectively even by the radar of that age.

That acceleration can be stated in Tellurian gravities; but the figure, by itself, would be completely meaningless to the mind. Everyone knows all about one Earthly gravity. Everyone has seen a full-color tri-di of hand-trained men undergoing ten and fifteen gees; has seen what it does to them. But ten thousand gravs? Or a hundred thousand? Or two hundred thousand? Such figures are entirely meaningless.

Consider instead the bullet in the barrel of a magnum rifle at, and immediately after, the instant of ignition of the propellant charge. This concept is much more informative. Starting from rest, in a time of a little over one millisecond and in a distance of less than three feet, that bullet attains a velocity of more than four thousand feet per second. Those missile-killers moved like that, except more so and continuously. They were the highest-acceleration things ever put into production by man.

The first killer struck its target and both killer and target vanished into nothingness; a nothingness so inconceivably hot that the first thing to become visible was a fire-ball some ten miles in diameter. But there was nothing of fission about that frightfulness; GalFed's warheads operated on the utterly incomprehensible heat generated by dead-shorted Chaytor engines during the fractional microsecond each engine lasted before being whiffed into subatomic vapor by the stark ferocity of its own performance.

Missiles by the hundreds were launched; from EastHem, from WestHem, from the poles and from the oceans and from the air; and in their hundreds they were blown into submolecular and subatomic vapor. Thus it made no difference what kind of a warhead any missile had carried. Fission, fusion, chemical, or biological; all one: no analysis, however precise and thorough, could ever reveal what any of those cargoes had originally been. Nor did any missile reach its destina-

167

tion. Admiral Dann had ships enough, and missile-killers in thousands to spare.

Meanwhile hundreds of small, highly-specialized vessels had been flying hither and yon above certain areas of the various oceans. They were hunting, with ultra-sensitive instrumentation, all Earth's missile-carrying submarines. They didn't bother about the missiles launched by the subs – the boys and girls upstairs would take care of them – they were after the pig-boats themselves. Their torpedoes were hunters, too. Once a torpedo's finders locked on, the sub had no chance whatever of escape. There was a world-jarring concussion where each sub-marine had been, and a huge column of water and vapor drove upward into and through the stratosphere.

This furious first phase of the 'police action' lasted – except for the sub-hunt – only minutes. Then every missile-launching site on Earth was blasted out of existence. So also were a few subspacers attempting to leave EastHem – all Earth had been warned once and had been told that the warning would not be given twice.

Then the immense fleet re-formed, held position, and waited a few hours; after which time Dann ordered all civilian ships to return to their various ports. The navy stayed on in its entirety. It would continue to destroy all ships attempting to leave Earth.

Twelve hours after Earth's last missile had been destroyed, two-hundred-odd persons met in the main lounge of the flag-ship of the fleet. Maynard, his face haggard and drawn, called the meeting to order. After the preliminaries were over, he said:

'One part of the operation, the prevention of damage to any important part of Earth, was one hundred percent successful. Second, the replacement of EastHem's dictatorship by a board of directors was also successful – at least, the first objectives were attained. Third, our attempt to replace WestHem's government by a board of directors which, together with that of EastHem, would form a unified and properly-motivated government of all Earth, was a failure. The Westerners did not try to leave Earth, but decided to stay and fight it out. For that reason many key men changed their minds at the last minute and remained loyal to WestHem's government instead of supporting us. Thus, while we succeeded in evacuating most of our personnel, we lost one hundred four very good men.

'The fault, of course, was mine. I erred in several highly important matters. I underestimated the power of nationalism and patriotism; of loyalty to a government even though that government is notoriously inefficient, unjust, and corrupt. I underestimated the depth and strength of the anti-Galaxian prejudice that has been cultivated so assiduously throughout the great majority of Earth's people; I failed to realize how rigidly, in the collective mind of that vast group, Galaxianism is identified with Capitalism. I overestimated the intelligence of that group; its ability to reason from cause to effect and its willingness to act for its own good. I thought that, when the issue was squarely joined, those people would abandon their attitude of "Let George do it" and take some interest in their own affairs.

'Because of these errors in judgment I hereby tender my resignation, effective as of now, from the position of Chairman of this Board. I turn this meeting over to Vice-Chairman Bryce for the election of my successor.'

He left the room; but was recalled in five minutes.

'Mr. Maynard, your tendered resignation has been rejected by an almost unanimous vote,' Bryce told him. 'It is the consensus that no one else of us all could have done as well. You will therefore resume your place and the meeting will proceed.'

Maynard sat down and said, 'I thank you, fellow Galaxians, for your vote of confidence; which, however little deserved, I am constrained to accept. Mr. Eldon Smith will now speak.'

The meeting went on for hours. Discussion was thorough and heated; at times acrimonious. Eventually, however, the main areas of discord were hammered out to substantial agreement. The Board of Directors of the Galactic Federation concluded its first really important meeting.

Earth's communications systems were restored to normal operating conditions and Maynard, after ample advance notice, spoke to every inhabitant of Earth who cared to listen. He covered the situation as it then was; what had brought it about, and why such drastic action had been necessary. Then he said:

'At present there are ninety-five planets in the Galactic Federation. Earth will be admitted to the Federation if and when it adopts a planetary government acceptable to the Federation's Board of Directors. We care nothing about the form of that government; but we insist that its prime concern must be the welfare of the human race as a whole. Earth now has two directors on our board, Li Hing Wong and Feodr Ilyowicz. Earth is entitled to three more directors, to represent the regions now being so erroneously called the Western Hemisphere. They must be chosen by an honest, stable, and responsible authority, not by your present government of corrupt, greedy, and self-serving gangsters and plunderers.

'We will allow enough freighters to land on WestHem's spaceports to supply WestHem's people with its usual supply of food and of certain other necessities, but that is all. Our milk-truck drivers have been recalled and we will do nothing whatever about the general strike. If you wish to let an organized minority starve you to death, that is your right. You got yourselves into this mess; you can get yourselves out of it or not, as you please.

'We will not broadcast again until three qualified representatives of WestHem have been accepted by us as members of the Board of Directors of the Galactic Federation. Until then, do exactly as you please. That is all.'

There is no need to go into what happened then throughout the nations of WestHem; the many nations whose only common denominator had been their opposition to the East. Too much able work has been done, from too many different viewpoints, to make any real summary justifiable. It suffices to say here that the adjustment was not as simple as Maynard's statement indicated that it should be, nor as easy as he really thought it would be. The strife was long, bitter, and violent; and, as will be seen later, certain entirely unexpected events occurred.

In fact, many thousand persons died and the Galaxians themselves had to straighten WestHem out before its three directors were seated on the Board.

170

There is no agreement as to whether or not the course that was followed was the right course or the best course. Many able scholars hold that the Directorate was just as much of a dictatorship, and just as intolerant of and just as inimical to real liberty and freedom as was any dictatorship of old.

It is the chronicler's considered opinion, however, that what was done was actually the best thing – for humanity as a whole – that could have been done; considering what the ordinary human being intrinsically is. By 'ordinary' is meant, of course, the person to whom the entire field of psionics is a sealed realm; the person in whose tightly closed and rigidly conventional mind no supra-normal phenomenon can possibly occur or exist. And the present state of galactic civilization seems to show that if what was done was not the best that could have been done it was a very close approximation indeed thereto.

At what exact point does liberty become license? What is Freedom? Is Ethics an absolute? Can any system of ethics ever become an absolute? The conclusion seems unavoidable that until human beings have progressed much farther than they have at present – until supra-normal abilities have become normal – the 'liberties' and the 'freedoms' of many will have to be abridged if the good of all is to be served.

Newmars was the first planet to be colonized and it was designed from the first to become completely independent of Earth in as short a time as possible. Thus, as well as being longer-established than the other planets, it grew faster in population. Therefore Newmars had a population of about a billion, whereas the next most populous planet, Galmetia, had scarcely half that many people and all the rest of the colonized planets together did not have many more people than did Earth alone.

Geographically, Newmars had somewhat more land than Earth and somewhat less water, but the land masses were arranged in an entirely different pattern. There was one tremendous continent, Warneria; which, roughly rectangular in shape and lying athwart the equator, covered on the average about ninety degrees of latitude and about one hundred fifty of longitude. There were half a dozen other, much smaller continents, and many hundreds of thousands of islands ranging in size from coral atolls up to near-continents as large as Australia.

Most of Newmars' people lived on 'The Continent', and some seven millions of them lived in and around the coastal city of Warnton, the planet's only real business center and the capital city of both the Continent and the whole Warner-owned world.

In establishing the University of Psionics, then, Adams did not have to think twice to decide where to put it. Earth, even though it would furnish most of the students, was out of the question; the U of Psi would have to be in Warnton, Newmars.

Within a day of landing, however, Adams realized that the business of starting such a project as that was not his dish. He simply could not spend important money. He had never bought even an expensive scientific instrument; he had always requisitioned them from some purchasing department or other. He had never in his life written a check for more than a few hundred bucks; he had no knowledge whatever of the use of money as a tool. Wherefore the *Explorer* landed at Warnton Spaceport and Barbara Deston took over. It had been Adams' idea to buy – or preferably to rent – a small apartment house to start with, but Barbara put her foot down hard on that.

She bought outright a brand-new forty-story hotel that covered half of a square block, saying, 'We don't want large class-rooms – the smaller the better, since it will be small-group work – so this will suit us well enough until the architects get our real university built. Then we can either sell it or form an operating company and merge it into the hotel chain.'

When the project was running smoothly, and after the eight had developed a nucleus of some fifty psiontists, the Destons took the *Explorer* to Earth and the Joneses and the Trains, in two Warner-owned subspacers, started out to cover the other planets, in descending order of population.

The Destons took up residence in their suite in the Hotel Warner and went to work. They scanned colleges and universities, whether or not any such institution of learning had ever shown any interest in psionics. They scanned Institutes of this and that, including several of Psychic Research. They scanned science fiction fan clubs and flying-saucer societies and crackpot groups and cults of all kinds and psychic mediums and fortune-tellers. They attended – unfelt – meetings of the learned societies. They scanned the trades and the professions, from aardvark keepers and aerialists through electricians and jewelers and ophthalmologists and spacemen to zymurgists.

Detecting a psionic latent, however weak, was now easy enough. There was an aura, if not an actual radiation, that was perceptible to the triggered mind at almost any distance. Any mind possessing that unique and unmistakable characteristic could and did feel and respond to the touch of a directed thought. Or, more exactly perhaps, a focused or tuned thought. Any such mind could and did (under such expert tutelage as theirs now was) learn telepathy in seconds; and, with very few exceptions, all persons with such minds became Galaxians and went to Newmars.

Since the operators knew what to do and exactly how to do it, the work went fast; and, very shortly after its beginning, a definite pattern began to form. Every possessor of a strong latent talent was at or near the top of his or her heap. If a performer, he or she had top billing. If a milliner, she got a hundred dollars per copy for her hats. If a mechanic, he was the best mechanic in town.

It need scarcely be said that Maynard, Lansing, Dann, Smith, Phelps, DuPuy, Hatfield, Spehn, Miss Champion, the seven leaders of the Planetsmen and their assistants, and hundreds of others of the Galaxians were found to be very strong latents. Or that, even though most of them were too busy to go to Newmars to study, each was given everything that he could then take that his teachers could then give.

On the other hand, not even the Adamses could at that time get into touch with a non-psionic mind. It was not that that mind refused contact or blocked the exploring feelers of thought; it was as though there was nothing there to feel. It was like probing with sentient fingers throughout the reaches of an unbounded, undefined, completely empty and utterly dark space.

And the conservative ('Hidebound', according to Deston),

greedy capitalists of Earth were non-psionic to a man.

The response to this psionic survey was so tremendous that the hotel building, immense as it was, was jammed to overflowing before the first real University building was ready for use.

As Barbara had foreseen, the psionics classes were small, but there were plenty of teachers; people whose former titles ranged from Instructress-In-Kindergarten to Professor Emeritus of Advanced Nucleonics. And these classes were being driven. They wanted to be driven. Each person there had been – more or less unconsciously – unhappy, discontented, frustrated. The few who had known that they had psionic power had been hiding it or disguising it; the others had known, either definitely or vaguely, that they wanted something out of life that they were not getting. Thus, when their minds were opened to the incredible vistas of psionics, they wanted to be driven hard and they drove themselves hard. They graduated fast, and either went right to work or formed advanced-study groups – and in either case they kept on driving hard.

When the *Explorer* emerged near Newmars, Barbara did not wait for the slow maneuvering of landing at the spaceport and then taking the monorail into town, but 'ported herself directly into the main office of the University. Five minutes later she drove a thought to her husband. 'Babe, come here, quick! Here's something you've simply got to see!'

He appeared beside her and she went on, 'I knew they were working fast, but I certainly didn't expect anything like *that* so soon.' Her mind took his up into a small room on the thirtieth floor. 'Just *look* at *that*!'

Deston 'looked' at the indicated group of four; who, heads almost touching, were seated at a small square table. One was a gangling, coltish, teen-age girl in sweater, slacks, and loafers, with braces on her teeth and her hair in a ponytail. The second was an old friend of Deston's – a big, taut, trim space-officer in a uniform sporting the insignia of a full captain. The third was a lithe and lissome brunette made up to the gills; the fourth was a bald and paunchy ex-banker of seventy.

'And *that* combination picked *itself* out?' Deston marveled.

'Uh-huh,' she said, gleefully, pressing his arm tightly

against her side. 'All out of their own little pointed heads and Stella says they're the prize group of the whole University. Dig in. Look. Just see what they're actually *doing*.'

'Uh-uh. I don't want to derail their train of thought.'

'You won't. Maybe if you grabbed 'em by the scruff of the neck and the seat of the pants and slammed 'em against the wall a few times you could, but nothing any gentler than that.'

'They're *that* solid?' He went in and looked, and his whole body stiffened. He stayed in for five long minutes before he came back to Barbara and whistled through his teeth. 'Wow and *wow* and WOW!' he said then. 'All of us Big Wheels are going to have to look a little bit out – we're going to have competition. We may have to demonstrate our fitness to lead – if any.'

'That's what I mean, and isn't it just *wonderful*? The University doesn't need us any more, so we can start doing whatever it is that we're going to do right now instead of waiting so long, like we thought we'd have to.'

'They've done a grand job, that's sure. Let's do some long-distance checking – see how Spehn and Dann are making out.'

They were making out all right. Since both were now psiontists, Intelligence and Navy were barreling right along. Graduates from the University of Psionics had been pouring into both services for weeks. Both services were expanding rapidly, in both numbers and quality; and, since the opposition was practically non-psionic, the Galaxians' advantage (Spehn and Dann agreed) was increasing all the time. Also, the opposition was not really united and could never be united except superficially because its factions were, by their very natures, immiscible. How effective *could* such opposition be?

Unfortunately, Spehn and Dann were wrong; and so were the Destons. It is a sad but true fact that a college graduate at graduation knows more than he ever did before or ever will again; and so it was with these young new psiontists. They thought they knew it all, but they didn't. They had a long way to go.

CHAPTER SIXTEEN

Strategic Withdrawal

Since the Galactic Federation claimed authority over all explored off-planet space, and since InStell still wanted to get rid of the job of policing all that space, GalFed took the navy over. (It had a tremendous war-chest, and the financial details of the transaction are of no importance here.) What had been the Interstellar Patrol was now the Grand Fleet of the Galactic Federation.

Fleet Admiral Guerdon Dann, being a psiontist, could understand and could work in subspace. Therefore he could perceive subspace-going vessels before they emerged into normal space, a feat no non-psionic observer could perform. Thus he perceived a very large number of vessels so maneuvering in subspace as to emerge in a roughly globular formation well outside his own globe of warships. He perceived that they were warcraft and really big stuff – super-dreadnoughts very much like his own – and that there were four or five hundred of them. That wasn't good; but, since their purpose was pellucidly clear, he'd have to do something. What could he do? His mind raced.

He wasn't a war admiral – pirates didn't fight in fleets. He didn't know any more about fleet action in space than a pig did about Sunday. There'd never been any. Missile-killers were new and had extreme range, and no repulsor except a planet-based super-giant could stop one after fifteen seconds of flight at 175,000 gravities. However, they carried no screen, so they'd be duck soup for beams, especially lasers – if they could spot them soon enough, and he'd have to assume that they could.

Torps had plenty of screen, but they were slow; hence they were duck soup for repulsors. What he *ought* to have, dammit, was something with the legs of a killer and the screens of a torp, and there was nothing like that even on the drawing boards. Before leybyrdite nothing like that had been possible.

Beams, then? Uh – *uh!* They'd englobe shipwise, four or five to one. His ships could then immerge – if they were fast enough – or get whiffed out.

He got into telepathic touch with his officers. 'I don't know whether we can do anything to those boys or not. Probably not. We certainly can't if we let them get close to us – they'll englobe us four or five to one if we make like heroes, so we won't. Be ready to immerge when I give the word. Try killers at fifteen seconds range as they emerge and send out some torps on general principles, but that's all. We're going to execute a strategic withdrawal – in other words, run like hell.'

Computers computed briefly; impressed data upon mechanical brains. Missile-killers and torpedoes hurtled away. The first strange warship emerged and the first missile-killer flashed into a raging, space-wracking fireball miles short of objective.

'I was afraid of that,' Dann thought on, quietly. 'I don't think they'll follow us – I think I know what they're after – so we'll run. Numbers one to fifty, to Galmetia; fifty-one to one hundred, to Newmars; and everybody, get under an umbrella, just in case they do follow us.'

En route to Galmetia – the flagship *Terra* was of course Number One – Dann had a long telepathic conversation with Maynard, and on landing he went straight to GalMet's main office. Maynard was waiting for him, with a staff of some fifty people. Maynard said:

'You all know that the purpose of the enemy fleet was not specifically to attack our fleet or our planets, but to break our blockade of Earth. They broke it, and announced that any planet refusing to resume full trade with Earth would be bombed. So,' he shrugged his shoulders and grimaced wryly, 'we give in and it is now business as usual. We have of course taken the obvious steps; we are beefing up our repulsors and are developing a laser that will cut an eighty-mile asteroid up into thin slices at half a million miles. We've also started on your special torp, Guerd, on a crash-pri basis. "TIMPS" is the name: Torpedo, Improved, Missile-Propelled, Screened. But we haven't been able to do anything more than guess at the answers to such questions as: Who are they? Where do they come from? No known planet, of that we are sure. Capital, Communism, Labor, or what? Hatfield, have you anything to offer?'

The meeting went on for four hours; but beyond the obvious fact that there was a planet – and not a Johnny-Come-Lately planet, either, but one long-enough established to have plenty of people, plenty of industry, and plenty of money or its equivalent – the meeting got nowhere. At adjournment time Maynard flashed Deston a thought to stay behind, and after the others had gone he said:

'You told me you didn't know anything. I didn't ask you then and I'm not asking you now what you're figuring on doing about it. But you're going to do something. Correct?'

'Correct. I don't know what anybody *can* do, but we're going to work on it. They have leybyrdite; but they almost certainly did not develop it themselves.'

'Cancel the "almost". We've never limited its sale – we can't. Anyone could have bought any amount of it. Dummy concerns – untraceable – is my guess on that. We know that a lot of Tellurian capital has always operated on the old grab-everything-in-sight principle, and everyone knows what Communism does. Either of them could and would run a planet as that one has obviously been run for many years – in a way that would make the robber barons of old sick at the stomach. But since it doesn't make sense that Labor has been doing it ... it almost has to be either Capital or Communism.'

'It looks that way.' Deston frowned in thought. 'But I don't know any sure-fire way of finding out, which, if either ... so I'd better go get hold of some people to help me think. 'Bye.'

Deston did not walk out of the room, but 'ported himself to Barbara's side in the University office. 'Hi, pet,' he said, kissing her lightly. 'I got troubles. How about busting in on that squirrelsome foursome that Horse French is in? I want to cry in their beer.'

'Uh-uh, let's not bust in; they'll have to come up for air pretty soon. Let's wait 'til they do, then 'port up there with some lemon sour and Gulka fizz and cherry sloosh and stuff for a break.'

The foursome did and the Destons did and Deston said:

'Well, well, Frenchy old horse, fancy meeting *you* here!' and four strong hands gripped and shook hard. This was the Communications Officer to whom Deston had reported the survival of the liner *Procyon* so long before. 'Nobody ever even suspected you of having a brain in your head. All beef – nothing but muscle to keep your ears apart, I always thought.'

'Hi, Runt! You? Think! What with? But I'll tell you how it was. So many captains got married that they couldn't find room for enough desks for 'em all to sit at, so they loaned me to this here Adams project – on pay, too. Nice of 'em, what? – but you've never met my wife. Paula, this renegade fugitive from InStell is Babe Deston – the unabashed hero of subspace, you know.'

'I know.' The slender, graceful, black-haired, black-eyed girl with the almost theatrical make-up, who had been watching and listening to this underplayed meeting as intently as Barbara had, gave him a firm, warm handshake and turned to Barbara. 'And you're Bobby, of course. These men of ours . . .' She raised one carefully-sculptured eyebrow, 'but *we* don't have to insult each other to prove that we're . . .'

'Hey!' Deston broke in then. He had been studying the way Paula walked – he'd never seen anybody except Barbara move with such perfect, automatic, unconscious coordination as that – 'Wha'-d'ya mean, *Paula*?' he demanded. 'She's Angelique de St. Aubin!'

'*In Person*, not a tri-di,' French bragged. 'But Paula's her real name. The only things about her that are French are the name she married and her professional accent. This psionics stuff is the only way I could lure her down off of the high wire – she wouldn't come to ground, even after she got her Mrs. degree, just for the honor and privilege of being Mrs. Captain Horace French.'

'Let's spread this around a little, huh, and give the rest of us a chance.' The coltish but attractive teen-ager, having gulped the last syrupy bits of a full half-liter of cherry sloosh, came in. 'I'm May Eberly. I can't tell you two wonderful people how glad I am that you started this and let me in – I never *dreamed* – well, anyway, it's *exactly* what I was born for. The others, too. You know what they call us? The Effeff – the Funny Four, no less – but I don't care. I *love* it! And this,' she waved a hand at the oldster, 'is Titus Fleming. He's got pots of money, so we call him "Tite", but of course he isn't, just the opposite, in fact he spoils us all rotten, and . . .'

'Hush, child,' Fleming said, with an affectionate smile. Then, to Deston, 'May has an extraordinarily brilliant and agile mind, but she is inclined to natter too much.'

'Well, why not?' the youngster demanded, engagingly. 'When we're on rapport I don't talk at all, so I have to make up for it sometime, don't I? And Mr. Deston – no, I think I'll call you "Babe", too. Okay?'

'Sure. Why not?'

'Horse, there – I never heard him called that before, but I like it – says if everybody's forbearing enough to let me keep on living long enough to grow up, which will surprise him a megabuck's worth, I'll be a gorgeous hunk of woman some day.' She executed a rather awkward pirouette. 'I can't do this anywhere near like Paula does yet, but I'm going to sometime, just see if I don't.'

'I'd hate to bet one buck against Horse's megabuck that you won't,' Deston agreed. The girl was certainly under fourteen, but the promise was there. Unmistakably there. 'Or that you won't live to break a hundred, either.'

'Oh, thanks, Babe. Oh, I just *can't* wait! I'm going to be a *femme fatale*, you know – all slinky and everything – but you prob'ly didn't come all the way out here just to chatter – I think Tite's word "natter" is cute, don't you? – so maybe before Horse bats my ears down again I'd better keep still a while. S'pose?'

'Could be – we're in a jam,' Deston said, and told them what the jam was. 'So you see, to get anywhere at all, we've got to do some really intensive spying, and the only way to do that is to learn how to read non-psionic minds, and the poop is that if anybody in total space can deliver the goods on that order, you four are most apt to be the ones.'

'Oh?' May exclaimed. 'That's a really funny one, Babe – we must *really* be psychic ...' She broke off with a giggle as the others began to laugh. 'No, I mean really – much more so even than we thought – because that's *exactly* what we've just been working on – not to be just snoopy stinkers, either – or stinky snoopers? – but just to find out why nobody could ever do it before – we aren't very good at it yet, but it goes like this – no, let's all link up and we'll show you. Oh, this is going to *really* be fun!'

The four linked up and went to work, and the Destons tuned themselves in; very slowly at first, more as observers than as active participants in the investigation. The subject this time was a middle-echelon executive, the traffic manager of one division of far-flung Warner Oil. He was a keen-looking young man, sharp-featured, with a very good head for figures. His king-size desk was littered with schedules, rate-books, and revision sheets. From time to time his fingertips flicked rapidly by touch over the keys of a desk-type computer.

The four were getting a flash of coherent thought once in a while, but that was all.

The Destons watched, studied, analyzed, and compared notes until their fusion finally said, in thought, 'Okay, Effeff, come up for air and take a break. Time out for discussion.' They emerged as individuals and Deston said, 'You aren't making contact and I think I know why. Horse, do either you or Paula know consciously that you're trying to work the Fourth Nume?'

'My God, no,' Paula said. 'We were exposed to that stuff a long time ago, but it didn't take.'

'You weren't ready, so Doc wouldn't have tried to give it to you, so who did?'

'Mr. and Mrs. Throckmorton.'

'They would,' Barbara said then. 'Fortunately, they've learned better now.'

'But *you* two can give it to us.'

'We could make a stab at it, but we'd rather not. We need

more practice. We'll call Adams and Stella and watch.'

The Adamses came in, and wrought; and this time, since the pupils were ready, the lesson 'took'.

'*Now* we'll git 'im!' May exclaimed. 'Come on, what's holding us up?'

'I am,' Deston said. 'Don't go off half-cocked; we've got a lot to do yet. Before anyone can do a job he has to know exactly what the job is and exactly how to do it, and we don't know either one. So let's examine your four-ply entity – the tools you're using. There's no three-dimensional analogy, but we can call Horace and Paula an engine, with two vital parts missing – the spark-plug and the flywheel . . .'

'But I want to learn that fourth-nume stuff *now*!' May declared. She was, as usual, 'way out ahead. 'I don't *want* to wait until I'm old and decrepit and . . .'

'Tut-tut, youngster.' Fleming reached out and put his hand lightly over the girl's mouth. 'That attitude is precisely what makes you the spark-plug; but if you and I had the abilities we lack instead of the ones we have, neither of us would be in this particular engine at all.'

'That's right,' Deston said. 'Now as to what this engine does. Postulating a two-dimensional creature, you could pile a million of him up and still have no thickness at all. Similarly, no three-dimensional material body can be compressed to zero thickness. The analogy holds in three and four dimensions. However, there are discontinuities, incompatibilities, and sheer logical impossibilities. Hence, ordinarily, a four-dimensional mind, which all psionic minds are, can not engage any three-dimensional, non-psionic mind at all. All possible points of contact are of zero dimensions . . .'

'But wait up, Babe,' French broke in. 'We can see three-dimensional objects, so why can't we . . .'

'We can't really see 'em,' Deston said, flatly. 'We can see what and where they are, but they're absolutely immaterial to us. So forces, already immaterial, become imperceptible. Clear?'

'As mud,' French said, dubiously. 'There's a . . .'

Paula broke in. '*I* see! The Fourth – they just showed us – remember? Manipulate – immaterial . . . non-space-non-time?'

'Oh, sure.' French's face cleared. 'What we were doing, Babe, was blundering around in the Fourth, making a contact once in a blue moon by luck?'

'That's about it. Now, another analogy. Consider transformation of coordinates – polar into Cartesian, three-dimensional into two-dimensional, and so on. What a competent operator in the Fourth actually does is manipulate non-space-non-time attributes in such a way as to construct a matrix that is *both* three- and four-dimensional. Analogous to light – particle and/or wave. You follow?'

'Perfectly,' the Frenches said in unison. 'Four on our side, three on the non-psi's side, with perfect coupling.'

'You lost May and me there,' Fleming said. 'However, you would, of course . . . but I understand much better now why we four work together so well. I'll venture an analogy – poor, perhaps – May scouts out ahead, in a million directions at once. I follow behind, sometimes pushing and sometimes putting on the brakes.'

'And steering the sled!' May exclaimed. 'I see, now, too – that's the way it works!'

'Close enough,' Deston said. 'Now. Thought patterns are as individual as fingerprints or the shape of one snowflake or one instantaneous pattern in a kaleidoscope. What two telepaths do is *not* tune one mind to the other. Instead, each one of a very large number of filaments of thought – all under control, remember – touches its opposite number, thus setting up a pattern that has never existed before and will never exist again . . .'

'I get it!' French exclaimed. 'Reading a non-psi's mind will be a strictly one-way street. We'll have to go *through* the matrix – which doesn't exist in telepathy – and match whatever pattern we find on the other side – which won't change.'

'That's right – we hope! Now you can go.'

They went; and this time the traffic-manager's mind was wider open to inspection than any book could possibly be. To be comparable, every page of such a book would have to be placed in perfect position to read and all at once!

Paula stood it for something over one second, then broke the linkage with what was almost a scream. 'Stop it!'

She drew a deep breath and went on, more quietly, 'I'm

183

glad it's you who will have to do that, Babe, not I. That was a worse thing than anything a Peeping Tom could ever do. It's shameful – monstrous – it's positively obscene to do a thing like that to anyone, for any reason.'

'Why, Paula, that was *fun*!' May exclaimed.

'But Babe,' Paula said, 'that was *nothing* like telepathy ... but of course it wouldn't be.'

'Of course. In telepathy the exchange of information is voluntary and selective. This way, the poor devil doesn't stand a chance. He doesn't even know it's happening.'

Paula frowned. ' "Poor devil" is the exactly correct choice of words. Are you going to have to use us like that on the other poor devils you are going to ... I can't think of a word bad enough.'

'No. I just tried it. I can do it alone now, perfectly. But that's the way it is; opening new cells and learning new techniques. I had the latent capabilities. You others did, too?'

'I *can*, but if you think I ever *will* you're completely out of your mind,' Barbara declared, and Paula agreed vigorously.

'But I want to and I *can't*!' May wailed. 'Why oh why can't I grow up *faster*!'

'We don't want you to grow up at all, sweetie,' French said. 'We don't want to lose our spark-plug. Ever think of that angle?'

'Babe, will I *really* have to leave this Funny Four then?'

'You'll not only have to, you'll want to,' Deston replied, soberly. 'That is one of the immutable facts of life.'

'Okay, this is lots more fun than being old would be, anyway. What'll we try next, Paula?'

'I'd like to go back up into the Fourth Nume and really explore it – turn it inside out – that is, if there's nothing more important at the moment?' Paula quirked an eyebrow at Deston.

There was not. Goodbyes were said, and promises were made to meet soon and often, and the Destons 'ported themselves away.

Maynard called a special meeting of the Board to order and said, 'Since you all know what the Tellurian situation is, politically and otherwise, I won't go into it. It seems to some of us however, that this recent disaster may not be a disaster at all; that, if we play our cards properly, we may be able to secure much better results than if our blockade of Tellus had succeeded.

'With all threat of nuclear warfare removed, WestHem's so-called defense spending will stop; in fact, much of it has already stopped. Ordinarily, this would not be a blessing, since business would slump into a rapidly-accelerating downward spiral. A bad recession, or even a severe panic, would follow. Any such result *could* be avoided, of course, if WestHem's government would cut taxes in the full amount of defense spending; but has any one of you an imagination sufficiently elastic to encompass the idea of that government giving up half its income and firing *that* many hundreds of thousands of political hangers-on?'

There was a burst of scornful laughter.

'Mine isn't, either. As you know, defense stocks are already plummeting. They are dropping the limit every day. Due to public panic, they will continue to drop to a point below – in some cases to a point much below – the actual value of the properties. I propose that we start buying before that point is reached. Not enough to support the market, of course; just enough to control it at whatever rate of decline the specialists will compute as being certain to result in our gaining control.

'Having gained control of the largest – excuse me, I'm getting ahead of myself. I assure you that this program is financially feasible. I am authorized to say that in addition to Gal-Bank, whose statements you all get, Deston and Deston, Warner Oil, InterStellar, and Galactic Metals will all put their treasuries behind this project.'

There was a burst of applause.

'Since we are very large holders of these stocks already, there is no doubt that we can obtain control. We will then re-hire all the personnel who have been laid off and convert to the production of luxury goods, preferably of the more expensive and less durable types. We will finance the purchase of these goods ourselves . . .'

This time, they clapped and whistled and stamped their feet.

'... and put on a massive advertising campaign for such basic spending as modernization, new housing, and so on. All of this, however, will be secondary to our main purpose. None of you have realized as yet that this is the first chance we have ever had of forming a political party and actually *electing* a government of WestHem that will govern it...'

There was a storm of applause that lasted for five minutes. Then Maynard went on:

'The Board seems to be in favor of such action. Mr. Stevens Spehn, who has done a great deal of work on the political aspects of this idea, will now take the floor.'

CHAPTER SEVENTEEN

Punsunby's World

Many parsecs distant from the remotest outpost of civilization there was a planet known to its inhabitants only as The World. The World and everything pertaining to it, including the People and the Sun and the Moons and the little nightlights in the sky had been created by The Company on Compday, January First in the Year One; and this day – also a Compday, of course – was the two hundred twenty-sixth anniversary of that date Jan. 1, 226. There was no celebration or ceremony – in fact, there were no words in the language to express any such concept – but, since it was Compday, all Operators worked only half a shift.

In the Beginning the Company had decreed that there were to be three hundred eighty-four days (plus an extra Compday, to be announced by the Highest Agent, once every few years) in each year. Each year had twelve months; each month four weeks; each week eight days – Compday, Sonday, Monday, Tonday, Wonday, Thurday, Furday, and Surday. All Operators were to work exactly half of each of those days except Compday, upon which they were to work only a quarter; the other quarter was to be devoted to being happy and to thinking pleasant thoughts of the Company, of its goodness in furnishing them all with happiness and with life and its comforts.

No other World had ever been created or even would be, nor any other People. The Company and The World comprised the Cosmic All.

The World had not changed and it never would change;

The Company had so decreed. Not to the People directly, of course; The Company was an immaterial, omniscient, omnipotent entity that, except in the matter of punishment, dealt with People only through Company Agents. These Agents were not People, but were supermen and superwomen far above People; so far above People that the lowest-caste Company Agents had qualities that not even the highest-caste People could understand.

Upon very rare occasions the Company, whose symbol was A A A A A A A, appeared in a form of flesh to the Highest Agent, the Comptroller General of The World, whose symbol was A A A A A A B; and, emitting the pure mercury-vapor Light of the Company and in the sight and the hearing of the highest-caste Company Agents, uttered sacred Company Orders.

Company Agents of various high castes transmitted these Orders to the Managers, who were the highest-caste people of the World. The Managers told the Assistant Managers, who told the Chiefs, who told the Assistant Chiefs, who told the Heads, who told the Assistant Heads, who told the Foremen, who told the Shift Bosses, who told the lower-caste People who were the Operators what to do and saw to it that they did.

At the time of the World's creation The Company had issued a three-fold Prime Directive; which was immutable and eternal: ALL PEOPLE MUST: 1) Be happy. 2) Produce more and more People. 3) Produce more and more Goods.

If a Person obeyed these three injunctions all his life, his immaterial Aura – the thing that made him alive, not dead, and that made him different from all other Persons – when he became dead was absorbed into the Company and he would be happy forever.

On the other hand, there were a few who did not follow the Prime Directive literally and exactly. These were the mals – the malcontents, the maladjusts, the malefactors – the thinkers, the questioners, the unbelievers – the unhappy for any cause. They were blasted out of existence by the Company itself and that was the end of them, auras and all.

And that was fair enough. Every Person was born into a

caste. He grew up in that caste. He was trained to do what his ancestors had done and what his descendants would do. He had children in that caste, all of whom became of it. He lived his whole life in that caste and died in it. That was, is, and ever shall be the way of life, and that is precisely the way it should be: for in pure order, and only in pure order, lies security; and in security, and only in security, lies happiness; and happiness is the First Consideration of the Prime Directive. Mals of all kinds are threats to order, to security, and to happiness; therefore all mals must die. So it was, is, and ever shall be. Selah. It is written.

Following the Prime Directive was easy enough; for most people, in fact, easier than not following it.

Since happiness was simply the state of not being unhappy, and there was nothing in the normal life to be unhappy about, happiness was the norm.

Producing People, too, was a normal part of life. Furthermore, since the Company punished pre-family sexual experience with Company wrath just a few volts short of death, the family state brought a new and different kind of happiness. Every female Person's job assignment was to produce, between the ages of eighteen and thirty, ten children, and then to keep on running her family unless and until she was transferred to some other job. Since every nubile girl wanted a man of her own, and since children were a source of happiness on their own account, not one woman in a thousand had to be brainwashed at all to really like the job of running a family.

And as for producing Goods – why not? That was what People were created for, and that was all that men were good for – except, of course, for fathering children. Also, there was much happiness to be had in keeping a machine right at the peak of performance, turning out, every shift, an over-quota of passes and an under-permittance of rejects – zero rejects being always the target.

No Person in his right mind ever even thought of wondering what the Goods he produced were for, or what became of them. That was Company business and thus incomprehensible by definition.

On this Compday forenoon, then, in a vast machine-shop in

City One of the World, a young man was hard at work — sitting at ease in a form-fitting chair facing an instrument-board having a hundred-odd dials, meters, gauges, lights, bells, whistles, buzzers, and what-have-you.

Occasionally a green light would begin to shade toward amber and a buzzer would begin to talk to him in Morse code; whereupon he would get up, walk around back of the board to his machine, and make almost imperceptible manual adjustments until the complaining monolog stopped. If, instead of stopping, the signal had turned into a Klaxon blare, he would have been manufacturing rejects, but he was far too good a machiner to make any such error as that. He hadn't turned out a single reject in eighteen straight shifts. He knew everything there was to be known about his machine — and the fact that he knew practically nothing whatever else had never bothered him a bit. Why should it have? That was precisely the way it should be in this, the perfect World that was precisely what the all-powerful Company had decreed.

He was of medium height and medium build; trimly, smoothly muscular; with large, strong, and exquisitely sensitive hands. He had a shock of rather unkempt brown hair, clear gray eyes, and a lightly-tanned, unblemished skin. He wore the green-and-white-striped coveralls of his caste — Machiner Second — and around his neck, on a hard-alloy chain, there hung a large and fairly thick locket. This locket, which had been put on him one minute after he was born and which his body would wear into the crematorium, and which — he firmly believed — could not be opened or removed without causing his death, had seven letters of the English alphabet cut deeply into its face. This group of letters – V T J E S O Q – was his symbol. As far as he knew, the only purpose of the locket was to make him permanently and unmistakably identifiable.

At exactly twelve o'clock noon the machine stopped; for the first time in exactly one week. At the same time he heard the sound of fast-stepping hard heels and turned to see a Company Agent approaching him — the first Agent to come to him in all his twenty years of life. This Agent was a young female, whose spectacular build was spectacularly displayed by a sleeveless, very tight yellow sweater and even tighter black tights. Her boots, laced to the knees, were of fire-engine-red leather. Her short-bobbed hair was deep russet brown in color. Low on her forehead blazed the green jewel of her rank. This jewel, which resembled more than anything else a flaring green spotlight about the size of a half-dollar piece and not much thicker, was mounted in platinum on the platinum drop-piece of a plain platinum headband. Under her sweater she, too, wore a locket; upon which was engraved the symbol A C B A A B A.

'Be happy, Veety!' the Agent snapped.

'Be happy, Agent.' The machiner raised his arms and put both hands flat on the top of his head.

'At ease, Veety! Follow me!'

Whirling on the ball of her left foot, she led the way down a narrow corridor; sharp right into a wider one; sharp left into the main hall and straight into the crowd of operators going off shift. She did not even slow down – the crowd dissolved away from her like magic. They fell all over themselves to get out of her way; for to touch a Company Agent, however accidentally or however lightly, was to receive a blast of Company wrath that, while not permanently harmful, was as intolerable as it was inexplicable.

Through the huge archway, along a wide walkway she led him, to the second archway on the right. She stopped and whistled sharply through her teeth. The exiting operators stopped in their tracks, put hands on heads, and stood motionless.

'V T J R S Y X – forward!' she snapped, and a green-and-white-coveralled, well-built girl – People had to be good physical specimens or they did not live to grow up – came up to within a few feet of the Agent and stopped. She was neither apprehensive nor pleased; merely acquiescent.

'Be happy, Veety!'

'Be happy, Agent.'

'Job transfer. Come with me and this other veety to that aircar over there.'

The Agent slipped lithely into the single front seat of the vehicle, at the controls; the two Machiners Second got into the back seat. The aircar bulleted upward, screamed across City

One to Suburb Ten, and dropped vertically downward to a high-G landing on the beautifully-kept grounds of a small plastic house.

'Out,' the Agent said, and led the couple into a large, comfortably-furnished living-room. 'Stand there ... hold hands ... V T J R S Y X – job transfer. You're eighteen today, so you stop machinering and start running a family. Permanent assignment. The Company knows that you two know each other and like each other. That liking will now become love. The Company knows all.'

'The Company knows all,' the two intoned in unison, solemnly.

'Press your right thumbs here ... you are mated for life. This house is yours – permanently. Four rooms and bath to start. It's expandable; one additional room per child. Here are your family coupon books; throw your single-person ones into the disposer. This special mating coupon gives you free time from now until hour seventeen, when you go to the band concert at Shell Nineteen. Amuse yourselves, you two.' The Agent smiled suddenly, a smile that made her hard young face human and beautiful. 'Have fun – in the bedroom, perhaps? Be happy, both of you.' The Company Agent executed a snappy about-face and strode toward the door.

'Be Happy, Agent,' the newlyweds said; and, as the door closed, went into each other's arms.

They amused themselves and were very happy indeed. They were still very happy while, as hour seventeen neared, they walked, arms around each other, toward Bandshell Nineteen. A man of their own caste, an older man, fell into step beside them.

'I'm V T B L Q Q M,' he introduced himself. 'I found out a thing after bed-hour last night that *everybody* has got to know ...'

'Shut up!' the young man barked. 'We don't want to know one single damn thing that we don't know already.'

'But listen!' the stranger whispered, intensely. 'This is *important*! The most important thing that ever happened in the World! There's a meeting tonight – I'll pick you up – but I tell you this right now. There ain't any such thing as the Company. It's just those damn snotty Agents and they're just as human as we are; they've been suckering us all our lives. If we had the gadgetry they've got we could knock them all off and take . . .'

'*Shut up!*' the girl screamed, and sprang away from him in horror. 'You're a mal – you're unhappy – that means *death*!'

'Death, hell!' came the whispered snarl. 'I got the straight dope – the real poop – last night and I'm still alive, ain't I? We're going to get some special insulation tonight and I'm going to grab one of those high-nosed bitches of Agents and choke her plumb to death after I . . .'

The man stopped whispering and screamed in utterly unbearable agony. His every muscle writhed and twisted, convulsively and impossibly. After a few seconds his body slumped bonelessly to the pavement; limp, motionless, dead.

'How terrible,' the girl remarked, in a perfectly matter-of-fact tone of voice. Then, with arms again around each other and as blissful as before, the two lovers stepped over the body and went on their interrupted way. Mals had no right whatever to live. Therefore the All-Wise, All-Powerful Company had put that mal to death. Everything was perfect, in this their perfect World.

And in one minute flat a ground-car, a light-truck type, came up beside the corpse and stopped. Two husky men, wearing the dark-gray-on-light-gray of Sanitationers Fourth, got out of it, picked the body up, and tossed it nonchalantly into the back of their truck.

Perce and Cecily Train 'ported the *Explorer* to a point in space well outside Pluto's orbit; well out of detector range of any of the strange warships englobing Earth. Aboard ship this time, in addition to the regular complement of spacemen and psiontists, were a couple of dozen graduates of the University, who were making the trip for advanced study.

'If any of us'd thought of it and if we'd stayed and if we'd had the techniques we've got now, we could've 'ported bombs aboard those jaspers and blown 'em clear out of the ether,' Train said, while they were getting ready to go to work.

'One if's enough, why use three?' Deston countered. 'But I

got a lot better idea than that one, especially since Bobby is just slightly allergic to killing people in job lots. We'll find out where they come from, 'port each one of 'em back to his own house, tuck him gently into his own bed, and present all those nice subspacers to Fleet Admiral Guerdon Dann, with the compliments of the University of Psionics – for a small consideration, of course.'

'*Now* you're chirping, birdie!' Barbara exclaimed. 'You *do* get an idea once in a while, don't you? That one is really a dilly. Ready, everybody? Let's go.'

They went ... and they studied ... and the more they studied the more baffled they became. The captains of the ships were, to a man, from Tellus. They were based on Teneriffe...

Deston shot the linked minds to the planet Teneriffe. The base was there – an immense one – but that was all it was. Just a base. There were no facilities to build much of anything; to say nothing of such an immense complex as would be necessary to produce any important part of that fleet.

Few of the captains had even wondered where the warships had been built. What difference did that make? That, or anything else pertaining to logistics or supply, was none of their business.

The Vice-Admirals and Admirals had wondered; but, since they had not been told, none of them had ever asked. Asking impertinent questions was a thing that simply was not done.

The Fleet Admiral did not know; neither did the Base Commander on Teneriffe. They got their orders via non-directional subspace radio from the Company of the World – 'World', of course, meaning Earth. It wasn't only a company, really, it was a new government, still very QT and TS, that was going to take over Tellus and all the planets, they both supposed. They had the power to do it, so why not? To any hard-nosed man of war might is right, and if they wanted to play it cosy and call themselves The Company of the World that was all right, too.

And as for the lower echelons...

'My ... God ...' Cecily said slowly, aloud, into the dense silence that had lasted through a long fifteen minutes of stupefied investigation. 'The Eternal, Omniscient, Omnipotent,

Omnipresent Company created the World and the People on Compday – Company Day, that is – January First of the Year One. No other World nor any other People – capitalized, please note, even in thought – ever were created or ever will be. Will some or one of you nice people please tell me what in all the infinite reaches of all the incandescent and viridescent hells of all total space we have got ourselves into now?'

'I'll never know, Curly.' Deston, who had been holding his breath for a good two minutes, let it all out at once. 'And the poor dumb meatheads *believe* that comet-gas with every cell of their minds ... and take everything that's going on right in stride – it's all Company business and as such is naturally incomprehensible to the mind of man ... "My God!" is correct, Curly. Check.'

'But look! Look in here!' Barbara put in, excitedly. 'Not the caste system – above it – Company Agents! Angels, suppose? Or something? None here with the Fleet; all back on the World. Those spotlight-jewels – *gorgeous*! I'd love to wear one of those myself. Power-packs, do you think?'

'Maybe,' Jones said. 'That's certainly something we'll have to look into. But what do we do now, Babe?'

'I know what *I'm* going to do – report to the boss in person – you people stay right here 'til I get back.' Deston disappeared.

Maynard was alone, so Deston 'ported himself unceremoniously into the private office. 'I don't want even Doris in on this until you let her in,' he explained, then reported everything.

As he listened, Maynard's face turned gray.

'So you see, chief,' Deston concluded, 'it's an unholy mess. What was it you said? A planet ... "run for years in a way that would make the robber barons of old sick at the stomach". You said it. You *certainly* said it. Have you got any idea as to who could be monster enough to pull a stunt like that?'

'More than an idea, son. This explains a lot of things I've wondered about, but I couldn't let my mind run wild enough. Two of 'em are why Plastics, one of the biggest of the big, never played ball, and how they got that way. It's Plastics, and Lord Byron Punsunby is head man.'

'That makes sense, so I'll do a flit ...'

'Not yet ... that's such a staggering thing ... what year is it, of theirs?'

'Two hundred twenty-six.'

'Um ... um ... m. Call it nine generations. At their breeding rate, with a start of only a few hundred thousand, they'll have population. The first three or four generations would know something, but by falsification of records, history, and so on ... and no press ... brain-washing and hypnosis ... it could be done. Definitely. So they've had at least five generations of ... of ...'

'Of serfs. A perfect serf set-up.'

'Check. And one of their castes is of top-notch engineers who don't know anything else and put everything they've got into it. And castes of scientists and so on.'

'That's right. As a 'troncist I'm here to testify that that locket is one beautiful job of work. Transmits everything except what the guy ate for breakfast, and maybe even that.'

'To Central Intelligence ... each checked as frequently as desired ... or even recorded ... God, what a system!' Maynard shook his head. 'And those Company Agents. Special castes, too. Charged, of course. Insulated boots. Magic no end. They could even *live* in a charged environment.'

'Could be. I told you, it's a mell of a hess.'

'One more thing. You've never thought of the real problem here, apparently. How can we – how can *anybody* – rehabilitate any race that has been driven that far off course?'

Deston's jaw dropped. 'Huh? Wow! It's a little soon, though, isn't it, to have to think about that?'

'I'll have to think about it, I'm afraid, whether I want to or not ... but that's more in my department than yours, I suppose ... well, I'll let you go now. Thanks for reporting. Good luck.'

'Luck, chief. 'Bye,' and Deston 'ported himself back into the main lounge of the *Explorer*.

Since the Plastics Building was one of the largest office buildings on Earth, it was very easy to find; and it was even easier to find the blatantly magnificent private office of 'Lord' Byron Punsunby, the president of Plastics Incorporated. Deston got into his mind and put it through the wringer. Punsunby knew a great deal that was new. He knew all about the business end – by what devious routes the goods were smuggled into the markets of Earth, how and through what underground channels they were sold, how incredibly vast the hidden holdings of Plastics were, and how all this skullduggery had been performed – but even he did not know even the general direction from Sol of Plastics' ultra-secret planet, The World, which had never been given a name.

It was and had always been Company policy that no Tellurian should know The World's coordinates. Only two living men were to know them; the Comptroller General of the World, who came to Earth to report to Punsunby after the close of business of each of The World's calendar quarters; and the captain – who was also the only navigating officer – of the one ship that ever made the direct run from The World to Earth and back. There were only two records of those figures in existence; one in each of the personal safe-deposit boxes of those two men.

Deston kept on reading. Yes, there were a few unscheduled visits; more than he liked of late ... he didn't like to use subspace radio, it *could* be tapped ... changing conditions ... trouble ...

Ah! That was what Deston wanted. There hadn't been enough generations yet to wipe out all the genes of throwbacks to the independent, intractable type. Conditioning might not hold; it was possible that some of them were even smart enough to pose as tractable, although the electronicists swore that their instruments were far too sensitive and comprehensive for that. Whatever the cause, in any case of real trouble checking the lockets even once every day wasn't enough. Occasionally Punsunby himself had to go to The World to order whatever steps might have to be taken to be sure of the elimination of all mals before too much harm was done.

Deston pulled back and set his jaw. 'Now ain't *that* a damn something!' he gritted. 'Well, the regular quarterly visit is only twelve days away – and maybe there'll be an emergency – I hope! – so we'll sit here and keep Lord Byron under surveillance every minute. I know you girls don't like this kind of Peeping Tomming, so you'll be excused. Perce?'

'Sure.'

'Herc?'

'Okay by me.'

'That's three. Talk to some of the graduates, will you, Perce, so we won't have to make the shifts too long? I'll take the first shift, starting now.'

CHAPTER EIGHTEEN

Hunchers

Company Agent A C B A A B A was a busy girl. She mated a dozen more couples that afternoon, then shot her aircar out to Suburb Fourteen, which was under construction. It was a beautiful layout, the girl thought, as she brought her car to a halt and looked the suburb over from a height of ten thousand feet. Rolling, heavily-wooded hills, a nice lake sparkling in the sunshine, and two winding streams. Lovely landscaping and curving, contoured drives. Over sixteen hundred of its two thousand homes should be done now – but were they? There wasn't a single house on Thirtieth Drive yet!

Frowning, she took a map of the suburb out of a compartment and scanned it. Then she compared it carefully with the terrain below. There was no one at work there this afternoon, of course, but she knew the call-code of the foreman of the project, so she punched it forthwith.

Her screen brightened, showing the head and shoulders of a man, who put both hands flat on his head and said, 'Be happy, Agent.'

'Be happy, Kubey! You're 'way, 'way behind sked on Sub Fourteen. How come?'

'I know, Agent, but there wasn't a thing I could do about it. Five of my best people went mal on me last week and the replacements they sent me were absolute gristleheads. All five of 'em fouled up their machines so bad I had to get a whole crew of . . .'

'That's enough. Be happy, Kubey!'

'Be happy, Agent.'

She snapped the set off and gnawed at her lower lip. An Agent didn't yap at damn stupid dumb jerks of People – it wouldn't do any good to, anyway, they didn't know anything – A B F A D A A was the lout who'd let this job get all fouled up – she'd do her yapping high enough up so it might do some good. She punched buttons viciously and a blue-jeweled, billiard-ball-bald man grinned at her.

'Keeps your tights on, Acey,' the Blue advised her, before she could say a word. 'The World is *not* coming to an end.'

'But what the hell's with it, Sub Fourteen being so damn far minus on sked?' she demanded. 'Keep on fouling off and I'm going to have to start installing on it before it's finished!'

'So what? There'll be all the finished houses you'll need, long before you'll need 'em, so...'

'"*So what?*"' she almost screamed. 'Because it never happened before with anybody else and because it's absolutely contra-Regs, *that's* what! And you know it as well as I do! It's your business to keep ahead of me, and by...'

'Shut up!' The man's grin had disappeared; his face was stern and cold. 'I know my business as well as you know yours, Acey.'

'Well, then, why ... Oh! But Abie, if you're having as much mal trouble as *that*, why didn't you tell me?'

'You just said why not. It's Abie business, not Acey, so just keep your tights on. And keep all this under your headband if you don't want to get bopped bow-legged.' He cut com; and, after a moment of lip-biting indecision. she did the same.

Then, shrugging her shapely shoulders, she set course for Suburb One and the immense apartment house in which she and eight-hundred-odd other AC's lived. She landed on the roof, parked her little speedster in its stall, and walked a hundred yards or so to a canopied, but unguarded hole with a stainless-steel pipe emerging from it. She slid unconcernedly down the slide-pole's three-hundred-foot length to the thirty-fourth floor, where the general offices were. She walked seventy yards along a main corridor, turned left into a narrower one, went fifty yards along that, and turned left again into a large room half full of desks. Some twenty girls, of about her

200

own age and size – and with pretty much her own spectacular shape – and as many young men, were already there. Some were at desks, working; some were at scanners, studying; some were sitting or standing by couples or in groups, talking or playing games; some singles were reading. All wore the head-light-like green jewels. The girls all wore the same uniform she did; the men all wore yellow whipcord battle-jackets, black whipcord breeches, and high-laced red leather boots.

'Hi, Bee-ay!' one of the men called. (Since everyone in the house was an Acey, other letters of each symbol were used intra-house.) 'You jump a mean knight; come on over and play me some chess.'

'Not enough time on the chron, Apey, I've got to red-tape it for a good hour yet,' and she strode purposefully to her desk.

She had hardly seated herself, however, when a big, good-looking, fair-haired young fellow came over and perched hip-wise on the corner of her desk.

'Hi, beautiful,' he said, swinging one big boot in a small arc. 'What do you know for real sure that's new?'

'Hi, Crip – mental, that is – nothing at all. Should I?'

'Nope. Everything is perfect in this our perfect World.' He squared his shoulders as though he had made a momentous decision and glanced quickly around. No one was within ear-shot; no one was paying any attention to their customary *tête-à-tête*.

Reaching into his pocket, he took out two soft, almost transparent pouches. He bent over, pulled his locket out from under his jacket, said, 'Well, beautiful, I'll see you, after,' slipped one of the pouches over his locket, tightened its drawstring, and put the now insulated locket back where it had been. Then, handing her the other pouch, he indicated silently that she was to do the same.

The girl's eyes widened and her face went suddenly stiff, but she pouched the locket and replaced it under her sweater, between her boldly outstanding breasts. 'So we're *both* mals,' she said, quietly. 'Mals of the worst type – hunchers. I've been afraid you were, too ... and you, too, for me, I suppose ... well, there goes the last secret between us – I hope? Except I mean of course ...'

He managed a grin. 'Of course. As far as I know, sweetheart. What held me up was – well, I may get flamed for this, and I didn't want you to be, too ... but you've been flirting with the flamers and if you go there's nothing left for me. That's the way you look at it, too, isn't it?'

'Of course, darling. I wouldn't live an hour, after. You came out because you noticed I was going off the beam?'

'How could I help but notice? But I wonder – is your hunch the same as mine? Something so wild – so utterly utter – that there are no words for it? That goes, some way or other, clear up to the Company itself?'

'That sounds like the same pattern, so I guess it's the same hunch. Something 'way out; beyond all understanding, sense, or reason. I can't get even a clue to it. But these...?' She indicated the lockets. 'Coms? Up to the Three-A's, maybe? And you blocked 'em? I'd never have thought of anything like that – but of course girl Sciencers First don't really ...'

'I don't *know* that they're coms; I was afraid to do any testing. But I knew something was riding you and I had to do something. But all I blocked was audio – if anybody is on us they're getting everything else and the well-known fact that we're in love will account for tension and so on – I think. I suppose you've heard the gossip that twelve Aceys from this house went absento – probably mal and probably flamed?'

'I've heard – and with that and this horrible hunch I've been jittering like a witch. It got so bad that I yapped at a Blue this afternoon – Old Baldy A B F A D A A himself.'

'Almighty Company fend you!' he gasped. 'You *are* asking for a flame!'

'Not in that, Beedy. No fear of *him* howling. He *can't* howl. He's so far minus sked on Sub Fourteen that I'm going to have to go contra-Regs ...' She explained the housing situation, '... so I could kick him right in the face and he couldn't even kick me back because I'm strictly on sked. He *said* he'd bop me bow-legged if I leaked about it, but that was all.'

The man whistled softly through his teeth. '*That* much mal trouble?' He thought for a moment, then threw off his dark mood. 'Retrieve the insulator and slip it to me when I get back.'

He moved quietly away, then came back with appropriate noise. He resumed his former position, put both pouches into his pocket, and said, 'I just had a cogent and gravid idea, my proud and haughty beauty. How about us taking five and going downstairs and tilting us a couple of flagons?'

'I'd love to, my courteous and sprightly knave, but I've simply *got* to get this red tape out first. An hour, say?'

'An hour's a date, you beautiful thing, you.' He took his leg off the desk and straightened up. 'I've got some-red-taping of my own to do. So, as Old Baldy would say, keep your ...'

'*Beedy!* Is *that* nice?' She laughed up at him; two deep dimples appeared. 'Besides, as you very well know, I *always* do!'

In an hour the paper-work was done. (While People all got half a shift off on Compday, Company Agents got theirs on any day other than Compday.) Bee-ay and Beedy tilted their flagons, ate supper together, and went to their rooms. Not only to separate rooms, but to separate wings of the immense building.

She, however, did not sleep at all well; and when she went to work Sunday morning she was still keyed up and tense – for no real reason whatever.

The job went along strictly as usual until, at hour sixteen plus fifty, she had just finished installing her last pair of newmates of the day and was getting into her aircar to go home. While she was getting into the front seat a pair of heavily-insulated arms went around her and a strong gloved hand went over her mouth. She bit and fought, but the glove was bite-proof and the man was big and fast and immensely strong. He dragged her out of the driver's seat and into the back, where he let her struggle; holding her only tightly enough to prevent her escape. In the meantime a smaller man, also dressed in a full-coverage suit that looked like asbestos but wasn't, cut three wires of the aircar's power supply and got into the front seat. The car shot straight up out of sight of the ground, darted northward, and came to ground on the flat top of a high, bare-rock mesa.

'Are you going to behave yourself?' the big man asked.

She nodded behind the glove and he released her completely.

'What the hell goes on?' she demanded, sitting up properly and putting her hair to rights with her fingers. 'You'll get the flame for this.'

'I think not,' he said, quietly. 'You're not frightened, I'm very glad to see.'

'*Frightened? Me?* Of any person or People ever born? High Company beyond!'

'Good girl. We've made a few poor picks, but you and your friend A C B D will make out.'

'Beedy? You've got him, too? Where are you taking us, if I may ask?' The last phrase was pure sneer.

'You may not ask,' was the calm reply.

Then the big man, working very deftly despite his heavy gloves, lifted the girl's locket and cut its chain with a heavy angle-nose cutter. He then twitched the band from her head, tied the locket to the band with the chain, and threw the bundle, in a high arc, out and away. When it came down there was a flare of greenish brilliance brighter than the sun, the white glare of a small pool of incandescent lava, and after a few seconds, the odor of volatilized rock.

'So?' the girl asked, quietly. 'So there goes a bit of Company power. But you ... Oh!' She broke off sharply as she saw the smaller man touching the aircar here and there with the looped end of a heavy wire held in one gloved hand. 'Oh? High resistance? How high?'

'One point two five megohms,' the big man said. 'We have no intention whatever of doing you any harm whatever.'

'You know, some way or other, I've rather gathered that?' and she extended a beautifully-shaped bare arm for the wire's touch. A minute later, while both men were shedding their insulation, she spoke again. 'You're going to give me some explanation of all this, I suppose?'

'We are indeed, Miss Acey Bee-ay, as soon as we get to where we're going and your friend joins us. It's altogether too long and too deep and too involved to go into twice for the two of you. We'll take off now.'

The aircar went straight up to twelve thousand feet, then hurtled north north east at its top speed. It held course and speed for over three hours. It crossed mountain ranges, lakes,

forests, and rivers. Finally, however, it slanted sharply downward, slowed, stopped, and descended vertically into a canyon
– a crevasse, rather – but little wider than the car was long and
half a mile deep.

It landed near a man wearing a greenish-gray uniform, who
had a sidearm in a holster at his hip. This guard saluted
crisply and put his hand against a slight projection of the rock,
whereupon a section of the canyon's wall swung inward, re-
vealing a long, straight, brightly-lighted tunnel. The three got
out of the car and the guard stepped aside, drawing his weapon
as he did so.

'As usual,' the big man told the guard. 'It's harmless and its
transmitters have been cut. You won't need the artillery.' He
glanced quizzically at the girl. 'Will he?'

'No,' she said, flatly. 'I know that you can handle me alone.
You know as much judo as I do and you're a lot bigger.'

'Excellent! In, then. It's about a mile. We walk.'

The three walked into and along the tunnel; with the girl,
under no restraint, between the two men.

After walking the indicated mile they came to what looked
like – and in fact was – the entrance to a thoroughly modern
building. They went in and the big man, after dismissing his
smaller companion, ushered the girl into a small, plainly-
furnished office.

'They aren't here yet, I see. Take a chair, please.' He sat
down behind the desk. 'We'll wait here; it won't be very long.'

Nor was it. In about fifteen minutes the door opened and
three gray-uniformed men, one of them pushing a wheeled
chair, entered the office. Beedy, without headband or locket,
was chained to the chair. His uniform was torn half off, both
eyes would soon be black-and-blue 'shiners', and his flesh was
puffy and bruised, but he was still full of fight. When he saw
the girl, however, he stopped struggling instantly and stopped
her with a word as she leaped to her feet, screamed, and ran
toward him.

'If you'd used your brain, meathead,' he said, glaring between swollen lids at the man behind the desk, 'and told your
gorillas to tell me you had *her* here, it would've saved all five
of us some lumps.'

'Well, I can't think of everything,' the big man admitted. 'I did tell her we had you, come to think of it, which perhaps accounts for her cooperation.' He studied his three men. The smallest one of them was of B D's size, but each of the three bore more marks of battle than did the captive. 'I was not informed that you are such an expert at unarmed combat. Free him, you, and get out. With the chair.'

'*Free* him?' one of the captors protested. 'Why, he'll ...' and one of the others broke in

'But he damn near *killed* Big Pietr, boss – they're taking him up to sick-bay now, and ...'

'You heard me,' the boss said, without raising his voice a fraction of a decibel, and the three obeyed.

As the door closed, the two went into each other's arms, the girl moaning over her lover's wounds.

'It's all right, now that I know *you* aren't hurt. You aren't, are you?'

'No, not the least bit, in any way,' she assured him. 'But they hurt *you*, and if you think ...'

'Hush, sweetheart, listen. I got more of them than they did of me, so, with you here safe, if they won't carry a grudge I won't.' He cocked a blood-clotted eyebrow – with a slight wince – at the man behind the desk. 'No grudge, I take it?'

'Splendid! No grudge at all.'

B D turned to B A. 'Wasn't this in your hunch?' he asked.

'Your getting all beat up certainly wasn't, but the rest of it ... well, I guess it could fit the pattern ... but don't try to tell me it was that clear in yours, either!'

'I won't; but it does fit the pattern.'

'You two are far and away the best we've found yet,' the man at the desk said then. 'Since I'm going to be your instructor, you may as well start calling me "Basil".'

'Bay-sill? That doesn't make sense,' the girl said.

'It's my name. We don't use symbols – I'll go into that later. You are beginning to realize that your knowledge and experience have left you almost entirely ignorant of man, of nature, and of the cosmos. Exposure to that knowledge will be such a shock to your minds that you will feel much better together than apart. To that end, would you like to be married

– "mate", is your word for it – immediately?'

'But we can't,' the girl said. 'Not for half a year yet.'

'Sure we can, and we will,' B D said. 'My hunch is that the Company is getting the flame . . .' He hesitated slightly and shivered, but went on doggedly, 'and that you have already captured at least twelve other Company Agents without getting flamed yourselves. Is that right, Bay-sill?'

'Very pleasingly right. Twenty, so far, have been able to withstand the impact of the truth and remain sane . . . but none of them are anything like in your class . . . you must both be mals.'

He glanced at them questioningly, but neither made any response and he went on. 'If so, I hope to persuade you to help us look for others like you. Now, before I take you upstairs to the sick-bay and thence to your suite, where you will find clothing and so on, I am going to give you some of the basic elements of the truth. I shall give them to you brutally straight. You will be shocked as you have never believed it possible to be shocked. You will not be able to understand any part of it at first, but you must not ask me any questions until tomorrow morning, when I will begin instructing you in detail. By that time you will have given the matter sufficient thought so that you will be able to ask intelligent questions. You wish to marry each other, you said?'

'We certainly do!'

'Splendid! You can make decisions, as well as think. I have very high hopes indeed of you two. After the short visits I mentioned I will arrange for your wedding. Then, if you wish, you may dine and retire to your suite until eight hours tomorrow.

'Now for your first introduction to the truth. This world is not the only world in existence and you people – you upper echelons are just as much people as those you call People – are not the only people. There are thousands of millions of other worlds, more or less like this one, throughout an immensity of space so vast as to be beyond imagining. There are thousands of millions of human beings – members of the human race, to which both you and we belong – inhabiting many of those worlds. One such world, my native planet Earth, has a population of almost seven thousand million people.

'Your concept of the Company is completely false. There are hundreds of thousands of companies, each a self-perpetuating group of men. Not supermen in any sense, but ordinary men like me. Your company was and is only one of the multitude of companies of Earth. It was founded by and is still operated by a group of greedy, utterly callous capitalists – money men – of Earth. It was founded and is being operated specifically as a world of slave labor. Every person born on this world is a slave; a slave without freedom, liberty, or personal rights of any kind.

'We, on the other hand, represent a society of worlds of freedom-loving people. We have come here to liberate all the inhabitants of this world from slavery; to enable you to take your rightful place – and that place *is* yours by right – in the fellowship of all the civilized worlds. Our creed, the creed of all free peoples everywhere, is this:

'We hold these truths to be self-evident, that all men are created equal, that they are endowed by their Creator with certain inalienable Rights, that among these are Life, Liberty, and the pursuit of happiness.

'These things I have told you, young friends, are fundamental. They are basic. They are absolutely necessary prerequisites for any learning of the truth; so think them over very carefully until tomorrow morning.

'When your instruction is complete, I am sure that you will be glad to work side by side with us to unite your world with our society – The Union of Soviet Socialist Republics.'

CHAPTER NINETEEN

Double Agent

Back on Earth, affairs political and financial moved so fast and in such quantity that Upton Maynard had more work on his hands than any one man could possibly do. He *had* to sleep five or six hours almost every night. Also, he could handle those Tellurian affairs much better if he were there in person – especially if he could drop GalMet entirely for a while – and why not? Young Smith had plenty of jets ... wherefore he called Smith and Miss Champion into his inner office.

'Miss Champion, take notes, please. Mr. Eldon Jay Smith, I believe, the Executive Vice-President of Galactic Metals, Incorporated?'

'That is precisely what I have the honor and privilege of being, sir.' Smith put his right hand over his heart and bowed. 'As of the present moment, sir; that is, sir, I mean, sir.'

'You'll start executing as of the present moment, sir,' and Maynard told him what he had in mind, concluding, 'So sit on the throne, bub, 'til I get back – and don't let the block line drop down through the bottom of the chart.'

'Drop? You kidding? Now we can get something done – it'll zoom right up through the top. How about it, Dorry?' He winked at Miss Champion, who, always the perfect First Secretary – always, that is, in Maynard's presence – did not wink back. She merely smiled.

'But suppose I take her along?'

'Go ahead. Do that. Wreck the outfit. I've been wanting to quit and go fiishing, anyway.'

'Yeah. I know. I know just what I'd be wrecking – anyway, I'd bet on the fish. 'Bye, Don; 'Bye, Doris,' and Maynard strode blithely out.

The girl gave Smith a long, level look. 'You're the only human being alive with the sublime nerve to give *him* the needle that way. Just suppose he climbs your frame for it some day?'

'He set the pace, didn't he? Anyway, I'd get along.'

'Pfooie! Nobody could blast you out of here with an atomic bomb and everybody knows it. You really know him, don't you? I've always thought I was the only one who did.'

'I know he's the universe's best – and that these damned yesmen and toadies around here make him just as sicka da bel' as they do me – and that's a great God's plenty.'

'That's what I meant, Don ... and you're not *too* bad a stinker yourself, in some ways.' For weeks, ever since they had become psionic, a current of something – like electricity plus – had been flowing between these two, and it was getting stronger all the time.

'Thanks for them kind words, Dorry. You're slipping. First thing you know you'll...'

'I'm not slipping and whatever it was you were going to say, I won't. No telepathy, no rapport. I've been a career business women ever since I was fifteen – a good one – and I'm going to keep on being just that.'

He smiled; more a grin than a smile. 'That's the way to talk, Dorry. Strictly business. If there's any one thing in this wide fat world I really love, it's business.'

'Let's get at it, then.' Miss Champion, now all briskly efficient FirSec, picked up her book. 'I'll remind you, Mister Smith, that you are wasting time that is costing the company a dollar a minute. In exactly four and one-half minutes you have an appointment with Felton of Barbizon about enlarging the operation there; at nine plus forty-five with Quisenberry of Belmark, ditto; at ten plus ten with Anderssen of Pharmics ...'

Maynard landed on Earth at Chicago Spaceport. He took a copter to the big old building on Michigan Avenue that was GalFed's headquarters. Stevens Spehn's office was on the twenty-sixth floor, in front, affording a splendid view of Lake Michigan – all water clear out to the horizon.

Having sent a thought ahead, Maynard strode straight through the main office and the FirSec's office. That smart girl, who of course listened in on everything, even – or especially? – on thought, merely glanced up with a smile from the tape she was reading and exchanged greetings in thought with him as he went past.

Spehn's office, vastly unlike his previous one, was small and plainly furnished. Even his desk was small; he could, with a little stretching, reach anything on its plate-glass top. He was leaning 'way back in his swivel chair, with both feet perched up on the corner of his desk. When Maynard came in Spehn pointed his cigarette at a huge overstuffed chair near the desk, but facing the huge front window. Maynard sat down, lighted a long, thin cigar, crossed his legs, and spoke aloud. 'So you're rolling, Steve. So you like your PsiCor, eh?'

'Oh, brother!' Spehn got up, walked around to the older man, shook him solemnly by the hand, and resumed seat and pose. Then: 'Oh ... broth ... *therr!* One hundred percent convictions so far and not a possible miss in sight. Psionic Intelligence agents are things that ... well, maybe some cloak-and-dagger men have dreamed about such things, but we've *got* 'em. Over ten thousand already and more coming and they're all batting a thousand. Boss, the Big Brains claim that while ethics is related to psionics, ethics is not and can not be made an absolute. Do you buy that?'

'In the abstract, as a generalization, yes. In practice, and in the specific case of our own culture as it now is, perhaps not. I might almost say probably not.'

'Very, very cautious about going out on a limb, aren't you? So bite yourself off a piece of this and chew on it and give your taste-buds a treat. The opposition hasn't got any psion-tists worth a tinker's toot and never will have any.'

Maynard did not question this statement. All experience had shown that any psychics of much ability, immediately upon perceiving the vastnesses of psionics, went to Newmars and the University of Psionics as a matter of course. Spehn went on:

'It's a truly wonderful thing to *know*, for certain damn sure, everything that goes on. So we're steam-rolling 'em to the queen's own taste. The next election will be honest; the kind of election the Founding Fathers had in mind. GalFed should be in the saddle shortly after that. Of course there'll be some fuss, but Guerd should be ready by then. You're sticking around?'

Maynard nodded. 'Longer than that, Steve. Until GalFed is, both in name and in fact, THE GALACTIC FEDERATION; until Tellus – a united Tellus – is both in name and in fact the capital of all civilization.'

Spehn thought for a moment. 'That's a big order, boss, but I wouldn't wonder if we might be able to deliver the goods.'

After half an hour more of discussion, Maynard went up one floor and had a long discussion with Fleet Admiral Guerdon Dann.

He then tuned his mind to that of Li Hing Wong, who brought Feodr Ilyowicz in for a three-way. Things were going as well as was to be expected. The Iron Curtain and the Bamboo Curtain, which had faced outward, had been replaced by Psionic Curtains facing inward. Since the fleet englobing Earth, whatever it really was, did not seem to care what happened to either Russia or China, there had not been very much effective opposition. People were dying, but that couldn't be helped. The only way progress could be made was by killing off the commissars and the warlords and all such corruptionists; and, since corruption had been the way of life for centuries, reclamation would necessarily be a slow process.

As each district was reclaimed and put under a psionic Peace-lord its people were given as much self-government as they could handle – which wasn't very much. They would have to grow up to self-government, and that would take a long time. If famine and pestilence did not take care of the population problem, population control would; by birth-control and logic if possible, by sterilization if necessary.

It was not a cheerful report; but Maynard had not expected it to be. He shrugged his shoulders and went on to interview every one of the men and women who were handling the political campaign. Then, last of all, he turned his attention to the financiers who were operating in the stock market.

The Plastics Building, in Chicago, Illinois, WestHem, Tellus, occupied the entire eight hundred block west; bounded by Halsted and Peoria Streets on the east and west, and by Washington and Randolph Boulevards on the south and north. Its main bulk, built of steel-reinforced synthetics of various kinds, was eighty-five stories high, and a comparatively slender tower reached up fifteen stories higher still. This tower housed the private offices of the Biggest of the Big of Plastics, Incorporated; and its entire top floor, the one-hundredth of the building, was devoted to the series of exceedingly private offices, in ascending order of privacy from the private elevator, of the least accessible man on Earth – President Byron Punsunby himself.

To say that these offices were sumptuous is to make the understatement of the year, but that is all that will be said. At three o'clock one Wednesday afternoon, while President Punsunby was sitting at his most sumptuous desk, alone in his most sumptuous, most private office, clear across the tower from the elevator, a call came in on a communicator that was his alone, in a mish-mash of noise and herringbone that he alone could unscramble. He stared at it angrily for a few seconds; his big, fat body tensing, his big, fat face stiffening, and his small blue eyes growing even harder than their hard wont.

He'd been getting altogether too damned many calls on that com of late and he hadn't liked any one of them. And this was the worst. It wasn't subspace, or even long distance; it was *local* – and this was one purely sweet-scented *hell* of a time for him to have to leave Earth ... why couldn't the ape handle a few things himself?

He unscrambled the mish-mash; Erskine Cantwell, the Comptroller General of The World, appeared.

'Where are you?' Punsunby snapped. 'Spaceport?'

'Yes. Just landing.'

'Come in. I'll be alone.'

Cantwell did not enter the Plastics Building by any of the usual routes. He approached it via subway, opened an almost invisible door into the second sub-basement, walked along a deserted hall, opened a completely invisible door by speaking a series of six coined words, and took the ultra-secret elevator straight up into Punsunby's ultra-private office.

'Well?' Punsunby demanded, savagely. 'I told you to take whatever steps might prove necessary. Why the hell didn't you do it, instead of coming here again?'

'What do *you* think?' Cantwell sneered. 'That I'm here for the fun of it? I'm only the Highest Agent, remember? Six A's and a B, with only a violet headlight. It takes the one and only discarnate God Himself – the one and only holder of seven straight A's – the All-Powerful and Eternal – the one and only being able to pour the pure mercury-vapor light of God onto his poor dumb creatures – *you*, you fat-head, are the only living human being who can modify Article Ninety of your precious Second Directive, and by all the devils in hell you . . .'

'Christ almighty!' Punsunby broke in. He had been turning not-so-slowly purple as he listened to this *lese-majeste*, but at the words 'Second Directive' his face began to pale. 'But that's the basis of the whole caste system – it's *never* been modified. Things *can't* be that bad, Ersk – there *must* be some other way of handling this trouble.'

'It's exactly that bad, and if you can find any other way to clean up the mess I'll roll a peanut from here to Buckingham Fountain with my nose. And I've had it. You can take this . . .'

'Don't say it, Ersk.' Punsunby got up, walked around the desk, and put a big hand on the slender man's shoulder. 'We couldn't operate without you. But such a change as that . . . God knows where a thing like that would end.'

'You're so right. That's the trouble with any rigid system,' Cantwell said, much more calmly. 'When it starts to crack it's apt to shatter. But that's the way you Tops have always wanted it, so you're stuck with it. So let's get at it.'

'All right. I'll have to make a couple of calls.'

There was no more talk of business until they were in SUITE ONE of the subspacer. Then Punsunby said, 'Go ahead, Ersk. What do you think it is?'

'I know what it is, now. Sabotage. Expert, organized, directed, and highly efficient sabotage. Worthy of the Commies at their very best.'

'The Commies? But I...'

'I didn't say it was and I don't think it is. I don't see how it could be. I can see only one possibility. I never have believed in mindreading; but what else can it be?'

'The Galaxians.' Punsunby thought for minutes. 'Mental stuff – that's why you want our mentalists to work openly with operators without losing caste. But no person has ever – knowingly, that is – has ever even seen a three-A, Ersk. It'd scare 'em to death.'

'It'll have to be worse than that. They'll have to shed their pretty colored spotlights, put on lockets, and *become* operators. How the hell else can we find out what is going on? All we're doing now is knocking hell out of production by killing thousands of dumb bastards who don't know whether Christ was crucified or shot in a crap game.'

'Well, how about hiring some of their psychics away from 'em? Price would be no object.'

'We can't. They're *ethical*. And if WestHem ever finds out what we're doing they'll stop the Earth in its tracks and throw us the hell off bodily. Don't kid yourself about this, Lord Byron, or you'll wind up square behind the eight-ball.'

Punsunby wriggled and squirmed all the way to The World; but his every idea was crushed by Cantwell's relentless logic. Therefore, as soon as the starship landed, the two Supreme Beings of The World went directly to the immense building housing Information Central and donned the gorgeously-colored, heavily-jeweled regalia of their respective positions. Punsunby sat on the splendidly ornate Throne of The Company; Cantwell on a much smaller and somewhat plainer throne at his master's feet.

Punsunby put on a wisely beneficent smile, Cantwell pressed a hidden switch, and each of the thousands of Agents in Information Central's vast building was bathed both in the pure mercury-vapor Light of the Company and in the warmth and abundance of the Company's good will. Each put hands on head; each was suffused with happiness at this all-too-rare personal contact with The Company Itself.

'Children of the Company – *my* children – be happy,' Punsunby told the raptly-listening thousands. 'In view of the unprecedented difficulties which the World is now experiencing, The Company decrees that Article Ninety of its Second Directive is amended by the addition to it of Section Fifty-Six, as follows: "All members of all Mentalist castes in category A A A are permitted and directed to work, with no effect upon caste, at whatever undertakings and in whatever fashions Highest Agent A A A A A A B shall set up and direct." Be happy, my children.'

The Company lights all went out, the golden thrones sank down through the golden floor, and Punsunby whirled on Cantwell.

'I hope to *hell* that does it!' he snapped. 'Now let's shed this junk and get me going back to Earth!'

Deston and his crew were not interested in Punsunby himself. What they wanted was the coordinates of The World. Thus they were on the lookout for, and were checking up on, every starship approaching Tellus. Thus, even before Cantwell's subspacer landed, they had learned everything that Cantwell himself had ever known about The World and had put the *Explorer* into orbit around The World's sun. And thus, long before the disguised psychologists of the World had made any significant progress in their investigations, the Galaxians were ready to go to work.

'Shall we take a quick peek at Information Central?' Deston asked, 'To see which of those colored-headlamped buzzards are doing what to whom?'

'We shall *not*!' Barbara declared. 'If I *never* know exactly which button a murderer pushes to kill a perfectly innocent person it will be three days too soon. We can cripple all the instrumentation of that whole Information Central without . . .' She paused and frowned.

'Exactly,' Jones said. 'That *would* tear it.'

'Well, maybe,' Barbara conceded. 'So we'll hunt up whoever's casing it and put *them* out of business, and *then* stop it. We know it isn't the Galaxians, so it must be the Communists.'

'If we couldn't find the place, how could they?' Deston

asked. His thoughts took a new turn then, and as he thought, his mind-blocks began unconsciously to go up. 'Okay, we'll hunt 'em up. We know how they work. They won't be close in – too easy to spot. They'll be 'way out somewhere, and quite possibly underground, It will be a job, fine-toothing that much territory, but there's a lot of us. We'll divide it up ... like this ...'

It was super-sensitive Bernice who finally found the Russians' carefully-concealed, deeply-buried headquarters.

'Good going, Bun!' Deston applauded. Then, after a quick probe, he went on. 'New Russia! That's really one for the book. First thing, let's get those Company Agents up here – those two there, I think, are going to be the answer to Maynard's prayer. Their language has been sort of – censored? – let's see how they take to telepathy.'

A C B A and A C B D, being very strong latents and well on the way to making psiontists of themselves without even knowing that such a science as psionics existed, learned telepathy in seconds. More, they went into a hammer-and-tongs mind-to-mind session with the Funny Four even while the six leaders were arguing with the other ex-Agents. All these were latents, however; hence, after the University of Psionics had been explained to them, they were more or less eager to go. They knew less of reality than even the little that the two 'hunchers' knew; but, like latents everywhere, they did want to learn.

Wherefore, after Barbara had had a flashing exchange of thought with Stella Adams, the new recruits were delivered to her in her office in the University. Beedy was still bruised and battered, but no one – except his new wife, of course – paid any more attention to that than he did himself. Everyone knew all about what had happened, and they all approved of him and he knew it.

'Babe!' Barbara burst out then. 'What's on your mind? You've been blocking solid – give!'

'I didn't mean to actually, but I wouldn't wonder. I don't like the only possible answer a bit, and you won't either. We never even *heard* of that planet New Russia. And how did they find this world? I've been racking my brains and the only possible answer I can come up with is that Feodr Ilyowicz has always been a double agent – suckering us but good, all along.'

'Oh, no!' came a storm of protest, and Jones added, 'I can't buy that bundle, Babe. There isn't a psiontist in the outfit. He'd be here himself – no, he couldn't, at that, but he'd have somebody on the job here.'

'You're wrong, Herc, he couldn't.' Cecily shook her head. 'Perfect Commie technique. When did a commissar ever trust a psychic as far as he could throw him? He'd use his knowledge, yes, but he wouldn't let him get out of sight.'

'That's true, Curly,' Deston said. 'Anyway, all . . .'

'But just look at what he's doing to Communist Russia!' Bernice broke in.

'He has to, or he wouldn't last an hour,' Jones said, grimly. 'All that means is that, compared to a planet and years of time, EastHem's expendable – for as many years as is necessary. So I'll buy it after all. What do we do next? Scout New Russia?'

'I don't think so; we need more dope first, and, as I started to say, we can find out. Flit us to one of Jupiter's moons, you Trains, and we'll put . . .'

'High it, fly-boy, and find the beam!' Jones snapped. 'We can't 'port those jaspers down there back to New Russia and we can't leave 'em here and we can't very well kill 'em in cold blood.'

'Okay, Control Six, I'll try it again,' Deston agreed. 'Um . . . um . . . mm. How about putting 'em – being sure we get 'em all, of course – into an empty hold here in the *Explorer*? Keep 'em in durance vile for the duration? Intern 'em?'

'That's a cogent thought, friend,' Barbara said, and the others agreed. 'I wish we could do a lot worse to 'em than that.'

It was done.

'Can I land now, Control Six?' Deston asked, plaintively, and the others laughed.

'Okay, fly-boy, you're on the beam now.'

'Thank you, Control Six. As I was saying when I was so rudely interrupted, let's flit to somewhere near Tellus and put the snatch on Ilyowicz and see if our guesses are any good. No, better let me do the grabbing alone – if he has any warning vhatever we'll never get him, and if I'm wrong about him I'll pologize abjectly.'

The Russian had no warning whatever. Before he could be-;in to think about setting up the psionic barrier through which io psionic force could act, he was in the *Explorer*. Nor did)eston have occasion to apologize. It became evident instantly hat Ilyowicz would fight to the death, and in another instant ;ix of the most powerful minds known to man were tearing at iis mental shields.

He held those shields with everything he had, but he did not lave enough. No human mind could have had enough. His ;hields failed; and, a moment after their failure, such was the rresistible flood of mental energy driving inward, Feodr Ilyo-wicz died. In that moment before death, however, the six learned much.

He had always been a double agent. He had always lived for Russia, he was dying for Russia. Not the Russia of Earth – that was expendable – no one cared what happened there for a few years or a few decades – but the great New Russia that already possessed one whole planet, was taking possession of another at this moment, and would very soon possess all the populated planets of civilization. Everything he had learned he had passed on to New Russia. It had a University of Psionics that would soon surpass that of Newmars. He had traced Pun-sunby to The World long ago, and had advised the Premier himself as to what should be done about it. If it had not been for that stupid oaf Ovlovetski he would have gone to The World himself and made such arrangements as to . . .

That was all. Feodr Ilyowicz was dead.

Thoughts flew for minutes, then Deston said, 'There may not have to be any scandal. I'll yank his first assistant – his nephew, Stepan Ilyowicz, you know – and we'll see what *he's* like.'

The nephew was deeply shocked at what had happened, but he opened his mind fully and completely. While his uncle had always been a solitary, secretive sort of man, one who never opened his screens fully to anyone, he had always believed him to be thoroughly loyal to the Galaxian cause. He had always acted that way; had never given any grounds whatever for suspicion.

Yes, he himself believed fully in Galaxianism and was completely loyal to it. Yes, if acceptable to the Board, he would be very glad indeed to take his uncle's place on the Board.

It was agreed that Maynard would have to know the whole truth, and would have to decide what to do with it.

Maynard was shocked, too; and for minutes deeply thoughtful. 'Well,' he said, finally, 'That teaches us something. There'll be no more gentlemanliness or courtesy on the Board with respect to mental privacy. Never again. No, we can't have a scandal at this point; it would be disastrous. I'll take care of it. Thanks, all of you – both for this and for the fine job you've done on the whole project.'

And Maynard did take care of it. It was announced with due pomp that Feodr Ilyowicz, the beloved, revered, and highly honored Second Tellurian Member of the Directorate of the Galactic Federation, had died almost instantly in his sleep of a massive cerebral hemorrhage.

CHAPTER TWENTY

The Election

'Oh, Babe, look!' Barbara laughed delightedly and hugged Deston's arm against her side. 'And she's four months pregnant, too.'

Deston 'looked'. Cecily Train was romping like a schoolgirl with Teddy and Babbsy. She was on her hands and knees on the rug in the main lounge, shaking her head and growling deep in her throat; the kids, with all four hands buried in her thick red mop of curls, were tugging at it and shrieking with glee.

'Uh-huh; nice.' Deston agreed. 'And you aren't quite as sylph-like yourself as you were a while back.' He glanced down at a slight bulge.

'Uh-huh. Bun, too. It's catching, I guess. There's some kind of a germ around, must be. S'pose we'd better fumigate the ship or something?' Her voice was solemn, but her eyes danced. 'But that wasn't what I meant, that she might hurt herself – I'm *so* happy for her. Who'd ever have thought that such an out-and-out stinker as she used to be would turn out to be such a wonderful person? Why, even Bun loves her now.'

'Something made her change her ways, that's for sure. Love? Psionics? It's a shame to break that joyous rough-house up, but we've got a lot of ...'

'We don't have to yet, my sweet and impetuous. It can wait a few minutes. I'm going to join that rough-house myself – the kids *need* exercise, you big dope.'

Wherefore it was fifteen minutes later that the Big Six went to work. The fleet englobing Earth was the first thing on the agenda, and disposing of the multitude of People aboard those hundreds of huge starships was a problem. So Deston shot a thought across space and – much to his surprise – Bee-ay and Beedy materialized beside him in the *Explorer*.

'You're *that* good already?' Deston marveled. The two were in perfect fusion. He had recovered fully from his fight with the Russians. Her face was no longer hard; it was beautiful. Both were again wearing platinum headbands mounting shining green jewels, but no lockets. 'And those? Reasonable facsimiles, I suppose?'

'No, duplicates. We felt – well, undressed – so the Four – we *won't* call those wonderful people funny even in fun – showed us all about 'em and we made 'em in about a minute. We aren't charged, though, now, of course; but we *could* be. On most things we're getting to be pretty good – the Fourth Nume, even. We can't do long distance 'porting yet, except on ourselves, but Stella says we'll be ready for anything in a couple of weeks. Then Mr. Maynard says we can go back to The World. He said "See if you can work out a program of rehabilitation that will begin to show results in the generation now being born." He's wonderful, isn't he?'

'He's wonderful at putting people to work, that's for sure. But what we wanted to know is, how can we put all those people back on your world without lousing everything up over there?'

'Oh, easy – that'll be perfect! It won't bother them a bit – "Acts of the Company", you know. There'll be enough of them, maybe...' the fusion scanned the fleet, '... almost enough, anyway, to put everything back to normal. The Three-A's will instruct and take care of caste, and the Aceys will give them all job transfers, housing, coupon books, and so on. Everything will be perfect. And that was a good idea, putting a psionic shield around The World, in case the Russians – but wouldn't it be a good idea to release it long enough to blow up their headquarters?'

'It would indeed...' Deston began.

'But no atomics!' Barbara said, sharply.

'Maybe not, at that. Half a dozen two-thousand-pound

222

charges of cyclodetonite will do the trick, with no more jar than a very small earthquake, and I know where they keep the demolition stuff...'

They placed the bombs; then watched a small mountain on The World erupt and then subside. They could find no trace of what had once been there.

'That's that,' Deston said then. 'Now if you two will show us exactly where to put each one of – but listen! There are *thousands* of 'em – your Aceys will be running themselves ragged – and those three-A's will smell – hell, *everybody* will smell a rat – they can't help but smell such a rough job as that.'

'Oh, no,' the two assured him, but they did grin at each other. 'The Ways of The Company are just as inscrutable to them as to everyone else. And after such a mal – such a disaster – it would be perfectly natural, wouldn't it, for The Company to do whatever is necessary to get its World right back into full production?'

'My ... God...' Cecily breathed. 'But that does make a weird kind of sense, at that.'

'Another thing,' the Aceys went on. 'It'd take simply forever to 'port them one at a time to the homes they used to have, even if they still have 'em. There's a great big recreation park back of our house – we'll show you where – so you can 'port 'em there in what you call job lots. That would be even more impressive and Company-like, don't you think?'

'I'll tell that whole cockeyed world it would,' Deston agreed, and that was how the job was done.

After it was done Train, who had been looking around on his own, laughed suddenly. 'Somebody did smell your rat, Babe. Cantwell. He called Punsunby and they're both having litters of kittens all over the place.'

They all looked, and Jones and Deston laughed, too; but the girls didn't think it was funny to see even two such men as those suffer so much.

'Well, whatever they decide to do, it'll keep 'em out of mischief for a while,' Deston said, 'so let's clean it up. Thanks a lot, you two,' and the Aceys 'ported themselves back to the University.

Then the six turned the entire fleet, together with its Tellurian officers – and also together with the whole group of Russian saboteurs to be interned – over to Fleet Admiral Guerdon Dann. All this, of course, was very much contrary to International and Interplanetary Law – but what else could they have done?

Deston turned then to Bernice. 'Bun, you're our supersensitive. We'd like to have you find out all you possibly can about New Russia without touching off any psychic alarms – I doubt very much if they've got anybody in your class for delicacy of touch. The rest of us will go along, to cover you if we have to, but you'll do all the feeling around. Okay?'

'I'll give it the good old college try, Babe,' silver-haired Bernice said, and Operation New Russia was begun.

While all these things were going on, and for some time before, the political campaign throughout all WestHem had been waxing warmer and warmer. It was now in full, hot swing. With full prosperity restored – and everyone who could either see or hear knew how that had come about and who had brought it about – the Galaxians were really making hay.

They had made so much hay that the Sociocrats and the Consercans, the two major parties before this unprecedented break-up, had merged as the only way of beating the snowballing Galaxians; and the Communists and the Liberals had joined them after being promised a place at the trough. This fusion party, the Party of Freedom and Liberty, was called the 'FreeLibs'.

'That old cliche about "strange bedfellows" was never truer,' Spehn said to Maynard one day. 'I never thought I'd live long enough to see renegade capital, labor, Commies, gangsters, radicals, and fascists all eating out of the same dish. How long can such an alliance as that last, even if they beat us this time?'

'It's up to us to see to it that they don't beat us even this time,' Maynard replied, comfortably, and lit another cigar.

Time went on; the campaign grew hotter and hotter, and at the calculated time the Galaxians filed criminal charges against almost a hundred Big Names of the opposition.

The 'Ins' screamed and howled, of course. They'd been framed. They'd been jobbed. Swivel-tongued demagogues ranted and raved about freedom and liberty and patriotism and motherhood; about tyranny and oppression and muzzling and dictatorship and fascism and slavery and corruption and soullessness and greed. They accused the 'upstarts' of everything they themselves had been doing and were still doing.

The Galaxian psiontists, however, had the facts. Events, names, dates, places, and amounts. They knew exactly what had been done, who had done it, and for how much, and they could prove their every allegation.

Truth and honesty and facts are much easier to present and to prove than are lies. Wherefore the Galaxians, in addition to publicizing their facts in newspapers, magazines, tapes, brochures, pamphlets, and flyers, also took a lot of time on the communications networks of vast InStell. According to law, InStell had to allot as much time to the FreeLibs as to the Galaxians – but it was probably neither accidental nor coincidental that little or no 'network' trouble ever developed on Galaxian time.

Psiontist-lawyers took solid facts to court and inserted them solidly into jurors' heads. Corruptionists, extortioners, boodlers, political and legal, and big-shot racketeers – lords of vice and crime – began to go one by one behind bars.

And the vast, lethargic, unorganized public began to stir ... began finally to move ...

As Election Day drew near, the 'fuss' predicted by Spehn did indeed develop. Nor was it merely 'some' fuss; there was a lot of it. There was a great deal of violence; there were more than a few deaths. Intrenched and corrupt power does not yield easily to displacement. The deeper it is intrenched and the more corrupt it is, the more difficult its ouster is, and WestHem's government had been corrupt to the core for a very long time. Thus, while some of the former incumbents were now in jail and more were on the way, the vacancies had been filled by people of the same stripe and the lower echelons, the boys and girls who got out the vote, had not been touched.

It was a thoroughly dirty campaign; nor were the Galaxians exactly lily-white. While most of the mud they threw was true

– even though some of it could not be proved except by psionic evidence, which of course was not admissible in court – they did at times do quite a little extrapolating: but not when they could get caught at it very easily.

The Galaxians had another great advantage in that every important political meeting was attended by at least one high-powered psiontist; and at these rallies, Galaxian or FreeLib, those experts inserted the truth into minds theretofore closed to reason. These minds thought, of course, that they had per-ceived the truth for themselves.

Registration soared to an all-time high of ninety-eight point nine percent of all eligible voters.

Maynard knew that the Galaxians would lose every strong-hold of organized Labor and every district controlled by ward heelers. He knew that they would win in all suburbs and 'out in the sticks'. It was in the middle regions that the issue would be decided, and he knew exactly where those regions were. He also knew that, in spite of all the illegal work the Galaxians had done in those regions, they would lose a lot of them. The decision would be close: altogether too close.

On the morning of Election Day, then, especially in those doubtful regions, tension hit its peak. Voting was far from clean, on both sides, but in that skullduggery the Galaxians again had two great advantages. First, their ringers and re-peaters had been set up so far in advance and so carefully as to avoid suspicion. Second, they had the psiontists. Not one in every precinct, of course, but one could 'port to any polling-place in less than one second of time.

And whenever a mind-reader stared into an imposter's eyes and told him who he really was, where he really lived, when and where and who had paid him how much, and dared him to sign that false name, the imposter ran: but fast.

Even so, it was very close. It see-sawed back and forth all night. Maynard and his staff were worn and drawn when, at ten o'clock next morning, it became mathematically certain that the Galaxians had lost the presidency and had not won control of either the Senate or the House.

'I can't say that I'm not disappointed,' Maynard said then, 'but – considering the lethargy of John and Mary Public, that we are a completely new party, and what the Free Libs promised everybody – we did very well. We elected such a strong minority that the opposition will have to maintain a solid front, which will be very hard for them to do. If we keep on working, and we will, we should be able to win next time.'

CHAPTER TWENTY-ONE

The Battle of New Russia

Bernice sat on the rostrum, at Maynard's right, when he called the Board to order and said, aloud for the record:

'Mrs. Jones, who is by far the most sensitive perceiver known to us, has made an intensive psionic study of New Russia. Her report is already on tape; but, since you are all psiontists, I have asked her to give you, mind to mind, everything she found out, so that you will be able to perceive and to feel the many sidebands, connotations, and implications that can not possibly be put into words. Mrs. Jones, will you take the floor, please?'

Bernice took Maynard's place in the speaker's box and an almost absolute silence fell; a silence that, even at the speed of thought, lasted almost half an hour. When she sat down, all two-hundred-odd members of the Board breathed gustily and stared at each other with emotions and expressions that simply cannot be described. Maynard resumed his place at the speaker's stand and spoke into the microphone:

'You see that Communism has not changed one iota in over two hundred years. It is a rule based solely upon violence and fear. It is a rule of terror, of spies, of informers, of secret police of the lowest, most brutal type – police who use by choice the most callous, the most hideous techniques of all the older regimes of the iron heel; those of the GESTAPO and the OGPU and the SLRESK and the KARSH. There are no civil liberties, no rights of any kind except those based upon the power to kill. There have been, there are now, and there will continue

228

to be assassinations and purges; slaughter at the whim of one power-mad man or of a group of such men.

'It is my considered opinion that Communism should have been wiped out before atomic energy was developed. It has never been willing to cooperate with any decent civilization. It was forced into a kind of coexistence by the certain knowledge that if it did not at least pretend to accept coexistence it itself would be destroyed in the worldwide holocaust that would inevitably follow any attempt at conquest by armed force. Its basic drive, its prime tenet, however, has not changed. Not in any particular. Its insane lust for dominance will never be satisfied until all civilization lies prostrate under its spike-studded clubs. Before colonization, it devoted its every effort, fair and foul, to the mastery of the entire Earth; since the first planet was colonized its innate compulsion was, now is, and will continue to be the complete mastery of civilization everywhere; wherever in total space our civilization may go.

'It is my carefully-considered personal opinion that this cancer in the body politic, if it is not extirpated now, will soon become inoperable. At the time when we acquired the fleet that had been englobing Earth, the Communists had built on their hidden planet a warfleet almost as large as our own. They were and still are building more superdreadnoughts. They intended to attack us as soon as their superiority was sufficient to warrant an all-out bid for supremacy. It was only the acquirement of that fleet that gave us our overwhelming superiority as of now. How long will our superiority last? They are building much faster than we can without converting to a war footing. Shall we do that, and try to perpetuate the cold war? An attempt that will certainly fail sooner or later? The only question, as I see it, is: Do we want war now, while by luck we have the means to win; or later, when we very probably will not have?

'I use the words "very probably will not" advisedly; with reference to our ultra-high-acceleration screened battle torpedoes, against which we ourselves have no defense except a planet-based repulsor. It is practically certain that the Russians do not have them in production yet. Ilyowicz knew about them and passed the information along; but he himself was

229

neither an engineer nor a scientist, and – fortunately – we kept the whole TIMPS project top secret and under psionic guard. The Russians will develop them in time, certainly; possibly in months, or even weeks. If we wait until they have them in production we may still be able to win, but I need not tell you at what appalling cost in lives.

'Mrs. Jones showed you the large portions of certain munitions plants, and entire areas that are probably munitions plants, that are hidden under psionic shields. The meaning of that is clear.

'I now ask the supremely vital question: Ladies and gentlemen of the Board – Shall we fight now or not?'

There was some discussion, but not very much. Every person in the hall knew the whole story with psionic certainty, and the spirit of Patrick Henry still lived. The vote was unanimous for immediate war.

The Galaxians' Grand Fleet, six hundred thirty-five superdreadnoughts strong, was in subspace on its way to New Russia. Fleet Admiral Dann, in his flagship *Terra*, felt happy, proud, and confident. Since bombs could not be teleported through competent psionic screening and the Communists had plenty of competent psionists, the battle would have to be fought along conventional lines. However, that was all right. He now had overwhelming superiority. He also had the TIMPS; which, he was sure, would win the battle. The worst that could happen was that he couldn't get them all. A lot of them would get away by immerging ... unless that thing Deston and Adams were working on would ... maybe ...

That was the only thing about this whole operation he didn't like. He called Adams, aboard the *Explorer*; which subspace-going laboratory, while travelling in the same direction as the fleet and at the same velocity, was in no sense any part of it.

'Doc,' Dann thought at him, 'I'm going to try again. I know there are only fourteen of you aboard this time, but Goddamn it, there's only one Andrew Adams. You're the most important man alive, and nobody in his right mind would call the Big Six expendable, either. The rest of us are – that's our business

230

– but if *you* get killed there'll be hell to pay and no pitch hot. I'd probably have to take cyanide or face a firing squad. So won't you please, *please* go back home and stay there?'

'We will not,' Adams replied. 'Your solicitude for us does not impress me, and that for yourself is absurd – it is on record that we are working independently of your fleet and against your wishes. We are conducting a scientific investigation, which may or may not result in the destruction of one or more Communist warships. It may or may not result in the loss of one or all of our lives, although we believe that we have a rather high probability of safety. In any case, the data we obtain will be preserved, which is all that is important. Whatever else happens is immaterial – the results of this investigation, young man, are necessary to science,' and Adams cut the telepathic line.

Dann sat back appalled. He had heard of selfless devotion to a cause, but this ... and not only himself, but also his wife and the other twelve top psionists of all known space ...

But Admiral Dann had very little time to ponder abstractions. Grand Fleet emerged. Not in tight formation, of course – really fine control was to come later – but most of the sub-spacers came out within a few thousand miles of where they had intended to. And every Galaxian ship, as it emerged, hurled death and destruction. The TIMPS were launched first, of course; they were the Sunday punch. Thousands of killers erupted, too, and hundreds of ordinary torps. They were not expected to do much damage – and they didn't – but they would fill the ether full of fireworks and they might keep the Communist needlemen busy enough with their lasers so that some of them might get through. At least, they'd give the enemy sharpshooters something to do.

Then, long before the end of the fifteen seconds it would take for the first TIMPS and killers to reach their targets, the big Galaxian battlewagons put out their every course of battle screen, torched up their every battle beam, and tore in at full drive to englobe the Commie ships and blast them out of the ether.

All space became filled with the unbearable brilliance, the incomprehensible energies of hundred-megaton warheads ex-

231

ploding as thick as sparks from a forging ram, and eight of the Communist ships of war were volatilized at that first blast.

But fifteen seconds at battle tension is a long time; plenty of time for a smart commander – especially one who has been warned that the enemy may have a weapon against which he has no defense – to push his IMMERGE button and flit for the protection of an umbrella. Therefore, five seconds after the first Commie ship had been blown to atoms – twenty seconds after the battle's beginning and long before Grand Fleet could begin englobing tactics against individual Communist ships – the Battle of New Russia was over. Not one Communist warship remained in space.

There was some defensive action, of course. The Commies had launched a lot of long-range stuff, too, but it was all ordinary stuff; stuff that could be handled. Defensive and repulsor screens flared white and beamers and lasermen were very busy men indeed for a few minutes, but not one Galaxian vessel was very badly damaged or had to immerge.

Admiral Dann had followed the last few Commies into subspace with his sense of perception, but they had simply disappeared – with no sign of damage or of violence. Okay: if they re-emerged to continue the battle that would be all right; if they never re-emerged that would be still better. Wherefore, after ordering full detection alert, both up and down, he relaxed – still strapped down at his con-board – and waited to hear from Maynard.

It is exceedingly difficult, as all psionists know, to work the Fourth Nume of Total Reality. What, then, of the Fifth? It had been known, theoretically, for many years, as the realm of two abysmally fundamental and irreconcilably opposed aspects of that Reality.

First, there was DISCONTINUITY. This was the aspect of complete unpredictability. The infinity-to-the-infinitieth power of all possible and impossible events could and would happen; simultaneously, in regular or in irregular sequence, or at complete random, or in all of these ways at once; completely without justification, reason, or cause.

Second, there was something that was called, for lack of a

better term, CREATIVITY. This was the hyper-volume locus of the basic male principle, although sex as such was only an infinitesimal part of it. It was the aspect or phase – Quality? Ability? Primal Urge? Power? Force? – backing and binding all being and all doing. It was the – the Will? The Drive? The Compulsion? – to be, to do, to develop, to grow – TO CREATE. It was the enormous 'natural tendency' toward the continuing existence of a universe of order and of law. Call it what you please, it is that without which – or without the application of which: language is *so* helpless in psionics! – this our universe could not have come into being and would not even momentarily endure.

Carlyle Deston, the only human being of his time to work the Fifth, reached it the hard way. He had a hunch, but he could neither show it nor explain it to his fellows. They got behind him a few times and pushed, but nothing happened. He, however, did not forget it. It kept on niggling at him, and he kept on nibbling at it, until the two Aceys graduated. They had something he needed and lacked; a subconscious – and therefore ineradicable by experience, education, or knowledge – innate conviction of superiority to any other race of man. He added them, and the Funny Four – *nobody* knew what that uninhibited foursome could do! – to his pushers; and the thirteen strongest psiontists of his time rammed his questing ego into and through the psionic barriers in the direction he *knew* he had to go.

He went: came back in zero time: and lay in a deep coma for forty hours. He could not explain, even to hysterical Barbara or to eagerly inquisitive Adams, where he had been or what he had done or what he had learned. However, he knew what he knew: wherefore a crew of the finest technicians of Galmetia, working under his minute supervision, built a machine.

It was like no other machine ever built by man. Everything, apparently, was input. It could take half the power of the gigantic leybyrdite-built generators of the gigantic leybyrdite-built *Explorer*, but there was no visible or perceptible output of any kind. There were no controls; no buttons or meters or dials or gauges. All the immense power of that machine would be controlled purely by thought. If that machine performed at all, it would perform at the immeasurable speed of thought.

His hunch was that the thing would work. Since he could work the Fifth Nume alone (no woman can even perceive that Nume) as well as he and Barbara together could work the Fourth, he was practically certain that it would work. Certain enough to let the others who had insisted on coming along, even Barbara, do so: but no one else. And most certainly not the kids. Something might happen.

Shortly after Dann's last protest to Adams, the psiontists aboard the *Explorer* gathered in the control room, around Deston's enigmatic 'Z-gun'.

'But what *could* happen, Babe?' Bernice asked, nervously.

'Don't worry, Bun. What is going to happen, as nearly as I can express it, is that I'm going to transform the coordinates of those ships from the continuous phase to the discontinuous phase of Reality; using just enough energy to control the balance.'

'You are not answering her question,' Adams said. 'There is an indeterminate and at present indeterminable probability that any disturbance of equilibrium will initiate an irreversibly accelerating transformation of the entire cosmos, so that...'

'Wow!' Cecily exclaimed. 'It's bad enough, thinking of destroying one whole planet, but the whole *cosmos*!'

'Compared to the discontinuous imbalances always there?' Deston protested. 'Have a heart, Doc! And you two gals, listen – what Doc calls a probability isn't even an actual possibility – it's out beyond nine sigmas – exactly as possible as that an automatic screw machine running six-thirty-two hex nuts would accidentally turn out a cash-register full of money. If it wasn't safe do you think I'd have Bobby here? Hell, I wouldn't be here myself!'

'Young man, your reasoning is deplorable,' Adams said. 'Your data is entirely insufficient for the computation of sigma in this case. Furthermore, the term "probability", in its meaningful sense, is defined by...'

'Meaningful sense and all, we'll drop all that stuff right now,' Barbara said, unusually sharply for her. 'Besides, it's about time to, isn't it?'

It was, and Deston stretched out on a davenport and closed his eyes. When the first Communist warship appeared in sub-space he stiffened suddenly and it vanished. As more and more warships immerged and were caught in whatever it was that Deston and his Z-gun were doing, nothing seemed to be happening in the *Explorer* at all. The machine never had done anything, apparently, and Deston's body was stiffly rigid all the time.

Adams, leaving Stella behind, bored into that psionic murk with every iota of his psionic might. He perceived much – no two of those disappearance occurred in exactly the same way – and he would remember every detail of everything he perceived.

When the ghastly performance was over Deston got up, jerked his head at Barbara, and the two walked out of the room with their arms tightly around each other. No words passed between them; or any thoughts except the knowledge of complete oneness. Neither words nor thoughts would do any good. It had had to be done and he was the only one who could do it. So he, had done it.

They would have to live with it. That was the way it was. Nothing could be done about it.

Adams, on the other hand – tall, lean, gray-haired, gray-eyed, gray-clad Adams – was purring like a tomcat full of canaries. 'Fabulous! Utterly priceless!' he enthused, to any-one who cared to listen. 'This is probably the greatest break-through of all time! The data we have obtained here will undoubtedly be the basis for a completely new system of science!'

Just before the adjournment of the board meeting following the fall of New Russia, Maynard said:

'Since science has not yet devised a recorder of thought, I will sum up briefly, for the minutes, the sense of this meeting.

'The political situation on Earth, while better than it was, is still bad. We have discussed strategy and have formulated plans by virtue of which we expect to win the next election.

'Plastics' serf world presents many problems, but they appear to be more a matter of time than of intrinsic impossibility.

The psiontists of that world are working out a program of rehabilitation that promises excellent results.

'The ordinary citizens of New Russia will not present any problems. The non-psionic commissars and hard-core Party members will not be allowed to present any problems. The New Russian psiontists do, however, present a very serious problem; one that has taken up practically all of the time of this meeting.

'Psionics is necessarily ethical, but ethics is not at present an absolute. Thus most of the New Russian psiontists, steeped from infancy in Communist doctrine and never exposed to any except Communist thought, are as thoroughly convinced that Communism is right as we are that it is wrong. This difference of opinion in these cases, while total at present, is probably not irreconcilable. It is believed that when these uninformed persons have studied all aspects of the truth they will of their own accord come around to our way of thinking.

'There are some well-informed Communist psiontists, however, who believe so thoroughly that Communism is right that they would rather become martyrs to its cause than renounce it. Feodr Ilyowicz, a man of wide learning, knowledge, and experience, was one. What can be done about such men as he was?

'Are we right? We do not know. We cannot know.

'All we can do – what we must do – is what eighty percent or more of this Board believes to be right.

'Our prime tenet, the solid bed-rock foundation upon which the Galactic Federation is being built, defines "right" as that which, in the opinion of at least four-fifths of the membership of its Board of Directors, is for the best good of humanity as a whole.

'It is a fact that about seventy percent of all known human population is non-Communist. This Board is in virtually unanimous agreement that about ninety-six percent of all people now under Communist rule as we know it would be vastly better off under Galaxianism; would live much fuller, freer, and better lives than under Communism. Thus, we believe that Galaxianism is for the best good of about ninety-eight and eight-tenths percent of all humanity known to us.

'More than the required four-fifths of us have agreed upon three points. First: each such psiontist as Feodr Ilyowicz was will be watched. Second: no general ruling will be made, but each such case will be decided upon its own merits. Third, the penalty of death will not be imposed.

'If there is no other business requiring our attention at this time, a voiced motion for adjournment is now in order.'

More Great Science Fiction Books from Panther

Panther Science Fiction — A Selection from the World's Best S.F. List

GREYBEARD	Brian W. Aldiss	40p	☐
THE MOMENT OF ECLIPSE	Brian W. Aldiss	35p	☐
THE DISASTER AREA	J. G. Ballard	30p	☐
THE OVERLOADED MAN	J. G. Ballard	30p	☐
THE DAY OF FOREVER	J. G. Ballard	25p	☐
UBIK	Philip K. Dick	35p	☐
DO ANDROIDS DREAM OF ELECTRIC SHEEP?	Philip K. Dick	30p	☐
THE GENOCIDES	Thomas M. Disch	30p	☐
CAMP CONCENTRATION	Thomas M. Disch	30p	☐
ALL THE SOUNDS OF FEAR	Harlan Ellison	30p	☐
THE TIME OF THE EYE	Harlan Ellison	35p	☐
THE RING OF RITORNEL	Charles L. Harness	35p	☐
THE ROSE	Charles L. Harness	25p	☐
THE COMMITTED MEN	M. John Harrison	35p	☐
THE VIEW FROM THE STARS	Walter M. Miller Jr.	35p	☐
MASQUE OF A SAVAGE MANDARIN	Philip Bedford Robinson	35p	☐
THE MULLER-FOKKER EFFECT	John Sladek	35p	☐
THE STEAM-DRIVEN BOY	John Sladek	35p	☐
LET THE FIRE FALL	Kate Wilhelm	35p	☐
THE KILLING THING	Kate Wilhelm	30p	☐
BUG-EYED MONSTERS	Edited by Anthony Cheetham	40p	☐

All these books are available at your local bookshop or newsagent; or can be ordered direct from the publisher. Just tick the titles you want and fill in the form below.

Name...

Address ....

....

Write to Panther Cash Sales, P.O. Box 11, Falmouth, Cornwall TR10 9EN.
Please enclose remittance to the value of the cover price plus 10p postage and packing for one book, 5p for each additional copy.
Granada Publishing reserve the right to show new retail prices on covers, which may differ from those previously advertised in the text or elsewhere.